Jericho

Ginger Jamison

Jericho

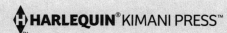
HARLEQUIN® KIMANI PRESS™

ROM
Jamison

Recycling programs
for this product may
not exist in your area.

JERICHO

ISBN-13: 978-0-373-09166-9

Copyright © 2014 by Jamie Pope

Printed in U.S.A.

www.Harlequin.com

To Tara Gavin for being so lovely and supportive.

And to my mother for being the strongest woman I know.

CHAPTER 1

"You're late. Again."

Georgia Williams nodded at her supervisor as she dumped her bag in her locker and slipped into her nonslip clogs.

Yes, she was late. Again.

Her whole day had gone to hell the moment she'd woken up. An annoyed landlord. A sick baby. A message on her machine from the sister whom she hadn't spoken to in years. And a car that had started spewing smoke on the highway. It was the type of day that made a person want to get back in bed and forget that the world existed.

"I'm sorry." She didn't even bother making an excuse. There was no use in explaining anything to "Nurse Ratched." The woman did not appreciate excuses, no matter how valid they were.

"That's the third time this quarter, Georgia." She tapped her clipboard. "If it happens again, I'm going to have to write you up."

Georgia nodded again. It was best not to point out that she was only four minutes late and that she often stayed well past the end of her shift to make sure her patients were settled. Nurse Drill Sergeant wouldn't care.

The woman had been on her case since she started working at Jericho Military Medical Center. And she wasn't sure why. It wasn't that she didn't pick on the other nurses, too. She treated them all like soldiers in her army. They weren't allowed to have a hair out of place, a shoe that was scuffed or an opinion that didn't agree with her own. She demanded perfection in everybody but she seemed particularly keen on pointing out Georgia's faults.

Georgia should be used to that by now. Taking orders from an unyielding, all-knowing ruler. She'd been taught to be obedient, to be seen and not heard, but for some reason her supervisor's superior attitude made her bristle. And a small part of Georgia wanted to rebel, to tell the woman to take her clipboard and shove it where the sun didn't shine.

But she couldn't do that. Going against the grain was what got her in trouble in the first place.

"I understand, ma'am," she said instead. "I'll try not to let it happen again."

Her sour-faced supervisor nodded, satisfied that Georgia was truly contrite. "See that you don't. I'm leaving for the night. I expect you know what you have to do."

"Yes, ma'am." Other areas of her life might be disastrous, but she took pride in her work. Taking care of other people was what she had been raised to do. "I'll get to it right now."

"And please pay special attention to Lieutenant Howard. He was just transferred here a few hours ago and he hasn't woken up yet. He'll need his bandages changed."

"I will." She brushed past her boss and escaped the locker room, eager to begin her shift.

"Hello, Miss Georgia," one of the soldiers called from his

opened room. She smiled and waved back to the private as she headed to the nurses' station.

When she first entered nursing school she never imagined that she would end up in a military hospital surrounded by young men. Her father would be appalled.

The only men an unmarried female should be around are the ones in her family.

And it was a rule he made sure they followed. Georgia and her sister were homeschooled while her brothers got to go to the local public school. They were made to wear long skirts or dresses that fell to their ankles while their brothers' clothing was never questioned. They were to be home before sundown, while their brothers got to stay out all hours of the night.

Their father was a minister, "a man of God," he called himself, but no other female who belonged to their church had to follow those rules. Only Georgia and Carolina, and Georgia learned firsthand what the punishment was for breaking those rules.

She checked the charts of her patients. It was after 7:00 p.m. For the rest of the evening it would just be her, a doctor and an orderly on duty in this ward. But even though the night staff was skeletal, the patients were never more than they could handle.

The hospital grew quiet during the night, almost peaceful. All the visitors had left. All the patients had been fed. All the occupational, physical and speech therapists had long ago delivered their services. And even though the ward was filled with grievously injured patients, they didn't require much care beyond the occasional dose of pain medication or a cup of water. Most of them only wanted a kind word. It was easy to get lonely there. Sometimes she would turn a blind eye when the ones who were able to move left their rooms to visit others during the night.

She understood a little about being lonely. She grew up in church. Around hundreds of parishioners. At choir practice on Tuesdays, bible study on Wednesdays and dinner on Thursdays. But all that had ended when her father found out that she was pregnant.

"Hello, Georgia." Dr. Allen placed his hand on her back, distracting her from her thoughts.

"Oh, hi, Greg," she said softly. She never felt comfortable around the handsome young doctor. He was a nice man and was never anything but courteous to her, but she could barely look him in the eye.

"I heard Bitchy McGee was giving you a hard time about being thirty seconds late for your shift."

She shrugged, embarrassed that news had spread so quickly. "I was late. I guess she didn't have a choice."

"You're a good nurse, Georgia. You don't deserve her crap. Try not to let it bother you." He patted her back.

"Thank you, Greg." She smiled at him, trying not to shrug away from his touch. "I'm going to get to work now. She might be lurking around the corner."

"Okay. I've been working a double. So I'm going to try to catch a few hours of sleep. I'll be in the break room if you need me."

She nodded and they went their separate ways. She stopped in every patient's room just to check on them.

It never got easier. She'd worked in a hospice facility for a short while and every day she went into work knowing that those people were going to die. They had cancer and Alzheimer's disease. They were old and frail and had no hope of survival, and yet seeing that daily wasn't as disheartening as seeing the men on her ward. They were more like boys, really. The youngest nineteen. All had been in their prime a few months ago, strong, healthy, patriotic. And now they were here. Some of them missing limbs, some who were blinded, all of them with scars. At least one night a week one of them would wake up screaming in the grips of some nightmare, reliving whatever horrible thing they saw while they were overseas.

It made Georgia think of her youngest brother. He was nineteen now and the last time she'd seen him he had been preparing to join the army. Even though she hadn't spoken to him in years, she hoped that he'd avoided this fate. Being stuck in the hospital was no life for a young man. Georgia hadn't considered herself a pacifist before, but the longer she worked at Jericho Medical the more she hated war.

"Hello, Miss Georgia. How are you this evening?"

"How did you know it was me?" she asked Tobias Clark as she entered his room. The lance corporal had been blinded in an explosion and had recently undergone his fifth surgery to restore his eyesight. So far nothing had worked. But he was one of the sweetest boys she had ever met and had the highest spirit among all the men on the floor.

"Because you always smell like sugar and baby powder. You're the best-smelling nurse in this whole dang hospital."

"You can thank my daughter for that," she told him as she made sure his bandages were snug. "I swear I get more powder on me than I do on her bottom. It's why I'm such a mess all the time."

"I know you're not a mess, Miss Georgia. You don't have it in you."

"How do you know that, Tobias? You've been talking to somebody?"

He grinned at her, his pretty white teeth making the room

seem a little brighter. "You know you're our favorite thing to talk about during the day."

She was jolted by his statement. "Why?"

"Because everybody has fantasies that the sweet little night nurse will turn naughty and make their dreams come true."

"Lance Corporal Tobias Clark! I cannot believe you just said that to me."

He flashed her another grin. "That's how I know you're never a mess, Nurse Williams. Because even though I can't see you, I know every inch of you is a proper Southern, church-going lady."

She shook her head but smiled in spite of herself. "See how much you know. I haven't been to church in years."

"And yet I know you pray every night, Miss Georgia. I know you pray for us."

She was speechless for a second. God and she weren't exactly on good terms at the moment. But she did think about the boys every day. She wished them well. She hoped for the best. It may not be praying, but it was the next best thing. "I pray for your mama. I'm not exactly sure how she put up with you for all those years."

"I'm her favorite, but don't tell my sister that." He turned his head toward her and was quiet for a moment. "If this operation don't take, I'm going to get me one of those dogs. Maybe even if it does take I will. I saw those therapy dogs on TV once. They're pretty damn cool. You think they'll let me have one?"

"I think so," she said quietly, suddenly feeling heavy about this boy coming to terms with never being able to see again. "I know there's some information about it somewhere in the hospital. I could find it and read it to you tomorrow. Would you like that?"

He smiled at her. "Yes, ma'am. It will give me something to brag about to the boys the next day."

Georgia squeezed his shoulder. "It's past ten o'clock. You need to be getting to sleep now."

She left his room and continued on to the next to find that serviceman sleeping. He would be leaving soon. He was one of the so-called lucky ones, only here because he got an infection after being shot in the arm. No permanent damage. No loss of limb. But he was one of the ones who woke up screaming sometimes. Post-traumatic stress disorder, they called it. The infection he could recover from. She wasn't sure how long it would take for the invisible scars to heal.

She entered the room across the hall, trying to shake herself out of her morbid thoughts. She was depressing herself tonight. Maybe it was time to look for another job. One in a maternity ward. Or a school. Her soul might feel lighter if she was handing out ice packs instead of tending to wounded soldiers. But she needed the money. She needed to give her baby girl a better life, and working nights here paid more than any other nursing job in the county.

A slight moan alerted her to the patient in the room, and Georgia froze when she saw him.

Lieutenant Christian Austin Howard. The man she had been warned about.

She wasn't sure why her hands trembled slightly when she set her eyes on him. He was just...so large. Bigger than any man she had ever seen. As he was lying down, she couldn't tell exactly how tall he was, but it had to be well over six feet. And yet it wasn't his height that caused her feet to become rooted to the ground. It was his width, his broadness, the way he made the bed beneath him disappear. The way he made the room feel smaller even though he was unconscious.

His face was harsh, with a wide jaw and a long straight

nose—plenty of hard angles. His brow was furrowed as if he was deep in thought. Everything about him screamed *commander.*

Obey me.

He reminded her of a sleeping lion—a powerful body under golden skin, with hair so dark blond it was nearly brown. He was terrifying. Some might say ugly, but she wouldn't describe him that way. There was something about him that made her not want to look away.

And he was burned. She hadn't noticed at first, but he was and it was disfiguring. The left side of his face, his cheek and jawline had taken most of the impact from the blast.

She had heard about him. About them. He was a war hero around these parts. He had led a unit that had been surprised by a rocket attack. The gossip was that he'd refused to be pulled off the field until the medics had seen to his men first. Still, he was only one of the three men who had survived. Ryan Beecher had been here before they'd sent him to Texas to be with his wife. Beecher had awoken with no memory at all. The final marine had escaped with no injuries and had never stepped foot in Jericho Medical.

Lieutenant Howard moaned again, scaring her. Reminding her that she had come in here for a reason. Her cheeks burned. She had been working here for eight months and had seen it all. Men who were hurt far worse than Lieutenant Howard, but she never had been unable to peel her eyes away from them.

"I could have stopped it," he croaked out. Georgia jumped at the sound of his voice.

He's just dreaming, you idiot. You're not afraid.

Still she made no move to get closer to him. She checked his chart, checking the last time he had been given medication.

But it seemed Lieutenant Howard wasn't going to let her get away with standing still.

He started to move, to thrash in his sleep. She took a step forward without thinking. The skin grafts. They must be kept very still. He could ruin any chance he had of healing.

She walked around to his good side and placed her hand on his shoulder to find his body rock hard and burning hot. She wanted to pull her hand away, but she knew it would be wrong. "Hush," she said, trying to comfort him into stillness. "You're not alone."

She squeezed his shoulder and murmured nonsensical things. The things she might say to her daughter when she was fussy. He turned his head toward her words. He calmed, and then he opened his eyes and blinked at her. He had the most brilliantly colored glass-green eyes. Her hand trembled again.

"Hello, Lieutenant." It was all she could think to say.

"Are you the angel of death?"

"I'm no angel. God wouldn't have me."

"I'm not dead." He said those words as though it was unbelievable to him.

"No, sir. You aren't."

He looked away from her for a moment, then went back to drilling his bottle-green eyes into hers. "Would you mind killing me?"

CHAPTER 2

The sound of distant laughter shook Christian from a deep sleep.

Something wasn't right.

It was past curfew. The base at nighttime always held a sort of eerie silence, an absolute stillness, but tonight it didn't. During his short time in the marines he had learned a lot, but the most important thing was that there was hell to pay for breaking the rules.

Looking around the quiet bunk, he realized that Gibbs, Johnson and Davis were missing. They were the guys he'd started basic training with a few months ago. They were his friends. His family now. His parents were gone. Dead in a crash the month before Christian enlisted. Those guys looked out for him. Helped him get through Hell Week. And if they were busted breaking curfew they would be in deep shit.

He got out of bed, shoved his feet into his boots and made his way toward the sound of the voices. He was hoping by some miracle that his friends wouldn't be there. But they were. Crowded around a Japanese girl who couldn't have been more than seventeen. He wasn't surprised to see her. Girls hung around outside the base all the time, hoping to get a chance to get to know one of the servicemen.

Christian stayed the hell away from them. He knew from some of the older marines that most of those girls were trouble. No matter what country they came from. Most of them were looking for a way out. He didn't care if his friends went out with them when they were on leave, but the girl shouldn't be on the base. Especially past midnight.

As he walked up, he saw Johnson push the girl against the wall and kiss her. She looked a little frightened but willing enough to be kissed by him, but when he saw Davis do the same thing mere seconds later, something inside of him screamed that it wasn't right.

"What the fuck are you guys doing? She's not supposed to be here."

"Relax, man," Gibbs said. His words were slightly slurred. He was drunk. They all were. They had to be. He couldn't think of any other reason they would be so stupid.

"You should join us." Johnson barely turned and looked at him. "Miko is fun. Aren't you, baby?" He grabbed her breast and Christian took a step forward. The girl laughed uneasily and tried to push Johnson's hand away but Johnson just squeezed harder.

"I don't want any part of this, and if you three assholes weren't shitfaced you would know that, too."

"You're such a fucking Boy Scout. That's why we didn't invite you in the first place."

He wouldn't have gone even if they had invited him. Three of them and one girl. It just didn't sit right. "You need to get back to the bunk." He took a step closer to the girl, who wasn't laughing now. She took in a quick breath as he neared her. He had that effect on some women. He knew he was a big, nasty-looking son of a bitch, but she was safer with him than the three idiots he thought were his friends. "Go home. Do you understand me? Go home right now."

Her eyes widened and she nodded.

"You three get your asses back in the bunk."

"What are you going to do? Rat us out?" Gibbs gave him a hard look. He knew that it wasn't in Christian's nature to be a rat, but they should also know he wouldn't have bothered to come and get them unless it was important.

"Just let the girl go home."

"All right, you stuffy son of a bitch." Johnson pushed himself away from her. "We'll be back in a few minutes. Just let us walk her out."

Christian gave them a hard look and then turned away. But something inside him told him to go back. To make sure the girl got off the base. But he didn't. He walked back to his bunk, hoping that his friends would do the right thing, but he had the sinking thought that they would just disregard everything he had said.

They didn't come back to the bunk for another hour and a half. He knew that because he'd lain awake waiting for them. The next day none of them would look him in the eye. The next week none of them were speaking to each other.

Four months later, Miko was back on base again. This time she was pregnant and sobbing. Christian wasn't exactly sure what had happened that night. He tried not to let his mind go there, but he never shook the feeling that he could have done more.

He looked at the crying girl, opening his mouth to say he was sorry when the explosion hit. Suddenly he was no longer a twenty-one-year-old kid on his first deployment in Japan. He was thirty-four on his third tour in Iraq, and the commander of his own unit.

One side of his face was on fire. No. It was melting. He turned his body away from the searing heat, the pain. The devil licked his skin. His men were everywhere, most of them dead already. He knew rocket attacks were a danger. He knew this day was coming but he didn't think he would lose his men.

This was supposed to be his punishment. He didn't do the right thing all those years ago. He'd failed her.

"You're not alone." A feminine voice, sweetened with a Southern accent, jolted him from his nightmare. "It's okay, sugar. I'm here. You don't have to be scared. Everything is going to be just fine."

The pain to the left side of his body was breath stealing. His skin felt tight, his face numb. His arm almost felt as if it belonged to another person. Opening his eyes was a struggle. He must be dying. There was an angel welcoming him to the other side.

No, scratch that. It couldn't be an angel.

He wasn't bound for heaven.

He managed to pry his eyes open and look at the creature who was trying to soothe him. Her honey-brown eyes went wide. Her mouth dropped open into a perfect O. He was in more pain than he could ever imagine, but he still took note of how plump and pretty her lips were. She was nice looking. With smooth coffee-and-cream-colored skin and dark auburn hair pulled tightly into a bun. There was a slight dusting of freckles across her small, round nose. Those features together should make her simply cute, but the woman standing before him was oddly beautiful. There was a softness floating around her. The kind that made him want to pull her into him just so he could feel it.

"Hello, Lieutenant." Her voice sounded breathless, almost as if she was afraid.

"Are you the angel of death?"

"I'm no angel. God wouldn't have me."

He was quiet for a moment, the realization coming hard and fast. "I'm not dead."

"No, sir. You aren't."

He should be. Why did they have to die when he got to live? He didn't deserve it. He had nothing left. No family. No home. And judging by the injuries to his body, he had no career. Those men, some of them no more than boys, had mothers and wives, children waiting for their homecoming. It wasn't right. He should be the one to go.

He blinked at her. "Would you mind killing me?"

"I've got enough sins to repent. Do you think I'm going to add another one by taking your life?" She placed the back of her hand against his cheek. "You don't want to die, Christian."

He blinked at her, and then leaned into her touch. Nobody had touched him like that in years. Nobody had called him by his given name in just as long. It was always *Howard,* or *Lieutenant.* Most of his men called him *sir.* "How do you know I don't want to die?"

"I've been working here for a little while now. I've seen hundreds of soldiers come and go. And I know if you had wanted to die you would have done so before they transported you all the way back to South Carolina. You must have something to live for."

He remembered now. He had been like this for weeks. Ruined. First in some hospital overseas, where he'd undergone a half dozen surgeries to try to repair whatever damage had been done to him. But he was never awake for very long. There had been nothing to stay conscious for. Sleep, no matter how disturbed it was, certainly was a better alternative to reality. Until now.

"Besides, you're too mean looking to die," she said softly.

"They would have to have a closed casket just so you won't scare off the mourners." She moved her efficient hands over his body to check beneath his bandages. "Beautiful," she murmured. "You know, I almost didn't come in here because you are so ghastly looking. I was afraid."

"I'm burned." He knew he must look bad. When his commanding officers had come to visit one of the few times he was awake, they wouldn't look him in the eye. They could barely look at him at all. "I haven't seen them yet. Are they that bad?"

"They aren't pretty, but I actually didn't notice them at first," she said in her soft, accented voice. "You are a very large man. A very, very large, scowling man. I bet you scare the living daylights out of all your men."

It was true. Sometimes he thought the only reason he moved up the ranks so quickly was because people were afraid of him. After the incident with Miko, he vowed that he would never be disobeyed again. But nobody but this little nurse had the balls to tell him that.

"Tell me who you are." He locked eyes with her for a minute. She tried to keep contact, but he knew he was making her uncomfortable.

"I'm Georgia Williams," she said, looking away. "I'm the night nurse."

She stepped away from him, but he reached out and grabbed her wrist. She was scared of him, but she tried not to let it show. She simply closed her eyes and breathed slowly.

"I'm not going to hurt you, Georgia. I just don't want you to go yet." Why the hell did he want her to stay? Yes, she was beautiful, but that had little to do with it. He knew she was a nurse, that she must be busy, but he needed not to be alone right now.

"I know you aren't going to hurt me. That would be very

foolish, because half of your body is one big painful wound and all I would have to do is poke you and you would start screaming like a little girl."

"I apologize, ma'am." He let go of her wrist. "I shouldn't have grabbed you. It won't happen again."

"Don't go all formal on me, Jarhead." She flashed him a quick smile. "I'm not upset. I wasn't leaving right now anyway. I was just going to grab some fresh bandages from the counter so I could clean you up a little."

"Thank you, ma'am."

"Georgia," she reminded him. "Or Nurse Williams if you have to be polite, but please don't call me *ma'am*. It makes me feel dreadfully old."

She went about changing his bandages, quickly but gently. She had the softest hands. He watched her while she worked, wondering what those hands would feel like if she wasn't being clinical. He wondered what they would feel like on him if he were making love to her.

That thought literally shook him.

"I'm sorry, sugar. Did I hurt you?"

"It's fine," he muttered. What the hell was his problem? Make love? To her? He hadn't ever made love to anybody. He had sex. He fucked. It had been over a year since he had any contact with a woman. That must be was what was making him insane tonight. A few touches from a pretty female had him thinking all types of stupid shit.

When he got out of here he was going to call Marguerite. She was who he always called in between tours. She never seemed to mind his brutish looks and she never said no. A few sweaty rounds with her and he would be back to normal.

"I'm all done, soldier." She looked at him with soft eyes. He knew why she was a nurse. She had this way about her that made a man want to be calm. "I have a few more patients to check on. But if you're hungry or need something to take the edge off the pain, I'll come back. Just press this button." She placed it in his good hand and held on to him for just a fraction longer than she should have.

And there it was again. The need to pull her beneath him and take in her warmth snuck up on him. His imagination had taken off again all because of a simple touch. He needed to get out of here as soon as possible. "I'll be fine, ma'am. Thank you."

"Georgia," she said to him. "Please call me Georgia."

"Good night, Georgia."

"Good night, Christian."

CHAPTER 3

Georgia climbed into her car after her shift ended and rested her head against the hot vinyl seat. She felt weary this morning. *Tired* wasn't the right word. Her shift had been fairly routine. No codes. No troublemaking patients. Nothing out of the ordinary, but this morning she felt as if she could barely move. It must have been the effects of the previous day still lingering in her mind.

What she needed was some sleep. Eight hours of glorious uninterrupted rest and maybe a long, hot bubble bath to ease the ache in her muscles.

She shut her eyes and let the sun shine on her face for a few moments, allowing herself to dream about the things she couldn't have. She opened her eyes before she fell asleep, willing her body to somehow become reenergized. She was going to need it to get her through the day. Her second and most important job started now.

It was time for her to be a mommy. She started her car and was at her next-door neighbor's apartment within fifteen minutes. Mrs. Sheppard was a widow in her mid-sixties and Georgia's lifesaver. It was she who looked after Abby while Georgia was at work. Every evening just before six-thirty Georgia would drop off Abby, who would be clad in her pajamas. Mrs. Sheppard would spend an hour or so with Abby before putting her to bed in the portable crib that Georgia had bought for her. Leaving her baby for some-body else to put to bed sometimes pained Georgia, but she remembered that she worked nights for Abby's sake. And that this shift was the only way she could spend the most time with her daughter.

"Good morning, Georgia." Mrs. Sheppard stepped aside and let her into her tiny apartment. "How was your night?"

"It was fine, thank you." She spotted her sleepy baby stand-ing up in her crib. Waiting for her. "How was my baby cakes last night?"

"She was delightful, as usual. You know, sometimes I feel downright rotten for taking your money. I don't do much at all. You won't even let me change her diaper for you in the morning."

It was silly but true. Georgia wanted to be the first person who touched her baby in the morning. She wanted to be the one to give her a bath and put on her clothes. She wanted her baby to have no doubt who her mother was.

"Hello, my love." She picked her up, burying her nose in Abby's curls. "How are you feeling this morning?"

"Let me fix you something to eat, honey," Mrs. Sheppard said, bustling into the kitchen. "I'll feel better knowing you had a good meal to get you through the day."

Georgia was tempted to take her up on her offer, but she shook her head. She only paid Mrs. Sheppard a hundred dol-lars a week to watch Abby. Mrs. Sheppard may claim to feel rotten, but it was Georgia who felt guilty for not being able to pay her more. "You do enough for me. You can't know how grateful I am to you that you keep her overnight. You know you are the only person I trust with her."

Mrs. Sheppard shook her head. "I know how hard this is for you. When my husband died I had two little ones to raise on my own. Thank God I had my mama to help me. I'm doing what's right. I just wish you would let me watch her for a little while longer. Just enough so you can get a few hours of undisturbed sleep. Look at you. You can't go on like this for much longer."

But she had to. "Don't worry about me. I get plenty of sleep," she lied as she slung Abby's diaper bag over her shoulder. "Go back to bed now. Abby and I are going to get ready for our day."

She had less than twelve hours to spend with her baby, so she kissed her neighbor's cheek and made her way back to her dismal-looking studio apartment. She needed a new car, but her first priority was to get a new apartment. There was paint flaking off the walls, the appliances were older than she was and the heat barely worked in the winter.

It was no place to raise a baby, but it was the best she could do for now. And despite the less than perfect living arrangements, she wasn't ashamed to live there. Getting this place and managing to pay the rent on her own for over a year now was a huge accomplishment. Two years ago she didn't know how to write a check or use an ATM card. Two years ago she hadn't been sure she could do anything without the aid of her father. How wrong she had been.

With Abby on her hip she scrounged around the kitchen to dig up something for them to eat. Oatmeal for Abby and some grapes that were on their way to being rotten for Georgia. She was going to have to go grocery shopping soon. She should probably go today, but she just didn't have time. She still had to sleep, shower, take Abby to the park and decide what bills she had to pay before things got shut off.

She'd never imagined being in so much debt. But when her father had kicked her out, he'd stopped paying her school loans, which was fine with Georgia. She could have managed them on her own, but the thing that had killed her was her lack of medical insurance. Abby had come early in an emergency C-section, and that had left Georgia with medical bills in the thousands. Whenever she thought about the amount, it was as though a large rock had settled on her chest.

So she tried not to think about it, or how Abby had come to be, because she couldn't change anything. And even if she could, she wouldn't change a thing. Life without her baby was unimaginable.

She cleared away their breakfast things, turned on PBS for Abby and crawled onto her mattress. Now it was time for her to snatch a few minutes of sleep. Her daughter usually lay quietly beside her. Georgia didn't know how an eleven-month-old understood that her mother needed to sleep, but she did and kept quiet while Georgia slept for a couple of hours.

Most days Georgia was so exhausted that she usually fell asleep as soon as her head hit the pillow, but today sleep didn't come even though her body was screaming for it. Now that she was home, now that she was finally away from anybody who might be able to read her thoughts, she let her mind wander to Lieutenant Howard.

Christian.

She had lied to herself when she'd said that her shift was routine. He'd asked her to kill him, and even though she was sure that he wasn't ready to die, his words had stayed with her the rest of the night. He'd stayed with her the rest of the night.

She had never met a man like him before. When she looked at him she felt all the air rush out of her lungs. It wasn't because he was enormous. Well, maybe that was part of it…or maybe because even in sleep, his face didn't relax.

She'd lied to him last night when she'd told him she wasn't afraid of him. She was terrified, but not because she thought he was going to hurt her. The moment he'd opened his eyes and looked at her she'd known that he wouldn't. She was afraid because she found herself drawn to him. Almost attracted to him. She hadn't been attracted to any man since she'd gotten pregnant. In fact, she avoided them.

But there was something about Christian. Something that made her wonder what it would feel like to climb in his lap and be held by him. To have those big hands stroke down her back. To make her feel something entirely different than she'd ever felt before.

She knew it was insane to think about him that way. He was a patient and he was injured. And she knew that being alone all this time was getting to her a little. She was missing her family even though she was mad at them, even though they'd turned their backs on her—they weren't all bad.

Her upbringing had been strict, but she'd enjoyed her siblings' company. And her mother had been sweet and gentle. Too docile to ever go against anything her father said.

"Ma?" Abby placed her chubby hand on Georgia's cheek and looked up at her.

"Yes, baby?"

Abby snuggled closer to her beneath the blanket, prompting Georgia to wrap her arms around her. It was as if she was reminding her to not think about them, to shut off her thoughts and use the precious little free time she had and go to sleep. She kissed Abby's dark curls and pulled her closer. Within moments they were both asleep.

★ ★ ★

Somebody was hovering over him as he slept. Years of training told Christian to stay calm, to strike when they least expected it. His hand itched to grab the neck of whoever was above him. He moved his left arm slightly, ready to defend himself, but when he felt the stiffness, the tight numbness in his fingers, he remembered where he was. Then the rest of his senses returned to him.

He could smell himself, a mixture of medicated salves and the musk due to not properly bathing in weeks. He could feel his hair brushing his forehead. He was so used to having it shaved that the feeling was foreign to him. He could hear his surroundings—beeping sounds from monitors in another room, the murmur of voices, the sounds of the place doing business as usual.

He was in Jericho Medical. Still. His fourth day. He had never been laid up for so long. But then again he had never been a prisoner in his own body.

He relaxed his hand and took his time opening his eyes. He could tell by the light on his face that it was daytime. That if he opened his eyes he wouldn't see Georgia. The night nurse.

After the first night he'd made a point to be as unobtrusive as possible. To get her to leave as soon as possible. To avoid her comforting touch. He was drawn to the woman and he wasn't sure why. She wasn't his type. She wasn't even the prettiest nurse in the hospital, but he looked forward to seeing her walk through his door every night.

So did the rest of the men on the floor. She wasn't flirtatious or overly friendly. She wasn't outwardly sexy. Most nights she wore prim cardigans over her scrubs. She never wore makeup, always had her hair ruthlessly pulled back. But maybe that was why they were all so drawn to her. The mystery. The curiosity of what it would be like to peel back all the layers of the sweet Miss Georgia and see what was on the inside.

He finally opened his eyes, surprised to see General Daniel Lee standing above him. The general was the only stable person in his life since he had joined the marines. For some reason he took a special interest in Christian. It was he who prompted Christian to want to rise through the ranks in the corps.

"Sir." Christian tried to sit up, but his ribs protested and his skin screamed out for him to stop.

"For Christ sake, Howard. At ease," General Daniel Lee barked at him. "You're half blown up. I think that gives you an excuse not to salute me."

"Yes, sir." He collapsed back on the bed, hating that sitting up was nearly impossible for him.

"I was wondering how long it was going to take for you to either kill me or open your eyes."

"Sir?"

"I saw your hand move. You were going to grab my neck and crush my windpipe."

There was no use in denying it. The general knew him too well. "I would have stopped the moment I saw it was you."

The general raised an approving brow. "Glad to see that even though you had the shit blown out of you, your training stayed with you."

"You trained me. If I hadn't attempted to kill you, I think you would be disappointed in me."

"I would. How are you feeling, son? You look like hell, but how do you feel?"

"Considering most of my unit is dead…like shit, sir."

"It wasn't your fault, Howard. You know that. There was nothing you could have done to save them. You are not to blame yourself. That is an order."

He looked away from his mentor. "Yes, sir."

"You don't have to call me *sir* anymore. Call me Dan." He sank his big body into the chair beside Christian's bed.

Christian wasn't sure he heard right. Nobody ever called the man by his first name. They hadn't dared. With the face of a bulldog and the temperament of a pit bull, he was the only person Christian had ever truly been afraid of. "I must be dying."

The general took off his hat and tossed it on the table. "Yes, you are, but I figure you got another fifty years left before you drop dead. I'm retiring, Christian. I'll be a civilian by the end of the month."

He sat back and let Christian process that for a minute. General Lee was retiring. It didn't seem possible. Christian thought the man was just like him. Thought the military was his world. Thought the man would die as a marine. "Why?"

"You almost died, son."

Of all of the things he could have said, that was the very last thing Christian expected. "I should have. I was their leader. I should have been the last man to come back alive."

The general rubbed his massive hand over his face, looking every bit of his nearly seventy-four years. "I've been a marine for over fifty years, enlisted right after my eighteenth birthday. I've seen a lot of men come and go. I've seen a lot of boys die. When you join, you go in knowing that you could die for your country. You know that the people you are friends with could die. You tell yourself you are going be detached, that when your friends die you're going to chalk it up to being a part of war. But that never happens. I was in Vietnam when I saw my best friend step on a landmine and die right before my eyes. I cried like a baby. That stayed with me. Every man that I saw die stayed with me. Every mother I had to send my condolences to stays with me."

Christian closed his eyes, but what he really wanted to do was cover his ears. This was General Lee he was speaking to. The man was a machine. If he was affected by it, then what chance did the rest of them have? "Why are telling me this?"

"Because when you got hurt, Christian, I—I was more… shaken than I ever expected to be."

Christian blinked at the man, unsure of how to respond to that.

"You know I've kept special track of you since you came under my command. You've been a model marine. You never screwed the local girls, you never got drunk or broke curfew. You've done everything right."

"That's not true, sir. I've made mistakes." He made one big one that he wasn't sure that even God could forgive him for.

"Not yet, son. But if you go back you will."

"You think they'll clear me to go back to active duty?"

"Don't know. But the fact that you want to after this worries me. You lost nearly your entire unit. You think going back is going to make you forget that?"

Nothing could make him forget that, but being a marine was all he'd ever known. If he didn't have that then he had nothing.

"I'm married," General Lee told him. "To one of those peace-loving hippie girls. Alma's her name. We met when she was protesting in D.C. She threw a can at my head, and when I turned around to let her have it I saw this beautiful, lanky redhead. It took six whole days to convince her to marry me." He smiled softly. It was the first time Christian had ever seen him do so. "And if we don't talk about politics we get along great. We have two daughters. I've spent most of their lives away. I've missed things. Big things, like first steps and proms. You don't have to miss those things."

"But I don't have a family."

"You can get one. Military life is hard on a family. I know about your background. You don't need the marines to support a family. You can do it the traditional way."

"The nurses can't even stand to look at me. What makes you think finding somebody to marry me is going to be easy?"

"You were a big ugly son of a bitch before and you're a big ugly son of a bitch now. You'll be fine."

He wasn't so sure about that. He never thought about having a family. It wasn't something that appealed to him. His parents were gone. The guys who he thought had his back turned out to be a bunch of drunken brutes. It was just better if he relied on himself. If the marines cleared him to go back, he would. There was no other option.

"Is that why you came here? To give me some advice?"

The general shook his head. "I know I'm not your father but I...I... It's..." He shook his head, flustered, and Christian watched in amazement as the man who always seemed so sure of himself seemed lost. "I don't want you to be one of those boys that doesn't come back. I don't want to attend your funeral." He got up and paced away from him. "I don't want you to go back. I like you, damn it. You satisfied?" He pinched the bridge of his nose. "I sound like a fucking pansy. I can't believe I'm actually saying this to you."

"You've grown sentimental in your old age, Dan. Now why don't you come over here, tuck me in and give me a kiss good-night," Christian joked, but General Lee's words hit him in the chest in a funny sort of way and he wasn't sure how to handle them.

CHAPTER 4

"You look like you're going to collapse."

Georgia stopped in her tracks besides Lieutenant Howard's bed and blinked at him, trying to figure out if she had heard him correctly. He was staring at her. His eyes swept across her face, seemingly taking in all her features.

The urge to turn her face away was overwhelming, but she kept her eyes locked with his because for the first time since he had been there, he had spoken to her first.

The man had barely said two words to her, though he was never rude. She could tell he had been raised right, or the military had beaten manners into him. He must have been the strong, silent type. She wasn't used to men like him. Her father always had endless words to say. Advice to give. Sermons to speak even at the dinner table. But Christian never spoke a word to her that wasn't necessary. She wondered what he was saving them up for.

She should be relieved that he didn't want to talk. Five nights she had treated him, and her reaction to him was the same every time she walked into his room. Fear mixed with excitement. The kind of feeling you get the night before school starts. There were other feelings, too, but she couldn't label them. She wouldn't let herself. But whatever this odd thing she felt for him was, she didn't want it to get any stronger. It was best that she kept her distance.

"I look like I'm going to collapse?" she said when she finally found her words. "Is that code for I look horrible, soldier? My, my—I can't imagine why you're single. With sweet talk like that you're sure to charm the pants off any girl in the county."

One corner of his mouth twitched, and if she didn't know any better she would have thought he almost smiled. And that made Georgia wonder what his lips would look like curled into a full smile.

All the other patients smiled at her. They teased her. They did what they could to get her to stay longer. And she knew it wasn't because of her, but to ease some of the loneliness and boredom of being stuck in the hospital for months.

Christian wasn't like that. It was almost as if he'd rather be alone. But nobody really wanted to be alone. It might be his higher rank, she thought, searching for a reason. Maybe his elevated position made it hard for him to interact with others. Or maybe he just didn't like her.

Or maybe you're just an overthinking idiot. Quit being so sensitive. He's probably just tired.

She had taken to checking on him last, making sure that every other patient was settled, even seeing some of them twice before she walked into his room. She wasn't avoiding him on purpose, she told herself. She wasn't putting off that little rush of feelings when she saw him. No, it was just that he was the most injured man on the floor. At the beginning stages of healing. His care would take more time than the other patients. And that meant she didn't get to his room until well past midnight.

He was always awake when she got there. In the back of her mind she always hoped he'd be asleep. It made her wonder if he was a night owl.

She wanted to ask the day-shift nurses about him. She wanted to know if he was different with them. If any of the other men visited him. If he seemed any happier than he did at night. If he had any family. Where he came from. Where he was going to. But she didn't ask. She didn't want anybody to know that she thought about this soldier more than she should.

"Your accent… Where are you from?" He turned the full power of his intense eyes on her, his gaze stopping on her mouth.

"Oakdale, South Carolina," she said, trying to keep the breathlessness out of her voice. "And don't try to change the subject, mister. You just called me ugly."

He stiffened. "I didn't, ma'am. You're not… I meant…" He shook his head. "You look extremely tired. I didn't mean any offense. I apologize."

She had flustered him, and it made her feel a little guilty. No wonder he didn't like her. "I was teasing," she said, giving him a little smile. "I guess I never learned my lesson as a kid. I used to send my father into fits because I never knew when to keep my mouth closed. You know I once told a deacon at my church that if he donated half the money he spent on belt buckles to the needy there would be no homelessness in the South. You can't imagine the kind of trouble that got me into."

Why couldn't she just shut up? She should do her job and get out of there like every other night. He made her nervous, but part of her wanted to get a little bit more out of him. Maybe if her curiosity was satisfied, she wouldn't spend so much time wondering about him.

"How are you feeling tonight?" She did her routine check of all his vitals. "How's your pain on a scale from one to ten?"

"About a four."

"Hmm. A four tonight? That means it must be a nine. The bigger you marines are the more macho you get." She handed him the medication he always refused. "Take these. And don't tell me no."

For once he reached out and took them from her. She couldn't help but notice how his face tightened as he moved his body. But he never complained. She didn't know if she admired him for it or thought he was plain stupid.

"If you're in pain, Christian, you need to call me. You don't have to suffer needlessly."

"Maybe I do," he said after he swallowed the pills. "What's that saying? Pain is just weakness leaving the body."

"That's ridiculous. Are you telling me that reason you are willing to suffer is because pain makes you stronger?"

His eyes shuttered but he nodded. "I'm in this pain because I was defending my country. There's no better reason than that."

"Well, you defended it and you survived," she snapped. "I still don't see the reason you have to suffer when I can help."

"Pain makes you grateful for all the times you didn't feel any. It makes you stronger."

She shook her head, his words striking a chord in her. "This must be one mighty grateful, mighty strong ward, then. Because there's about twenty boys on this floor who are suffering. They should be down on their knees thanking the good Lord because they are blind now, or legless or paralyzed. They are supposed to be grateful for those long nineteen years of good health? That they at least escaped childhood with their bodies intact? Damn it, Christian, their lives are drastically changed all because they went off to fight some war they don't even know why they are fighting. And you are telling me that they have something to be grateful for?"

"It's their job. It's my job. It's my life."

"Well, your life is stupid! Everybody is not like you. They are not as cold or as tough. Some of them can't handle the pain. Do you know how many servicemen turn to drugs after they leave here? Or alcohol? There's a suicide hotline for them that gets over three hundred calls a day. You can't tell me that pain is good. That this war is good. I won't believe it. I haven't seen one benefit from it yet."

She stared at his expressionless face for a long time, her chest heaving. It dawned on her how stupidly she'd just behaved. Of course he would defend it. His life's work. That was what soldiers did.

She turned away from him, covering her burning face with her hands. "You have to forgive me. My mouth always gets me in trouble. No wonder why my father kept telling me I should be seen and not heard. I never know my place."

He reached out and grabbed her arm. She shut her eyes for a moment, noting how cold his hand was. That this was another thing he suffered silently.

"Look at me," he barked at her. She turned slowly, seeing that he was sitting all the way up. His face was tightly drawn with pain; his brow glistened with sweat.

"Lie down," she cried. One more thing to be added to her guilty conscience. She was supposed to soothe him, not cause him more pain. She was ashamed of herself. "Please, Christian."

"Shut up! Your place with me—" he bored his eyes into hers "—is to say whatever you think. Don't you ever apologize to me for telling me what is on your mind. Do you understand?"

The burned side of his face twisted horribly, making

him look like a beast. She should be scared. He had her arm clamped tightly in his hand, the pressure uncomfortable. She hated being trapped. She hated feeling as if she couldn't get out, but for some reason she didn't feel that way with him.

"Answer me. Do you understand?"

"Yes. Yes! Please lie down. You're hurting yourself."

He looked at her for a long moment, his face still twisted in agony, his green eyes glowing with anger.

"I'm sorry." She didn't know what made her do it, but she stepped closer and smoothed a kiss across his forehead. She kept her lips there. "Please," she chanted into his skin. "Please lie down. Please. Please. Please."

It took a moment for him to comply, but when he did a cry of relief escaped her.

She left his bedside for a moment to get another blanket from the closet and covered him with it. His eyes never left her face as she wiped his brow and smoothed his growing hair away from his face.

He finally shut his eyes, and she stayed a few more minutes to make sure he was soothed. When his breathing evened and his huge body finally relaxed, she stepped away.

"Good night, Georgia," she heard him say just as she was about to leave his room.

"Good night, Christian."

Sweet little Georgia had a temper. Maybe *temper* wasn't the right word, Christian thought as he tried to shake off his encounter with her. She was passionate. And her passion was well hidden behind that sweet smile and good "Southern Miss" manners.

He hadn't minded her disagreeing with him over the war. He was used to that. He remembered how angry some people were when they first landed in Iraq, when servicemen, a lot of them kids, started dying. And even he sometimes couldn't find the words to defend why they went in. But he would always try to defend it. It was his job.

He was fascinated to see a spark ignite within her. Her whole face changed—away went that hauntingly tired expression. Her eyes lit up, her cheeks got color and he could barely process what she was saying because he was too busy looking at her. If she could get so heated just talking to him about pain then he wondered how she would be in bed. How she would feel with her thighs wrapped around him. How it would feel if she was uninhibited and hot and taking exactly what she wanted from him.

It was wrong to think about her that way, but he was in a hell of a lot of pain and stuck in the hospital until God knew when. And she was beautiful. With soft hands and a curvy figure that he could just make out under her loose-fitting scrubs. He was never a man prone to daydreams, but he decided tonight that he would let himself have that one little fantasy. It wasn't as if anything was going to come from it.

Before he was content to just get a little glimpse of her each night. He stayed up for arrival even when his body was begging for sleep. In the span of a few minutes everything had changed.

He hadn't meant to get angry with her. He hadn't meant to grab her again. But her words had shaken him.

I never know my place. I should be seen and not heard.

She had heard those words from her father. A world-class dickhead—Christian knew that without even knowing anything about the man. From those few words he realized that Georgia's true nature had been muffled. That the sometimes shy little thing had a lot more spice than even she knew. He wondered if she ever got to let herself free. Or if she was just waiting for the right man to show her how.

He definitely was not the man who was going to show her. But he wanted her to know that at least when she was with him she could speak freely, that she could be who she was without fear or condemnation.

As much as he liked seeing her sparked, he regretted what had happened between them tonight. She'd kissed him. Just on his forehead. Not in a sexual way, but sweetly, like a mother would kiss a child, and while it had soothed him, it had jolted him, too. It had made him realize how long he had gone without simple human touch. It had made him hungry for it.

Now, because of that simple little kiss, instead of just keeping his fantasies firmly in check he was going to have to keep the urge to pull her down, to kiss some of her sweetness out of her, ruthlessly under control.

Georgia walked into her apartment, Abby on her hip. For once she wasn't exhausted after her shift, which was odd for her. She had barely gotten any sleep yesterday. Abby refused to go down for her afternoon nap.

Maybe her blood was still humming from her encounter with Christian. She'd yelled at a patient. She'd let her opinions cloud her judgments. She'd upset him. She had done everything a nurse was not supposed to do. If her supervisor heard about it, she could be fired. But nobody knew about the heated words she had exchanged with Lieutenant Howard, because even though her blood was still heated when she'd left his room, the floor had been calm. All the other patients had been sleeping. The doctor on duty and orderly had been off somewhere probably trying to get some sleep.

The rest of her shift had been uneventful, but it went by in a blur. And now she was home, knowing that she should get some rest while she could, but she was too wired to do so. Instead, after feeding Abby, she went through the massive pile of unopened mail on her kitchen counter. Most of the letters were junk mail or bills, but one letter stuck out, because it was in a pink envelope and dressed with slanted feminine handwriting. Even after two years of not seeing her sister's handwriting, she would know it anywhere.

Last week Carolina had left a message on her machine. Georgia wasn't sure how she got her number, or why after all this time she had tracked her down, but instead of calling her back like she'd begged, Georgia had ignored the message.

Out of everybody, her sister's betrayal hurt the most. They were best friends. Carolina was the only person who knew what it was like to be one of Pastor Abraham Williams's daughters. Carolina had been the one she'd gone to after it had happened. She had been there with her when the results of her pregnancy tests had come clear. Carolina had held her while she cried. She'd promised that she would stand by Georgia's side. But it hadn't happened. Carolina had stood silent while their father cast her out.

Georgia stared at the letter for a long time, almost afraid to open it. But she took one look at her daughter and mustered up some strength. She had given birth alone, had spent nearly a month in the hospital with a sick baby. She had worked hard to get her own place, her own car, to carve out a life of her own. She had proved to herself long ago that she didn't need the help of her family.

It was okay to read the letter, she told herself. Because she knew that no matter what it said, she knew she would survive. She ripped open the envelope and unfolded the sheets of stationery that her sister was always so fond of writing on.

Out of it drifted five crisp one-hundred-dollar bills. Georgia stared at the money for a long time. She was shocked by the sight of it.

Where had Carolina gotten that kind of money?
She turned to the letter.

Dear Georgia,

I don't blame you for not returning my call. If I were you I would never speak to me again. What I did I can't even forgive myself for. I won't try to explain my actions away except to tell you that I was scared. I was never strong like you. I could never speak up. But I never once thought he was serious about making you leave. I thought that eventually he would believe you and ask you to come back, but he never did.

I don't want you to think that your absence has gone unfelt here. The town is not the same without you. The house is not the same. Mama is not the same. She misses you. I can see it in her face. It's killing her not to know how you are. Father banned her from speaking your name. He had us take your pictures down. She broke after that. She cried for days and hasn't been the same since. I don't tell you this to hurt you, but to let you know that even though she didn't do anything to stop him, she loves and misses you more than you could know.

I wanted to talk to you sooner, sister, but I couldn't. He barely let me out of his sight after what happened to you. But I'm not under his control anymore. I married Miles Hammond, that young dentist who came to town just before you left. He made me come in for more cleanings than a person should have in a lifetime, but that was the only way he could see me. He's a good man. He treats me kindly and encourages me to do what I want to do. I wanted to talk to my sister. He hired a man to find you.

We don't live in Oakdale anymore. We moved to
Southington to a big house with plenty of space. He
says you can come stay with us for as long as you want.
For forever if that's what I want. I do want that. I want
to see you again. I want to see my niece. But I can understand if you don't want to see me. Just let me know if
you are okay or if you need anything. I sent some money.
I know how you are. I know you have too much pride
to accept it, but please do. Please buy Abby something
nice and maybe something for yourself.

I want to hear from you. And if you can, please send
me a picture of my niece. I'm going to be a mama in
a few months and I want to show my baby its cousin.
Please, Georgia, don't let this letter go unanswered. I'm
starting a new life and I don't want it to be without you
in it.

Love you always,
Carolina

Georgia's head spun for a long time after she put the letter
down. Her sister wanted to see her again. She missed Carolina. There was so much she wanted to say, so much in that
letter she wanted to respond to, but the thoughts were too
big to put into words. Maybe she just wasn't ready yet—one
letter and five hundred dollars wouldn't magically cure all
the pain that lay just beneath the surface. It wouldn't make
her forget the past.

But even though she wasn't willing to make that big step,
she could make a small one. She would keep her sister's money.
For Abby's sake. Georgia had started a college fund for her
the day she got out of the hospital. Some weeks it was hard
to put money in there when there were so many other bills
to be paid but she did so religiously. Her daughter deserved

a good life. Despite the circumstances under which she was born, she still deserved the world.

Before Georgia could change her mind, she pulled one of Abby's photos out of an album, wrote *I love you* on the back of it and mailed it to her sister.

There would be a day she was ready to see her sister again, but it wouldn't be soon.

"Good morning, Lieutenant," a slender blond-haired nurse greeted him as she walked into his room.

"Morning," he returned, waiting for the nurse to look at his face. She didn't. She looked at his hairline, below his neck to his chest, but her eyes never once touched his face or even attempted to. He hadn't seen how bad his scars were, but every time somebody avoided eye contact with them he felt how disfigured he must be. Still, this woman was a nurse. A professional. She should be able to look at his face.

"I'm going to check your graft," she said quietly.

She was so unlike Georgia, even unlike some of the other nurses who asked him how he was feeling or at least pretended they cared how he was.

He expected better. He spoke again, setting his eyes on her face. "The doctor said that after the dressing comes off I still won't be able to stretch my arm for another three to four weeks."

She nodded, staring at his arm. "That's right."

"He also said I might need physical or occupational therapy to regain full strength in my arm."

Look at me. Look at me!

"It's possible." Her hands started to move quickly, but her eyes never strayed away from her task. She wasn't as gentle as some of the other nurses. Again his mind traveled back to

Georgia and her sweet hands and the smile she always man-aged to produce for him.

He knew what this nurse wanted. To get away from him as quickly as possible. Apparently, Jericho Medical's motto—We Treat Patients Like Family—didn't apply to him.

But he wouldn't accept that. "Can you explain to me ex-actly what occupational therapy might entail?"

"I can have someone explain it to you later." She moved her hand to re-cover his wound, but she had moved too fast, causing her hand to slip and slam into the rawest part of his arm. Searing pain shot up his arm and all the way to his neck, causing his body to spasm involuntarily.

"Shit." He gritted his teeth as waves and waves of pain traveled through his body.

"I'm sorry!" For the first time she looked at his face.

But it was too late for that. She had expected him to act like a beast. Now he would act like one. "Get the fuck out of my room."

She gasped, but he didn't care. He had been stuck in this godforsaken hospital for two weeks with no word of how long he was going to be there or if he was ever going to be able to go back to active duty. He was sick of it. Sick of the people not looking at his face. Sick of the shitty food and the drafty room. Sick of being sick.

"Lieutenant Howard, I need to finish."

He picked up his dinner tray and flung it at the wall. "You are finished. Get out of my room and don't come back."

She stared at him, unable to move.

"Now!" he roared, and she scampered out like a scared little rabbit.

He had never yelled at a woman before, but he wouldn't allow himself to feel guilty about it. If she didn't want to be around him, he didn't want her around.

A few moments later, people rushed his room. Three orderlies, two doctors and the nurses' supervisor. All prepared to subdue him.

Glenda Chestnut took over his care. By her demeanor he could tell she was the head nurse. She had no problem looking him in the face, but her touch lacked any warmth at all. He was mildly surprised that a woman so dour could have such a happy-sounding name.

"Nurse Paul apologizes for hurting you, Lieutenant. I will make sure it does not happen again."

"I don't want her back in here. I don't want anybody who can't look me in the damn face in here. I got blown to hell for this country and she won't even look me in the eye. She shouldn't be working here."

"I see," Nurse Chestnut said. "I will handle this immediately."

"Good. Now all of you get out. I don't want to be bothered."

They all stared at him, unmoving.

"Go!"

Once he was alone, Christian placed his uninjured arm over his eyes and went to sleep.

It only seemed like thirty seconds later before someone else was hovering over him. This time he didn't forget where he was. He knew it was her without even seeing her. He could smell her. Baby powder, sugar and something sensual he couldn't name.

He opened his eyes to see Georgia standing over him. Her pretty little face twisted into a frown.

"What do you have to say for yourself, mister? You caused one hell of a racket today."

"Where were you?" he demanded, ignoring her question. She had been gone for three days and he hadn't realized how much he had come to depend on seeing her until she didn't show up. She was the only perk of being stuck there.

She raised a brow at him. "Did you miss me?"

"Yes," he said without thinking. For a moment he wished he could take it back, but she smiled and her cheeks turned pink and his embarrassing honesty suddenly became worth it.

Christian never ceased to surprise her. Only a few hours ago he'd been throwing around hospital trays and cursing at nurses and now he was telling her he missed her. The little rush of pleasure she got out of his words was undeniable. And truth be told, she'd thought about him, too, while she was off.

Even though she had ordered herself not to, he snuck inside of her head at the most inconvenient times.

Like when she was alone in bed.

"I was off. Do you expect me to work seven days a week?"

"Yes. If I have to be here, so should you." He sounded like a petulant three-year-old. She wanted to take him in her lap and soothe him. She silently laughed at the image that popped into her mind. Him in her lap. She wouldn't survive it.

"You, sir, are a very cranky bear tonight. I'm almost tempted not to give you the present I bought for you." She moved around the foot of the bed and uncovered his feet. They were quite lovely for enormous man feet, smooth with neatly kept toenails, no hair to been seen. She absently stroked the soles of them with the back of her fingers. "You caused a lot of turmoil around here. Half the nurses refuse to come into your room now. But I can't blame you too much for kicking Alice out of your room. The woman has the personality of a dead fish."

He looked up at her, surprised, and for a moment she thought her big mouth had once again got her in trouble. But it wasn't that, she realized. She was touching him. More than touching him. She was stroking his feet, running her fingernails gently up and down his soles. She didn't want to stop even though she knew she should, so she ignored the questioning look he gave her look and stomped down the feeling that she might be doing something wrong.

His was feet were icy cold and she was just doing her job. She was bringing him comfort.

She stopped stroking only to take one of his feet in her hands to rub it. She had never touched a man's feet before. She never touched a man in any way that wasn't medical. But with Christian… He was different from the others. They had families to bring them comfort. To love them and touch them. The only person who came to visit him was his former commanding officer. He needed a little more than just rest.

That explained it, Georgia reassured herself. She was doing a good deed for a good man.

And when Christian closed his eyes and exhaled, she knew what she was doing was more than a good deed. It brought him pleasure. There was so little pleasure to be found in the hospital. To be found in life. And if she could give it to somebody, she didn't want to stop. She wanted to make this man feel good. She wondered what it would be like to touch her lips to the tips of his toes. She wondered how he would respond if her lips traveled farther than that. To his ankles, up his shins, to those powerful muscled thighs.

A shiver ran through her. Her nipples tightened. A slight throb settled between her legs. It was then that she dropped his foot.

Those thoughts were wrong. No, they weren't. It had taken her a long time to realize sex wasn't wrong, that thinking about it, that wanting to have it, wasn't wrong.

What was wrong was thinking about Christian that way. Yes, he was a man who was beautiful and strong and made her feel unlike any other man had before, but he was a patient and she was a nurse. This had to stop. These strange feelings for him had to stop.

They locked eyes for a heated moment and something she couldn't name passed between him. Her feelings didn't disappear like she had wanted them to. Looking into his intensely green eyes somehow made the emotions even stronger.

"My present," he said gruffly. His eyes settled on her mouth then traveled down her body before returning to her eyes.

"Oh, yes. Socks," she squeaked, her heart racing as she fumbled in her pocket for his gift. "I know how cold your feet get. This hospital's air conditioning is colder than the Arctic. These are the good kind. They are insulated." She quickly put them on his feet and continued to babble nervously. "I had to go to the army/navy store to get them. I checked two other stores before that but they looked at me as if I was crazy when I asked for thermal socks for a man with a size-fourteen foot. I even wasn't sure they would fit because your feet are so huge, but they do. I bet your mama was glad when you finally stopped growing. I'm not sure where they found you clothes."

She found herself running her hands over his now-covered feet. This time she wasn't sure if she was doing it to soothe him or herself. She forced herself to stop, and when she knew merely stopping wouldn't be enough, she stepped completely away from him.

"Thank you. That feels better."

Why did he have to look at her that way? As though he could see inside her.

Her cheeks burned. "You're welcome, Jarhead." She tried to inject some lightness into her voice. "Now that your feet are warm, there is no reason you should be so cranky."

"She wouldn't look at me, Georgia," he said, and the raw

pain in his voice shook her. "I know it's bad, but I deserve to be looked in the eye."

He didn't look so bad. At least not to her, but she knew how he felt. When she'd told her family she was pregnant they wouldn't look her in the eye. Her father and her brothers had treated her as though she was soiled. They'd made her feel unworthy.

"You deserve more than that, Christian." She wanted to wrap her arms around him and soothe his hurt away. Maybe the world thought that because he looked so big and fierce that he didn't have feelings like everybody else.

The world was wrong.

She took another step away from him, afraid that if she got any closer she wouldn't be strong enough to walk away.

"I have to go now."

He nodded. "Will I see you tomorrow?"

"Of course you will."

CHAPTER 5

Her skin was softer than he had imagined. He kept sliding his hands over her bare thighs, up and down, over and over, just because he couldn't get enough of the feel of her.

She lay waiting on the bed beneath him. Naked. Open to him. Not tense at all. Not nervous or in a hurry like some of the other women he took to bed. Instead she lay quietly with a small smile playing on her pouty mouth, her arms opened to him. She knew they had all night, had forever if that was as long as it took. He leaned down and kissed his way across her collarbone.

She gave a soft little laugh and breathed his name in that husky Southern accent of hers. His cock hardened, grew to epic proportions, and it made the struggle to stay outside of her, to prolong their lovemaking, that much harder. But he wanted to taste all of her tonight, every inch of the sweet skin that he had fantasized about for weeks. He took her nipple in his mouth, suckling her. She sighed and moaned his name.

Even her moans were pretty.

Her gentle hands touched him everywhere. They pulled

him closer. They held him to her. She wanted him and the knowledge of that made him want to shout from the rooftops.

"No more," she told him. "I'm ready."

He wasn't. He wasn't ready to stop kissing her curvy little body that had distracted him for so long. He peppered kisses down her stomach. He licked around her belly button, gave her little loving bites on the skin around her hips.

She laughed again. She was the only woman in the world who could be playful with him, who could laugh with him. Who wanted him just as he was.

He moved between her legs to enter her. She was ready for him, so wet he could feel it as soon as he touched himself to her lips.

Crash.

"Oh, shit, man. I mean, Lieutenant. I mean, sorry."

Christian's eyes popped open. He would joyfully murder whoever it was that had interrupted the best damn dream he ever had.

After Georgia had left him last night, he couldn't stop thinking about her. He always thought about her, but yesterday something had passed between them. Something more than he expected. She'd touched him, willingly, not because she was trying to make him feel better after what had happened, but because she'd wanted to. It was almost as though she couldn't help herself.

The rational side of him knew that she was just being sweet. To not think of her actions in any other way, but his brain and his body were telling him otherwise. Now seeing her would be the best and worst part of his day because he knew that from now on every time she left him she would leave him wanting her.

"What the hell did I bump into?" his visitor asked, rubbing his hip. He had gauze wrapped around his head and dark sunglasses covering his eyes. "Hey! Is anybody here or am I going through all this shit for nothing?"

"I'm here," Christian said. The kid, he couldn't be more than twenty, was feeling his way along the wall. He was one of the ones Georgia had talked about. The war had cost him his vision. "There's a chair to your left about six steps over. Watch out for the monitor. It's on your right side, three steps ahead of you."

"Thanks, sir." The boy breathed out a sigh of relief. "Getting used to this being-blind thing sucks."

"I can imagine." All of Christian's anger had melted away the moment he realized the boy couldn't see. "Who are you, soldier?"

He grinned and saluted. "I'm Lance Corporal Tobias Clark at your service. Although I guess I ain't gonna be a lance corporal anymore. They don't let blind men serve in the marines, do they?"

"I'm afraid not, son. I'm guessing they don't let burned and broken ones serve, either." The doctors were avoiding his questions. With each passing day Christian was losing hope he would ever return to duty.

"I'm not so sure about that, sir. You're a legend."

Christian shook his head. "You must have me mistaken with somebody else."

"Nope. They tell tall tales about you. Christian Austin Howard. The seven-foot-tall marine with three first names, fists the size of hams and the meanest face God ever created."

"I'm nowhere near seven feet tall," he said quietly. He was a full six inches away from it, but the rest wasn't too far off.

"They say you made every man who served under you cry."

"That's not true." It hadn't been all of them. He demanded excellence, and when he didn't get it there was hell to pay.

"They say you tried to pull every man in your unit away

from the wreckage after the rocket attack and that you refused to get treated until they saw to everybody else first."

That part he couldn't dispute, because he didn't remember anything that had happened the day of the blast. Only the spotty images he sometimes saw in his dreams. One doctor said that he couldn't remember due to a blow to his head. Another doctor said that he didn't remember because he didn't want to, because his brain simply couldn't handle the trauma of seeing so many of his men die.

"I couldn't tell you about that. I don't remember what happened."

"I believe it, sir. I knew you couldn't be as mean as they made you out to sound after hearing that. So what, you went all crazy on a nurse. I burned myself with a firecracker once and it hurt like a bitch for two weeks. I can't imagine how mean I might get if half my body was all burned up."

"Thank you, Tobias." There was something about this kid he liked immediately. He was open in a way that people never were with Christian. "How did it happen, son?" Christian made a motion toward his eyes that Tobias couldn't see.

"You mean the blind thing? On patrol in Baghdad," he said in a matter-of-fact tone. "Roadside bomb got me and a few civilians. I was in armor so my body was protected, but the damn blast burned my eyes."

"I'm sorry."

"Don't be. It's all a part of it, I guess. I'm actually kind of lucky. I can get out of bed. Word around here is that you can't yet."

"That's the thing about being seven feet tall—when you get hurt it takes more than one person to get you out of bed."

"How many does it take?"

"Ten."

Tobias chuckled. "Wish I could see that."

"What are you going to do now that you can't go back?" It was a question Christian had for himself.

"I don't know. I've been thinking about it. I'm only nineteen. Can't be sitting around for the rest of my life. Miss Georgia tells me that blind people can do the same jobs as everybody else, that I could go back to school and become whatever I wanted. But I never liked going to school. I wanted to join the marines the day I learned what one was."

"You talked to Georgia about it?" he asked, feeling a sinking little lurch in his belly. He knew that she was just being sweet to him, that he was no different than any other man on this floor, but a part of him wanted to be more to her than that. It was a foolish thought.

"Well, yeah." Tobias grinned. "I try to talk to her as much as I can. We all do. She's the best-looking nurse in the whole dang hospital. Or so I hear. But she's just real nice, you know? Them other nurses treat us as if we are just a part of their job. Miss Georgia cares. She got me some information on a Seeing Eye dog and she found a teacher that's gonna teach me Braille. She even called my mama and asked her to bring me my own pajamas just because she thought I needed a little bit of home."

"She's sweet."

"Yup, that's why her boss, Nurse Stick Up Her Ass, don't like her. Because we all do. She's always on her case. But Miss Georgia never does anything she's not supposed to. She would never risk her job. She's got her baby to feed."

"Baby?" Christian's head spun at that word. He had no idea that sweet little *young* Georgia was a mother. He'd never once heard her mention a child. But then again, they never talked about much of anything. He knew nothing about her.

"She's got a little girl, not even one year old yet. I'd bet she's a good mama, too. If she takes this good of care of us, imagine what she's like with somebody she loves."

"Tobias!"

He startled. "That's my mama looking for me. If you ever need anything, sir, some food that don't taste like dirt, an extra blanket, anything, you let me know. I'll have my mama bring it to you. I figure since we're neighbors we should be seeing each other from time to time."

"I don't get very many visitors. I would like that."

"Tobias!"

"Coming, Mama!" He stood up and felt his way along the wall. "It was nice talking to you, Lieutenant Howard. You helped me win a bet."

"What?"

"I bet Rivers that you were a decent man. He bet that I would leave here crying like a baby. It's nice to see that you didn't live up to all the hype."

"Mama, no!"

Abby woke up cranky from her nap. She had been fussy all evening. She wasn't sick. Georgia checked her temperature a half dozen times. She wasn't hungry. The child had more than enough to eat. She was just in one of those moods where she didn't want to be put down. And if Georgia had her way she would hold her until she settled. But she didn't have her way. If she didn't leave right now she was going to be late for work.

"Georgia, she'll be fine. Just give her here." Mrs. Sheppard held out her arms, but Georgia had a hard time handing her baby over.

"No." Abby buried her face in Georgia's neck and the working mother's guilt stabbed her a little harder.

"I have to go, baby cakes. Please be good for Mama and go to Mrs. Sheppard."

Abby gave her a mutinous look and shook her head. *No* was one word she had mastered quickly. There wouldn't be any reasoning with her today. As if there was ever any reasoning with an eleven-month-old.

"You make me feel horrible," she told her daughter. Stupid tears started to cloud her eyes. She never cried, but leaving her daughter, maintaining this life, was getting too hard. Sometimes she just wanted a break from it. Or somebody else to shoulder some of it. Just a little of it.

"That's the thing about being a mother," Mrs. Sheppard told her as she tugged the angry baby from her arms. "Your children will always make you feel horrible. If they don't, then that means you're not doing your job right. Now go on." She pushed her through the door. "You don't want to be late, and when you come back here to get her in the morning you are going to sit down and have pancakes and bacon with me. You hear?"

"Yes, ma'am."

Georgia tried not to glance at Abby as she turned away. She looked betrayed, as though she was two seconds away from breaking down, but there was nothing Georgia could do to fix it right now. Nothing besides stay. And she couldn't do that. In the end she did this all for Abby.

Her daughter's wails came just after Mrs. Sheppard shut the door. It took everything inside of her not to turn back. So she ran down the stairs to her car and cried all the way to work.

For the first time since he arrived at the hospital, Georgia didn't smile at him when she entered his room. Her eyes were a little red. She looked as if she barely had the energy to walk.

Christian sat up, ignoring the throbbing pain that traveled

through his ribs. If he could he would pick her up, carry her to the bed and tuck her in. Which was weird for him. It was an urge he'd never had with a woman before. When it came to beds and women, Christian didn't usually associate the two with sleeping, but Georgia looked so damned tired, and ever since he'd learned about her baby he wondered when she had the time to sleep at all.

Or more important, when she did sleep was she alone or was there a man there to keep her warm?

"What are you doing, Lieutenant Lunkhead? Lie back down."

He grasped her hand as soon as she got near and closed his fingers around her slender ones. She looked up at him with wide eyes, surprised by his move, but he didn't let go of her hand. "What's wrong? You were crying."

She nodded and gently rested her other hand on top of his. "That was hours ago. You shouldn't be able to tell."

He was able to tell because he spent so much time studying her face. He would know immediately if anything was different. "Did you get into a fight with your husband?"

He held his breath as he waited for her answer.

"I don't have one of those."

"Boyfriend?"

"Don't have one of those, either."

He exhaled. He didn't know why. It didn't make a damn bit of difference. Nothing was ever going to happen between them. "Then why were you crying?"

"My daughter," she admitted with a sigh. "Did I ever tell you about her? I have a baby girl named Abby, and she didn't want me to leave for work today. She never wants me to leave for work, but today she cried. I could hear her screaming all the way down the hallway. Every night I have to be here while somebody else puts my child to bed and it kills me. I'm not even the first person she sees when she wakes up in the morning. I work nights because we need the money. If I could change things, I would, but there doesn't seem to be any other way."

"What about her father? Doesn't he help out?"

Georgia stiffened at the question. "Abby doesn't have a father."

He should leave it at that. It was none of his business but something inside him needed to know more about her. "Do you have anybody to help you? What about your family?"

"No family, either." She shut her eyes for a moment as if she were in pain. "My next-door neighbor watches her overnight, but sometimes I worry. She never complains, but she's in her mid-sixties and retired. I wonder if leaving a fussy baby with her is the right thing to do." She shook her head. "Why am I telling you this?"

"I asked."

"Well, aren't you a nosy thing tonight? I'm a mess, Lieutenant Howard."

She absently ran the tips of her fingers across his knuckles for a moment. Damn her. Did she have any idea what her little absentminded touches did to him? If she ran her fingers over his knuckles and he felt it all over, what would they feel like running down his back, or his arms? What would they feel like on his naked chest? She looked into his eyes and seemed to read his mind because she blushed and pulled her hand beneath his.

"Get your big paw off me. I've got to check your grafts."

Since the incident with the tray, the other nurses wanted as little to do with him as possible. Georgia was the only one besides the doctor to touch him. She was the only one who didn't seem to mind.

"I'm a mess, Christian," she said as she worked. "A guilty-feeling, crying mess. I bet you would never let your life get so out of control. I bet you even put your clothes away in alphabetical order."

"Sit down, Georgia."

"What?" Her hands paused midaction.

"Sit. In that chair. Behind you." He knew when she was finished with her work she would walk out the door. But tonight, even though he knew he should let her go, he wanted her to stay.

Her eyes went wide again. "I'm not supposed to."

"Who's going to find out? I know you come to see me last."

She shook her head. "You're not supposed to know that."

"But I do. Everybody is sleeping. You can sit for a few minutes. You know you want to."

She looked unsure for a moment, but eased into the chair. "Why do I feel as if you are tempting me with forbidden fruit? You know I'm in a dangerous mood. I'm sleep-deprived and emotional. You could have a whole mess of trouble on your hands in a few minutes."

"I'll risk it. Just relax for a second. You look dead on your feet."

She shut her eyes and rested her cheek against her palm. "You're not supposed to be feeling sorry for me. You're the one who's bedridden in the hospital because you were defending my freedom. I've got my health, and my beautiful baby. I've got a roof over my head and a job. I have a lot more than most people. You shouldn't feel sorry for me." She yawned widely. "And I shouldn't feel sorry for myself."

And yet he did. She was a young woman, working a hard job and raising a baby on her own. He wondered what had happened to her family but knew it was wrong to ask. She had mentioned her father in passing a few times and not in the past tense. Where the hell was he now? How could he let his daughter struggle alone? And then there was her daughter's father. The bastard had left Georgia to raise a baby on her own. The man should be drawn and quartered.

"It's all right to complain sometimes, Georgia. You can't hold everything inside."

"You do," she countered without opening her eyes. "You don't complain at all. I know you must be mad about what happened. You're in pain. Your life will never be the same again and yet you never say a word about it."

He wasn't angry about what happened. In some ways he thought he deserved it, that this was his punishment for mistakes he'd made a long time ago. To make up for Miko. To make up for his parents, who had never gotten to see the man he became all due to his selfishness. "Marines don't complain."

A sleepy smile curved her lips. "Of course. Talk to me so I don't fall asleep, honey."

"About what?"

"Anything. Tell me a story. What's basic training really like?"

"You ever been to hell?"

She opened her eyes, and a combination of sleepiness and laughter played there. And he wondered what she would look like after he made love to her. Hopefully the same. Her face was the kind a man wanted to fall asleep staring at.

"Nope. Haven't been yet."

"Marine basic training is a little like that. Only not as hot."

She laughed and shut her eyes again. "Tell me more."

CHAPTER 6

The next day Georgia was feeling a little bit better. She tried not to think that her improved mood had anything to do with Christian. It couldn't have. Even though she'd spent nearly an hour in his room last night, he was just another patient.

No different from the rest of the men on her floor.

She needed to keep telling herself that. If she didn't, it could be dangerous. Her slight bump in happiness must have to do with how she'd started her morning. Mrs. Sheppard gave her a short stack of pancakes, four pieces of bacon and a big of cup of coffee with so much sugar and milk it made her teeth hurt. That much carbs, bacon and sugar would lift anybody's mood.

Plus Mrs. Sheppard had told her that Abby didn't sleep well the night before. Georgia wanted to feel bad about it but she couldn't, because her baby had taken a three-hour nap after breakfast, which meant Georgia got to sleep for three blissful hours in a row.

Feeling energized, she took her daughter to the park. Even if she didn't have any energy she would have made the trip.

It was important for Georgia to do as many things with her baby as possible.

Wednesday was the free day at the zoo. Fridays they went to the children's reading hour at the library. Some days they went down to the waterfront and fed old bread to the seagulls. And on weekends they went to the museum. It was a place that Georgia had never been allowed to go as a child. Her father, being a minister, was strictly against it. There were naked bodies there. Naked bodies performing acts of depravity. Or so he said.

When she was a teenager she had taken a book out of the library about Michelangelo's life. She had heard about the Sistine Chapel and was amazed by the amount of work it took to create such a masterpiece. She didn't see any lewd artwork. She only saw it as art, but when her father found the book, he got angry. He told her that looking at those pictures was a sin, that the only naked man a woman should see was her husband. And instead of making her return the book he threw it in the fireplace.

Her father wasn't always so radical. He used to be nicer. A friendly preacher who taught the word of God and welcomed everybody to church on Sunday. But that had all ended when her oldest brother, Abel, died when she was twelve. He had been murdered by his girlfriend's estranged husband.

She'd never known her brother well and she'd been too young to understand the circumstances around his death. Her parents had thought it was too sordid to explain to them, and maybe it was. But ever since then her father had become harsh. Strict. Even his sermons had changed. He no longer preached about love, but about sinners and repentance.

My daughters will not be the kind of women who lead men into temptation.

From that point on everything a normal teenage girl

thought or felt became a sin. They were barely allowed out of the house without an escort. They weren't allowed to watch TV, listen to the radio or see any movies. Georgia and Carolina were woefully ignorant about everything. And that had become clear when Georgia was finally allowed to attend college. It was a women's Christian college, but those girls knew a hell of a lot more about the world than she ever did.

She was not allowed to take up residence there. Only go to class and come back, but even then she relished her tiny bit of freedom. She stayed in the library as long as she could, looking at art books and studying classics. She was just trying to learn a little more about the world she was a part of. But while she did it she knew she was doing something her father disapproved of. She felt guilty then.

It took her nearly two months of counseling at the women's center to realize that what she had done wasn't wrong. It was normal to be curious about the world.

Now she made sure her daughter was exposed to as much as possible. She wouldn't have her feeling left out or less than others. And if she had questions about anything, Georgia would do her best to answer them. She wouldn't make her daughter feel guilty for wanting to live life.

"You want to go down the slide again, baby?"

"No!" she said, smiling. That was Abby's favorite word these days, and Georgia was never sure if she didn't really want something or she just liked saying it.

"No?" She took her daughter by the hand and led her to the bench. "Well, how about some juice, then? I brought some animal crackers, too."

"Oooo."

She placed Abby on her lap and cuddled her close while her daughter had her snack. She was so absorbed in watching her baby eat that she barely took note of the man sitting on the next bench.

"Conner!" He looked up from his laptop. "Please don't climb up the slide. I would like to make it through this week without a trip to the doctor."

Georgia spotted a little sandy-haired boy rushing up the slide as if he could outrun his father's order.

"I don't know why I'm surprised," he said to Georgia. "He's just like me when I was his age."

Georgia smiled and nodded and handed Abby another cracker.

"I think little boys are meant to get hurt sometimes, but my ex-wife will skin me alive if he comes back with even a scratch on him."

"You'd better go get him, then." She motioned toward the playground. "He's hanging upside down from the monkey bars by one leg."

"Connor!"

The man was off, and Georgia kissed Abby's shoulder. "Sometimes I'm really glad you're a girl, baby cakes."

Abby loved pretty sundresses and patent leather shoes, but even if she didn't, even if she wanted to play in the dirt, that would be okay. Whatever Abby wanted to do with herself would be okay.

The man came back slightly out of breath and stood before her. "That kid is going to be the death of me. Even when he was your daughter's age, he was running me ragged. How old is she anyway? About one?"

She nodded. "Her first birthday is next week."

"First birthdays are the best." He stepped closer and reached out to take Abby's hand. A tiny bit of panic seized Georgia. She had seen this man before. At this very park with his son. He seemed like a nice man. And they were in public, but for some reason, his nearness, his interaction with her daughter, made her breath come short. "What's your name, beautiful?"

"Her—her name is Abby," Georgia replied, forcing the words to come out.

"Hi, Abby." He looked up at Georgia. "I'm Rick. I've seen you here a few times, but we've never met."

"Georgia."

"Georgia." He smiled, showing off perfectly white teeth. "What a beautiful name."

"Thanks." She dug in her bag for baby wipes to clean Abby's hands and face. She needed something to do to distract her from his gaze.

"Are you named after somebody?" His face broke out into a mischievous grin. "Or is it something crazy, like you were conceived in the great state?"

He was hitting on her. The tips of her ears started to burn.

"My mother just liked the name, I guess."

She didn't get hit on very often, being homeschooled and going to an all-girls college. So when it did happen on the rare occasion, she didn't know how to handle it. Of course, the boys at the hospital flirted with her when she came to check on them, but that was nothing. Military men were the most respectful men she had encountered.

Rick was different, and not physically injured. And wasn't a bad-looking man. Most women would probably find him attractive, with his long, lean frame and dark hair, but Georgia could barely look past her anxious twitchy feeling to see that. Most men had that effect on her.

And then there was Christian, who was overpoweringly big, looked like a beast and tended to grab her when she least expected it. He had a totally different effect on her. He made her exceedingly uncomfortable, too, but not in the way Rick did. She should be scared of Christian. She shouldn't even be thinking about him now. Instead she should be flattered by Rick's attentions. She should want to get to know the nice man who seemed to enjoy spending time with his son at the park. But she didn't. She was royally screwed up.

"As you can tell, I'm no good at picking up women at the park." He grinned bashfully. "But there's something about you, Georgia, that captures my attention every time I see you. What do you say we get the kids together and get some ice cream?"

"I say…" *Say yes. It might be good for you. It's time for you to move on.* But she didn't say that. "Your son is standing on top of the swing set."

"Shit. Connor!"

He was off, and while his back was turned Georgia took her baby and went home.

"Okay, toss me another one."

Tobias held out his hands, waiting for Christian to throw him another object. They had been playing this game for the better part of a half hour. Tobias had somehow managed to make his way into Christian's daily routine, often spending hours in his room just talking or listening to baseball games on the radio. Christian wasn't the type of man who was easily impressed, but he had to admit he was amazed by Tobias. He was the type of soldier that he would have liked to have had in his unit in Iraq. The kid was good for morale. He always seemed so damn happy.

Christian never met somebody so damn accepting of his fate. He was nineteen years old and suddenly blind. Why the hell wasn't he mad? Or at least acting like a bratty teenager about it? But he took everything in stride. Christian wished he could feel the same way about his fate as Tobias.

"Ready?" He threw the item so it hit him square in the chest. "What do you think that is?"

Tobias rubbed his hands over it, then put it to his cheek for a feel before finally bringing it to his nose to smell. "Is it a plum?"

"It is. Good work, kid."

"Thanks." His grinned widely at the praise. "Throw me another, sir."

"Can't. Ran out of stuff." He had already thrown an empty water pitcher, a tube of toothpaste and the socks Georgia had given him that had been freshly laundered. Christian didn't have any other personal possessions.

"What you need is a mama. Mine brings me all types of stuff. My room is getting so full we're going to need a moving truck when I get out of here."

Christian thought back to his mother for a moment. He tried not to think about her often—the pain of her death, even after more than ten years, was still fresh. She would have brought him whatever he wanted. She would have made him chicken soup. She would have knitted him a sweater. She would have done anything.

As a kid, he'd never appreciated her mothering. He'd felt smothered by it. That was another thing he would change if he could go back in time. He would let her know how much he loved her. His dad, too. Joining the marines was the last thing his parents would have wanted him to do, but after he lost them there didn't seem like any other choice. But he didn't want to think about a past he couldn't change, so he turned the conversation back to Tobias instead.

"When are you leaving here?"

He shrugged. "Nobody's said for sure. They want to try one more surgery. A corneal transplant, but I don't know. Nothing's helped so far and they said this operation only has a thirty percent chance of working due to my type of injury. I'm not sure if I want to go through all of that for something that might not work."

"So you're going to give up on your eyesight?"

Tobias turned his head, his sightless sunglasses-covered eyes nearly connecting with Christian's. "Does it seem like I'm giving up, sir?"

He wasn't judging Tobias's choice. He just wanted to make sure he understood him. "Don't you want to see again?"

"You know I do." For the first time since they met, the boy's face grew stormy. "You know what's worse than not being able to see? Getting your hopes up that the next thing will work only to find that it only made things worse. I could see shadows before the last surgery. Now I can't. I can barely tell if it's day or night. What's the next thing that's going to happen? Total fucking darkness? And even if it does take, I have to be worried that my body's going to reject the transplant for the rest of my life, and where will I be then?"

"I don't know. But if it were me, I wouldn't give up until I knew there was nothing else left for me try."

"You think I'm a coward, don't you?"

"No, I—"

"I have to go." He got out of his chair a little quicker than he should have and knocked into Christian's nightstand, banging his hip. He didn't react. He just kept feeling his way along the wall until he was gone from Christian's sight.

Later that night, Georgia forced herself to sit at the nurses' station after seeing to her patients. She hadn't gone in to see Christian yet. She could have. She could have been in and out of there by now, because one of her patients had been discharged. But she made herself sit and complete her paperwork. She had the entire night to check on him.

Her shift was usually very quiet after she saw to all the men on her floor, and at times she often found herself scrounging for something to do.

There were other nurses in other wings there, too. They sometimes left the orderlies in charge while they congregated in the break room and gossiped about what was going on in the hospital. Georgia had joined them once, but she never felt as if she fit in. It must be another one of those drawbacks of growing up so isolated. She never had many girlfriends. There were the girls she used to go to church with, the children she would see in Sunday school, but as a child her best friend was her sister. Carolina was the only person she had really been able to speak to.

Ever since her letter showed up, Georgia had been missing her more and more almost to the point where it was painful. What would be the harm of talking to her sister? She could use a friend.

But just when she was about to break down and call her, some of the bitterness returned. The betrayal. She tried to pull up one of her father's old sermons about forgiveness but none came to mind. It must not be time yet.

Georgia threw down her pen. Paperwork wasn't enough to take her mind off her family. It was 12:15 a.m. The last of her patients seemed to have drifted off to sleep soon after eleven. Except for Christian. He never went to sleep until after she came. She didn't want to think that he waited up for her. But sometimes she would loop back around again and peek in his room one more time. She told herself it was just to check on him. Not to get one more glimpse of him. He was always asleep when she did. She wondered if the day would ever come when she walked into his room and he wouldn't be awake to greet her. So far that day hadn't come. And she was glad for it.

As soon as she walked into the room, his presence struck her. He had his bed in the upright position but she could barely see it behind his broad shoulders.

His massive hands rested on top of the thin blanket. Her eyes went to them before they settled on his face. She couldn't help but wonder how hands of that size would feel all over her body. Would they be tender? Would they feel rough and callused? Like the hands of the workingman she knew he was. Would his touch feel good? Could it be possible that under that huge, alarming exterior lay a gentle man? It had been nearly a month since they had met, but his bigness, his width, his underlying power, still affected her. Every time she saw him she felt dizzy.

Maybe it was because he waited for her. His tense features relaxed slightly when he spotted her. It was silly, but seeing that pleased her more than anything else had in a very long time.

"Hello, Lieutenant. How are you this evening?"

"You're late."

He frowned at her. Pouted at her, to be more accurate. And if Christian hadn't been over six and a half feet tall and the size of a linebacker, she would have said he resembled a pouting three-year-old child.

"I see you took your cranky pills this evening." She walked over to the foot of the bed and pulled the blankets from around his large feet. "What's the matter, sweets? Are you still cold?" She lightly ran her fingers over his socked feet. He wore the socks she'd given him. Another thing that pleased her more than it should. She'd made sure the hospital had provided him with more socks, but he never wore them. He had hers laundered so often she was afraid they were going to fall apart.

She absently stroked up the soles again, eliciting a little

moan from Christian. She barely heard it. She had set some of the money her sister gave her aside just for herself. But there was nothing she wanted. Maybe she would get Christian another pair of socks. Or some pajamas. Something that would bring him a little comfort.

Unlike all the other soldiers, no family ever came to visit. He had no love to get him through this. No support. If she could provide a little to him, it would help her sleep better.

"I can get you another blanket or bring you a cup of coffee. It won't even be hospital coffee. We got one of those fancy machines in the break room. You strike me as a man who would enjoy a good strong cup of light and sweet French vanilla roast."

The corners of his mouth curled into a slight smile. "I don't drink coffee."

"Hot chocolate, then? I could scrounge up some of those little marshmallows for you."

"I'm not cold, Georgia."

She re-covered his feet and went to his side to check on his wounds. "You're healing nicely. Are you in pain? Is that what's bothering you? You know I could get you something for it. Why didn't you call me?"

"I'm fine."

"Oh?" She knew he wasn't. She could tell by how stiff he held himself tonight. To the world he might appear emotionless, but she could see he was upset about something. Maybe it was the mother in her, but she wanted to make it better. "I bought you another present. I know you haven't been able to see yourself yet. So I went and spent a whole ninety-nine cents of my own money and got you this here hand mirror." She slipped the small folding mirror out of her pocket and handed it to him. "I'm sorry it's pink, but they didn't have any in camouflage."

He seemed hesitant to take it, and she understood why. This was a big moment for him. He hadn't seen his new face yet. She couldn't imagine how hard it must be to know you were never again going to be who you once were.

"Do you want to do this alone?"

He shook his head and took it from her. He just held it for a minute, his eyes closed as if he was bracing himself.

"Go on, honey."

He lifted the mirror and stared, his expression never changing. How could he do that? How could it be possible for him to give no sign of what he was thinking? She held her breath and watched him, waiting for some sign of emotion.

"My hair is long," he said, frowning.

She exhaled. How typical of a marine to be worried over the length of his hair.

"I kind of like it like this."

She ran her fingers through his thick, dark golden curls. It was softer than she expected. She studied the locks, noting how each individual strand was a different color. His hair was beautiful. It felt good beneath her fingers.

"You don't know how many women would kill for hair like this. They pay hundreds of dollars just to try to get this color."

"I guess I should keep it like this, then," he said, grimacing. "It seems I don't have much of an ear anymore—maybe this will cover it."

She touched the ear he was referring to, tracing what was left of the shell. It wouldn't be noticeable at all beneath his hair. In fact, none of his burns were that noticeable to her. "It's not so bad." She stared at him as he stared at himself. "What do you think?"

"It's terrible, but I guess I was imagining worse. You know that scene from that Indiana Jones movie, *Raiders of the Lost Ark,* where the guy's face melts off?"

"No. I've never seen that movie, honey, but tell me any-way." She stroked the backs her fingers down his cheek. The skin was leathery but still soft, and for a few minutes she marveled at the texture against her skin.

"I guess I thought I would be a man without a face. Just bone and blood."

"Can't you feel your skin?" She traced her fingers along his jawline. He may not feel it, but he was lucky. She had seen worse burns. She had seen men die from them. Christian's burns were oddly beautiful.

He looked at her. "I can feel your fingers on my face."

"Oh." She dropped her hand, embarrassed that she'd let herself get carried away. "I'm sorry. I didn't realize I was petting you like a dog."

He grabbed her waist, his hands reaching under her scrubs to touch the bare skin of her lower back. He stroked her there.

His hands. On her skin.

The heat of his fingers was like lightning bolts, shooting waves of warmth up her body. Her nipples tightened painfully in reaction. She lost her breath. The reaction scared her.

"Let go of me, Christian."

He did so immediately. The last time she'd asked a man to stop touching her he didn't. Christian did without hesitation. He was a gentle man behind his alarming exterior.

"I—I'm sorry, Georgia."

"It's okay." She grabbed his face with both hands, her breath still short, and pressed a kiss to the burned side of his face. She knew she should step away from him after that, but she couldn't make her feet move. "Thank you for listening."

Her lips seemed to be rooted to his skin. She kissed the other side of his face three, maybe four times before she dragged her lips down the bridge of his large, straight nose. He shut his eyes and she knew he felt like her in that moment.

Starved. For human interaction. For affection. For something they were missing. She kissed his eyelids, and for a moment she rested her lips against them.

"Thank you."

"Georgia." He said her name in a guttural way, as though it had been ripped from his chest. She knew she had to step away then. To leave him alone tonight. They had crossed a line, and she wasn't sure if she could pretend as if nothing had happened. She knew that after tonight they could never go back to the way things were before.

"Good night, Lieutenant."

Christian found it impossible to sleep that night. At first he thought worrying about Tobias was going to keep him up that night. But it turned out that Tobias hadn't entered his mind at all.

It was Georgia. He shouldn't have grabbed her. He knew it was wrong but she touched him gently, willingly, when he hadn't been touched in so long. He was never a man who needed it, but with Georgia, he craved it, and when she touched him and then pulled away, something had snapped inside of him. He wanted more. He had never lost control like that before. She must have put some kind of spell over him. And his body couldn't tolerate not having her close.

But the way she reacted when he touched her...

Fear. He could read it in her eyes. As if he was some monster who was going to take her away. And he'd felt like one. Especially when the gratefulness had spread across her face when he let her go. But she'd ended up surprising him, just when he was about to beat himself up, just when he was about to add yet another regret to his collection of many, she'd taken his face in her hands and kissed him. Kissed him all over his face. Sweetly, but not as sweetly as before. Not like a mother would kiss a child, but like a woman would kiss a man.

It confused the hell out of him and gave him one more reason to want to get to know her better.

Christian's next few days at the hospital seemed impossibly long. Georgia was off. He had his first painful session of physical therapy and Tobias didn't come to visit him.

At first Christian didn't know what to think. He knew the kid was scared about the surgery, about losing the tiny bit of eyesight he had left, but Christian didn't think that would end his visits. Maybe Christian had said the wrong thing to him. Maybe he should have kept his mouth shut. It was none of his business, but Tobias didn't seem like the type of kid who would give up so easily. Why should he just accept things when there was a chance to change it?

Christian wanted to ask the nurses about him, but his pride wouldn't let him. He had no business making friends with a nineteen-year-old lance corporal. If he were serving instead of stuck in bed it would have never happened. The boy would have never gained that level of familiarity with him. It was probably the reason Christian didn't have many people he could truly call a friend.

"Hello, Christian."

He opened his eyes to see General Lee walking through the door, which normally wouldn't be exceptional. The man tried to visit him at least once a week, but he always wore his uniform.

Today he didn't.

He was still neat. Not a hair out of place, but he wore khaki-colored slacks and a salmon-colored shirt.

Salmon.

It was damn close to pink.

"Your wife pick out that shirt for you, sir? Or have you come here to confess something to me?"

The general chuckled and eased his large body into the chair beside Christian's bed. "She bought this shirt for me six years ago for my birthday. I promised her I would wear it as soon as I retired. I didn't think she would remember, but when I got out of the shower this morning my clothes were laid out for me on the bed. I should know my Alma better by now."

"How's retirement treating you so far?"

"Today's my first day. I thought I would find myself wondering what the hell I was going to do with the rest of my life, but again my wife has that all planned out. She presented me with a thirty-item list this morning."

It was Christian's turn to chuckle. "And how did you respond to that?"

"I was relieved, actually. My wife may have been a hippie, but she's tougher than any drill sergeant I've ever had. The woman would have made a damn fine marine."

Christian could clearly see the admiration on the general's face. Again, seeing this side of the man was odd for him, but it made him realize that there was life outside of the marines. "What's the first thing on the list?"

"A cruise." He shook his head with a frown. "A one-week cruise around the Caribbean." He shuddered at the word *Caribbean* as though it was a dirty word. "I've spent the past few years in and out of foreign countries, and I swore to myself I would never leave American soil again unless I had to."

"Then why are you going?"

"Because I have to. Because my wife wants to, and after forty years of her supporting me it's time for me to do what she wants."

"That's very noble of you, sir."

"Dan," he reminded him. "And it's not noble. It's marriage.

After this she has me taking tennis lessons and a woodworking class. Ballroom-dancing lessons were on the list, but I drew the line at that. I'm still a man after all."

"I guess the watercolor class is out, then. I was hoping you were going to paint me a pretty picture to hang on my wall."

"Smart-ass," he muttered. "I'm leaving tomorrow. I won't see you for a while. My wife says I should stop by and make sure you don't need anything before we leave. She says I'm a bad visitor, that I should be bringing you things to make you more comfortable. The thought never occurred to me."

"I guess she should put learning etiquette on that list."

He shrugged. "Do you need anything, son? I see you've got good socks on. Who gave you those?"

"Georgia."

"Georgia?" He raised one of his bushy eyebrows. "You've got another visitor I don't know about?"

"She's a nurse."

"She wouldn't happen to be that pretty little thing who works the night shift?"

Christian nodded. He was mad at himself for saying anything. He didn't know why, but he wanted to keep whatever it was he and Georgia had going on private. He couldn't put a name on what he felt for her, but he didn't want to share it with anybody else.

"And she gave you socks?"

"She probably gives them to everybody."

"Not at fifteen dollars a pair." He stared at Christian for a long moment as if he was trying to figure out something. "She must like you. That's a good thing. After you threw that tantrum and smashed your lunch against the wall, you don't seem to have many fans."

"Georgia just wants to make everybody feel comfortable. She would do the same for anybody."

"But she didn't do it for anybody. She did it for you."

"What's your point?"

"Nothing." The general gave him a curious look. "A woman who will bring a man socks seems like the kind of woman a man would want to marry."

Christian's head swam for a moment. "Are you suggesting that I marry the night nurse because she bought me socks?"

"No. What I'm suggesting is you start thinking about things you might want in a wife. Pretty and cares about a man's comfort are two things I would put on my list."

"Did you have a list when you met Alma?"

"No, but she had legs that went up to her armpits and an ass that I wanted to get down on my knees and praise God for," he said, causing Christian to smile. "I'm just saying you need to start thinking about life after the marines. You don't have a wife to make a list for you."

Christian had wondered when this moment would come. The general had not been subtle when dropping hints about life after the military. He knew what was coming and he was prepared for the blow, but it didn't stop his heart from racing in his chest. "Are you telling me that I'm not going to be allowed to go back to active duty?"

"I'm not telling you anything. I'm retired."

CHAPTER 7

"Nurse Williams." Georgia heard her name called as she left the locker room and headed for the nurses' station. She froze, knowing the sound of that voice all too well.

"Yes, ma'am?" She turned around to face her supervisor and she almost regretted her decision. She had that expression again. The I'm-going-to-rip-out-your-soul-and-eat-it-for-breakfast expression that every nurse feared.

Her boss never wanted to speak to her when she did a good job, only when she did something wrong. And Georgia knew she had done something wrong.

Christian.

Somehow, without her meaning to, their relationship had traveled past that of nurse and patient. She had come to the realization that she felt things for him. Things she shouldn't. She could still feel the way his tortured skin felt beneath her lips, and while she'd been off for the past three days, she found herself pressing her fingers to her lips as if she was trying to recreate the memory, wondering what it would be like if she had been brave enough to press her lips to his.

She shouldn't have gotten so close to him, but there was no turning back now. She couldn't pretend he was just another patient. They were friends in an odd sort of way. And that odd friendship could put her job in jeopardy.

"You were late again today." The woman tapped on her clipboard. "We have talked about this. I'm writing you up."

Late? It took a moment for her brain to process this. This wasn't about Christian. She let out a hysterical bubble of laughter, relived that her secret was still safe.

"Is something funny?" The woman's stern expression turned into a frown.

"No, ma'am, it's just that I wasn't late today."

"Are you telling me that I'm mistaken? I saw you walk into the locker room at 7:06 p.m. You are supposed to begin your shift exactly at seven. Seven-oh-six is very late in my book."

The woman watched everybody like a hawk. Georgia was genuinely surprised that Nurse Chestnut had not noticed when she came in.

"I've been here since six. Nurse Cheng had to leave early because her son is sick. She asked me to cover for her."

"I can vouch for her," Dr. Allen said from behind her. "She walked in the door at 5:58, to be exact. You should be thanking her for covering part of another person's shift instead of taking glee in writing her up. Georgia's a good nurse. She works hard. The patients love her, and instead of telling her how good she is, you harp on little insignificant things like a few minutes here and there."

"Dr. Allen—" she narrowed her eyes on him "—I know Nurse Williams is very popular here with the male patients, but I wasn't aware you were so invested in her welfare. If you are engaging in an outside physical relationship, I need to know about it. I frown on my nurses engaging in workplace relationships, but there is nothing in the bylaws that says it is forbidden as long as Human Resources knows about it and you both do not let it interfere with your work."

"We are not sleeping together, ma'am," Georgia said in nearly a whisper. Her father had taught her never to raise her voice, but she wanted to scream at the woman. To rage, to slap the self-righteous look off her face. Her insinuation felt like a punch to the stomach. She almost felt as though she was standing in front of her father again, explaining in vain that she was not what he thought she was. "Just because somebody thinks I do my job well doesn't mean I'm sleeping with them."

"I think I might have to report *you* to Human Resources," Dr. Allen said. "You have just insulted us both. We are not sleeping together. And you aren't the only one who knows the bylaws here. Maybe Human Resources has to know, but you do not, and you are way out of line for trying to use your power to intimidate your subordinate."

"I wasn't..." Her face flushed red and she closed her mouth as she tried to compose herself. Georgia watched in awe. It was the first time she had ever seen her boss flustered. "Maybe this is something we need to discuss in private, Dr. Allen. Georgia needs to get back to work."

"So do I. I have no need to discuss anything further with you. Remember, Nurse Chestnut. You may be her supervisor, but I am an attending doctor here, and you certainly don't tell me what to do or how to behave. Got it?"

"Yes, Dr. Allen," she said stiffly. "If you'll excuse me, I need to be going now."

Georgia was torn between wanting to hug Greg Allen or slap him. "It's a little bit wrong of you to wave your doctor status in Nurse Chestnut's face. You doctors think you know so much, but we nurses run the hospital."

"I know it," he said, grinning. "But that woman has an

enormous stick up her ass, and I think somebody should knock her down a few pegs as often as possible."

"Well, thank you for coming to my rescue, but I have a feeling that you made things a lot worse for me. She's going to be on my case now more than ever."

"There are two ways to prevent that, Georgia."

"How?"

"One—you could ask to be transferred to another unit. Two—you could marry me and never have to work another day in your life. We've just had our first full conversation in nine months. I think our future looks promising."

Georgia blushed furiously. He was right. She was always so busy being uncomfortable around him that she never said more than two words to him.

"You're a beautiful woman, Georgia. I wouldn't mind having to go to Human Resources for you."

He walked away after that comment, leaving Georgia a little stunned.

He's just being sweet, she told herself. *He's just a flirt. Don't read anything into it.*

But if he wasn't just being sweet... She shook her head and went to back to work.

Christian had known the moment Georgia walked into the hospital that evening. He wanted to say that the air felt different, that he felt her presence in his blood, but he couldn't. The thing that gave away her arrival was the other soldiers shouting out greetings as soon as they saw her.

She was early that day, adding an extra hour to her long shift. He sometimes wondered how she did it. As a marine he knew what hard work was like. He knew the pain of waking up impossibly early to get a job done. But Georgia somehow seemed superhuman.

The general's words stuck in his mind.

Think about what you want in a wife.

The idea sounded absurd to him at first. And he knew that after he got out of the hospital and returned to his normal life, marriage would be the last thing on his mind. But since he had so much time on his hands he had a hard time not thinking about it.

What would he want in a wife?

He gave it some thought, right up until the moment Georgia walked into his room. Then all other thoughts ceased.

"Hello, Georgia."

She gave him a ghost of a smile as she approached him, and he had a feeling that something might be off in her world.

"How are you, Christian? You look better and better every time I see you."

She briefly touched her hand to the burned side of face. The skin felt tight but it didn't hurt much anymore. He spent a lot of time studying his face now that he had a mirror. He understood why some people had a hard time looking at him. One side was the same as it had been, but the other side... It resembled melted plastic, no longer smooth or just white, but raised with thick bands of pink and brown that used to resemble flesh. His eye was slightly distorted. The corner of his mouth was pulled down. It looked like a makeup job from a bad horror movie, but it wasn't. It was what he had to live with for the rest of his life.

"I bet you say that to all your patients."

"I don't." She froze and locked eyes with him. "Do you think I'm a flirt?"

For a moment he thought she was teasing, but when her face fell he knew she wasn't. "No." She was the type of woman who could drive any man insane with lust just by looking at him. But she wasn't a tease. She was sweet. There was something subtle about her that wrapped around a man and made him want to get closer, but he would never describe her as a flirt. If she was, he wouldn't be so attracted to her. "Why do you ask?"

"No reason." She broke eye contact with him and went about doing her routine examination.

"You're a bad liar." He grasped her hand, forcing her to stop and look at him. "Tell me what happened."

"My boss wanted to know if I was sleeping with Dr. Allen," she said in an explosion of words. "All he did was vouch that I got here on time, but the first thing she wanted to know was if we were sleeping together. She said she knew I was popular with the male patients, but I don't do anything but try to be kind. I'm not sleeping with anybody. Why would she think that about me? Is there something I'm doing wrong?"

The conversation he'd had with Tobias came rushing back to him. He'd said Nurse Chestnut didn't like Georgia because everybody else liked her. Christian knew the woman was probably just jealous.

He set his other hand over hers and ran his fingers across her smooth knuckles. "I don't know why she thinks that about you. You haven't done anything wrong."

Her eyes filled with tears and she stared up at the ceiling, trying to blink them back. "I've been trying not to let it bother me but—but it does. It brought me back to the last time I spoke to my father. He thinks the same thing of me. He said that I lead men into temptation. He blames me for what happened."

Suddenly Christian felt sick to his stomach and his grip on Georgia's hand tightened. "What happened?"

"I'm sorry. It's nothing." She pulled her hand from his and swiped at her eyes. "I shouldn't have said anything."

He sat up and grasped her hips. But unlike the last time

he grabbed her she didn't ask him to let her go. "What happened?"

She looked at him for a long time, saying nothing. Her face was full of misery, and for as long as he lived he would never forget how she looked tonight.

"I—I was raped. By my older brother's best friend, and nobody believed me."

"Georgia, no." There were a few times in his life that he almost felt his heart stop, and this was one of them. Her admission took his breath away. He wanted to tell her to stop talking, to take it back, but there was no going back after a revelation like that. Someone had hurt this beautiful, sweet girl. Someone had hurt Georgia.

"My father said that I was a liar. That I'd whored my body to a man. That I was just blaming it on Robert because he was a good boy and that I was doing this to get back at him." It was as if a dam had burst, each detail worse than the last. It was as though she couldn't stop her outpouring of words. "Robert told my father that I—I tried to seduce him. He stood in my living room and told my whole family that I had tried to tempt him into sinning. That I was trying to use him to cover up my mistake with another man. I watched my family turn on me. Nobody would look me in the eye. Nobody would believe me. I didn't tempt him. I didn't lie. Abby looks just like him. My baby is proof of that. But they'll never get to see her, because after they kicked me out, I'll never step foot in their house again."

The tears streamed down her face. He lifted his fingers to catch them, to wipe them away. Seeing her cry was physically painful for him. Knowing there was nothing he could do to fix it was worse than being hit with a bomb. "Why wouldn't they believe you?"

"My family is very religious. My father is a minister who

believes that unmarried women shouldn't be around men.
He had my sister and I homeschooled. We weren't allowed
to wear pants or listen to the radio. He thought the outside
world was full of sin and corruption for young women. Eve
tempted Adam with an apple. He thought all women were
the same way. Only on earth to tempt men to sin. Unless they
were trained not to."

"Your father sounds like an asshole." He was. How could
he not protect his daughter?

She let out a watery laugh. "Say that again."

"A big asshole. A huge one. The king of them."

"I used to think he was right. I let Robert kiss me. I was
twenty-one years old and had never been kissed before. I knew
I shouldn't have done it, but at first it was nice. But then it
wasn't and he wouldn't stop." She shook her head, as if trying to shake the bad memory out of her mind. "It took me
nearly a year with a counselor at a women's center for me to
believe that it wasn't my fault."

"Why didn't you go to the police?"

"My family wouldn't believe me. I didn't think the police
would, either." She ran her fingers through his hair, studying
him for a moment. "You look scary right now. Relax, honey."

She was petting him again. Giving him comfort when she
was the one in need of it.

"I could kill him for you. Tell me where to find him and
I'll do it for you."

"He's not worth it."

"What about your father, then? I almost think what he did
was worse. He's not a man in my book."

"Christian…" She rested her forehead against his. "Nobody has ever offered to commit first-degree murder for me.
I'm flattered."

"I'm not joking. He deserves to be punished. What about

child support? The court can prove paternity and make him pay. At least that way you'll be vindicated. The world will know he's a liar."

"No." She shook her head firmly. "I don't want anything from him. I don't ever want to see him again. He's not her father. I'd rather struggle to pay off her medical bills for the rest of my life and survive on peanut butter and jelly than take anything from him."

"Medical bills?"

"Abby came early. There were complications. She's fine now, but I'm hopelessly in debt."

"How old are you, Georgia?"

"I'll be twenty-four in a month."

She was a baby. He stroked his thumbs across her cheeks. "You're tougher than half the marines I know."

"We women are a tough bunch. You think getting blown up is bad, you should try childbirth."

"I'll pass."

He pulled her a little closer so that he could reach her neck. The cords were tight when he touched them. He massaged them, watching as her eyes drifted shut and her mouth open slightly in pleasure.

Protect her. The strength of that thought scared him. She was doing fine by herself, but who was there to take care of her?

"I can't believe I just told you all of that. You're the only person besides a counselor who knows."

"I won't tell anybody," he promised as he stroked down the length of her back.

She opened her eyes and grinned at him. "I hadn't pegged you as much of a gossip. Next time it's your turn to tell me your deepest darkest secret."

He paused for a moment and looked at her. His darkest secret was his biggest regret, and he was struck how similar her story was to Miko's. Christian could never be sure what had happened to that girl on base that night, but he was afraid his friends had done the unthinkable and he'd been too cowardly to do anything to stop them. If he could go back, he would change that. He would do his best to make it right.

"I once killed a man just to watch him die."

"Liar." She brushed a kiss across the burned side of his face. "It's your turn tomorrow. We're friends now. You are obligated to spill your guts to me."

"Am I?"

"Yes." She pulled away from his touch. "I have to get back to work. Good night, soldier."

CHAPTER 8

Georgia could barely sleep the next day. Strange energy flowed through her body and all she could think about was last night with Christian. Part of her couldn't believe she'd told him about her past. But a bigger part of her wasn't surprised that she had.

Christian made her act in ways she never thought herself capable. He made her body crave closeness, intimacy. He made her want to not be alone anymore. Her counselor had told her that this would happen one day. That she would be able to move on, that she would want to be with a man. But Georgia didn't believe her. Maybe it was time for Georgia to let somebody into her life. But she knew that person couldn't be Christian.

He was bound to go back to active duty. Yes, he was badly burned. Yes, his body sustained terrible injury, but he was healing. His appearance would remain changed forever, but his body would be well enough to serve again. She didn't need to hear it from a doctor to know that. He was going to walk out of her life one day soon. Maybe he'd been placed in her path to show her that it was possible. That being close with a man was something she could do.

What she felt for him was nothing more than a little in-fatuation. But...the way he rubbed her neck and wiped her tears, she knew that for as long as she lived, she would never forget the tenderness of those moments. She found it hard to imagine that another person could make her feel so safe.

She tossed and turned that morning until her baby climbed on top of her and forced her to be still.

"I'm sorry, Abby. Mama's disturbing you."

"Mama." She rested her head on Georgia's chest and the two of them managed to get an hour of sleep.

The lack of sleep caught up with her that night, and by the time she walked into Christian's room she was dead on her feet.

"Sit down and don't argue with me," he ordered.

She smiled. His soft, deep voice always sent tingles through her body. "Are you going to make me do pushups if I don't?"

"No. Suicide drills. Sit down."

She pulled the chair closer to the bed and nearly collapsed into it. Christian reached for her hand, tugging her forward so that she could rest her head on his mattress.

"I'm not sure I like you working the night shift when you have to go home and raise a baby during the day." He rested his hand on her cheek, causing her to shut her eyes and revel in the warmth of his skin on hers.

"Mmm. If I worked the day shift we couldn't be friends like this."

"I won't get to see you at all if you collapse from exhaustion," he said gruffly, and the protectiveness in his voice made her smile.

He lightly brushed his fingers along the curve of her jaw. She shivered. Her nipples tightened and that warm feeling coursed through her. But she also felt sleepy and safe, as if nothing or nobody could get to her while she was with him.

She realized that she had fallen asleep when she felt his thumb brush over her lips. Without thinking she kissed it.

He stiffened. "Go back to sleep."

"You know I can't." She sat up and then stood. The temptation to sleep in that spot was strong, but the temptation to crawl in bed with him and forget about the world was even stronger.

She looked away from him, as if that would stop the longing in her chest. "How much time was I out? You know if my boss caught me that would be the end of my job."

"It was six minutes exactly." He shook his head. "How much longer are you going to go on like this, Georgia? It's not good for you to be exhausted all the time."

"Stop fussing at me." She reached behind him to loosen his hospital gown and immediately realized her mistake. Her breasts brushed against him for a moment and the contact was almost painful. She glanced up at him to see if he had felt it, too, but he wasn't staring at her face for once. His eyes settled on her lips. She tried not to grow self-conscious under his examination, but she'd always thought her lips were just a little too full. It was one of the many reasons her father had forbidden her to wear makeup.

"Sit up." She tried to force herself back into being a nurse. Maybe these nighttime visits were a bad thing. Maybe her boss and her father were right. Maybe she was seeking trouble. "I've got an order to remove the bandages from your torso. The donor site from your grafts should be all healed up by now."

He quietly did as she asked. But her fingers grazed his exposed skin as she pulled the gown from around his shoulders. She had been a nurse for two years. She had removed patients' gowns countless times. She had never been affected by it. But none of her patients had a body like his. She couldn't help herself. Her fingers lingered a little longer than they should have. She was teasing herself with these little touches. She wanted to run her hands all over his back. She wanted to press her face there and kiss him. But she didn't. She couldn't.

When he was finally free of the gown, he lay back on the bed. All of her training went out of her head. All thoughts of the task she was supposed to be performing disappeared. She knew his body was hard beneath the gown, but she'd never imagined that it would look like this.

Tarzan.

There was something a little wild about the way he looked. His tousled golden curls combined with his big scarred body. He was the exact opposite of what she thought she might be attracted to. Growing up she always imagined the man she would marry would be slim and neat looking. Unobtrusive and kind. She never imagined she would ever find a man so large, a man others were afraid of, so attractive.

She drank in his body for a long time. It was as though her eyes couldn't get enough. It was as though they were hungry. She focused on his nipples, wondering if his were anywhere near as sensitive as hers. She wondered what it would feel like to run her tongue across one of them. She wondered what his mouth would feel like on hers.

That thought was a shock to her system. She was his nurse—she was supposed to be treating him, not fantasizing about him. She cleared her throat and looked back up to his face. This time he was staring at her. His intense green eyes were boring into her. It made her even hotter than before, and she hoped that he wasn't able to read her mind.

"Aren't you supposed to be telling me a secret tonight?" She carefully peeled off his bandages to reveal new pink skin, finally returning to her nursing duties. One more part of his body healed. He was one step closer to walking out of the hospital. She grew unreasonably sad. "Don't think I forgot about it."

Little by little, she exposed his entire torso. More beauty. Hard stomach with lines she wanted to trace with her fingers. Why couldn't he have had a jellylike gut instead of perfectly formed abs? Why couldn't one part of him be just a little bit unattractive to her? She swallowed hard. "Tell me about your family." Her voice sounded thick even to her own ears.

"I thought you wanted to know my darkest secret."

"Huh?"

"You asked me to tell you a secret. Then you asked about my family. Which one do you want?"

"I want all of it." *All of you,* she stopped herself from saying.

She turned away from him and went to the sink to fill a basin of water. His nearness was suffocating her. She should walk away now, go about the rest of her shift pretending that it was just another normal night, but she couldn't force herself to leave. "What are you doing over there?"

"I'm going to clean you up a little. You're sticky from the bandages."

"I stink. I don't know how you can stand to be around me sometimes. Is there any way I could take a shower?"

She turned to face him as the thoughts of his hard naked body in the shower invaded her. Heat and water and soap all over his body. She wondered if he touched himself in there. If he put his hands on his… She tried to stop herself from completing that thought. But lately when she showered she wondered what it would be like if she were ever to touch herself there, in between her legs. It was wicked, or so she had been taught. She had never touched herself, but lately she ached there. Her breasts felt heavy and her body yearned for some kind of relief.

"Georgia?"

"Hmm?"

"Can I take a shower?"

"No." She snapped back to reality. "Soon, honey. In the next couple of weeks or so. And you don't stink." She pulled a bar of soap out of the cabinet. "You smell like a man." She approached him with the steamy basin of water. "I'm going to give you a good washing. And you're going to tell me all about yourself while I do."

She needed to hear him talk to distract herself. When they were quiet her mind had a chance to wander.

"I don't have a family," he said as she dipped the soap into the water. She didn't bother with gloves, like she should have. She was going to allow herself this. Contact. Her skin on his.

"Lift your arm," she ordered. "You'd better not have any family. Or else I would have given them one angry phone call for not bringing their behinds here to visit you."

He smiled. "My mother would have liked you."

"Would she? Tell me about her."

She cleaned him, attacking him with the bar of soap and washcloth just like she did all of her other patients, but the whole time she kept telling herself that there was nothing more intimate or special about her cleaning him.

She was lying to herself.

"My mother was a tiny, bigmouthed New Yorker."

"What?" She looked up at him as she ran the wet cloth across his chest.

"Yeah. She was from Queens and barely reached five feet. She met my father in a strip club in New York City, where she was a cocktail waitress."

"You're kidding."

A slight smile curled his lips. "Nope. My father was there for a bachelor party and he took one look at my mother and they were a couple from that day on. They were mismatched. My father grew up Westport, Connecticut. He was quiet and reserved and everything my mother wasn't. But they fit together."

"What happened to them?"

"Car accident. The morning I graduated from college. I was supposed to pick them up from the airport but I was too hungover. My father rented a car and just before they turned on to campus, a tractor trailer smashed into them, killing them on impact."

"Christian…"

His story took her breath away. He told it so matter-of-factly, as if he was reciting the weather, but she could tell by the tightening of his features that he was deeply hurt.

She dropped the washcloth and took his face in her hands. "You know that wasn't your fault." She searched his face for an answer. "Don't you?"

"I was selfish."

"You were twenty-one." She kissed his long nose.

"Georgia," he said, his voice sounding choked, "don't kiss me."

She slid her lips across his face and down to his jawline, where she left behind a half dozen soft kisses. "Why not?"

"You know why." His injured hand had found its way under her scrubs again and she feel could his burned fingers stroking across her lower back. The sensation of his rough fingers against her smooth skin sent goose bumps up her body. She didn't want him to stop. She wanted to feel that sensation all over.

And when a little moan escaped her lips she realized that she was doing it again. She was getting too close. She was taking things too far. "Okay." She stood up. "I won't do it again."

He looked at her almost helplessly for a moment before he shut his eyes.

She picked up the washcloth and continued to wash his chest. They didn't speak anymore after that. She just concentrated on washing him, clearing the soap off his body, washing down the hard planes of his stomach.

She was so in tune with what she was doing that she didn't realize that this was the longest time she had ever spent bathing a patient. She didn't realize the effect it had on him until he grabbed her hand.

"Stop," he groaned.

"What?"

He didn't have to answer because she saw it. The blanket had tented. His erection was so big she was lost for words.

Heat climbed her up neck. Her hand twitched and she had to order herself not to touch the blanket, to pull it down and reveal the things that caused her so much fascination.

Her eyes shot to his face. He still had her hand in a vise grip. She could tell he was mortified, but she wasn't. She felt... She didn't know how to put it in words.

"Don't be embarrassed, honey. It's a natural reaction. This happens to a lot of nurses. It's never happened to me, but I must say I'm quite flattered."

He opened his eyes and scowled at her. "This is not funny, Georgia."

"I know. What do you want me to do?"

"Leave."

"Leave?" She was hurt by his request.

"Yes. Go." He let go of her hand.

"Okay. Let me put back on your gown."

"Please, Georgia. Just go."

She didn't say another word or give him another look. She just left the room.

CHAPTER 9

Christian didn't get any sleep that night after Georgia left. It was impossible. What the hell was she doing kissing him like that? Touching him like that? Making it nearly impossible for him to behave himself. She had no idea how close he was to hauling her off her feet and pulling her on top of him. No woman had ever touched him like that before. No woman had ever wanted to.

She was no practiced seductress. In fact, everything she did was sweetly innocent in a way, and it made him want her more. It made him crave her. What the hell was he going to do? He could barely look at her now without wanting her. How was he going to be her friend now that he knew what her hands felt like on his body? He should ignore her. Pretend like he was sleeping when she came in. But he knew he couldn't do that. She was the only thing he looked forward to, the only thing that made his stay in the hospital bearable.

"Sir, you in here?"

Tobias appeared in his doorway, his hands on the wall, his eyes bandaged.

"Where else would I be?"

The boy's face broke out into a grin. "You mind if I stumble my way in?"

"Get your ass in, soldier, and sit down."

"Did you miss me?"

"No. Where were you?" he asked when Tobias sat down.

"Got that surgery I told you about."

"Oh?"

"Yeah. I figured what's the worst that could happen? I was already blind."

"So the surgery didn't take." Christian couldn't keep the disappointment out of his voice for the boy. He had his whole life of ahead of him, and it didn't seem fair that he couldn't experience everything it had to offer.

"Not the way they wanted it to. But when they take these things off my eyes I can see some. It's blurry as shit, but I can see light and I even can see color."

"That's good. I'm happy for you, Tobias."

"Thank you, sir." He was silent for a moment. "And I'm sorry for getting all bitchy on you. I didn't mean to. It's just... You know."

He did know. Life had thrown them both for a loop. "Don't worry about it. But you do realize that if I wasn't laid up in this bed I would have stomped your ass into the ground."

"Yes, sir." He saluted with a grin. "So what's new with you? Are you any closer to getting out of here?"

"I haven't heard yet. Nobody will give me an answer. But I'm getting damn sick of being here."

"I'm past sick of being here. The doctor told me I might be getting out of here soon...." Tobias turned his face away from Christian. He didn't sound happy about finally getting some sort of life back.

"What is it?"

"Nothing. It's just, what the hell am I going to do when I get out of here?"

"According to Georgia, anything you want."

"Miss Georgia." He smiled. "I wish I could take her with me when I go."

"You're not the only one."

"You've got a crush on her, too?"

"I don't," he said truthfully. He didn't. What he felt for her couldn't be classified as a crush.

"What does she look like? I've got this picture of her in my head. Sort of a mix of the good witch from the Wizard of Oz and Audrey Hepburn."

"What do you know about Audrey Hepburn? You're barely out of diapers."

"My sister's got a big black-and-white poster of her in her bedroom. I saw her every day until I went to basic training. Am I close? What does Nurse Williams look like?"

"She's pretty," he began, unsure about how to describe her. "She's got honey-colored skin and dark reddish-brown hair that she always wears in a bun. Her eyes are big and light brown and you can tell how smart she is just by looking into them. And her nose…" He smiled to himself. "It's little and cute and she has a half dozen freckles sprinkled across it. And her skin is…" He stopped talking realizing that he sounded like a complete jackass.

"Yeah, but what's her ass look like?"

Christian threw his head back and laughed. He had forgotten what was important to a nineteen-year-old.

"What's the matter, Georgia?" Mrs. Sheppard asked her as soon as she walked through the door. "You don't look very happy this morning."

"I'm fine," she lied, plastering a smile on her face. "I just had a rough shift last night. All I need is a little bit of sleep."

Mrs. Sheppard frowned at her. "I'm guessing you're not going to let me keep this baby so you can get more than two hours of uninterrupted sleep."

Georgia genuinely smiled at Mrs. Sheppard this time. "You know I won't." She draped her arms around the older woman. "But I will allow you to give me a hug."

"I can do that, you sweet girl." She squeezed Georgia and smoothed her hair. "You miss your mama. Don't you?"

"I do. Some days more than others."

"Why can't you call her? I'm a mama and I know that there is very little that my daughter could do that would make me not want to hear from her."

Georgia wanted to call her mother. She wanted to hear her voice so badly some days she ached. But she couldn't pick up the phone. She didn't even think about it. Her father controlled everything, including her mother. He would never allow his wife to speak to his outcast daughter. Even though she wanted to. Even though, according to Carolina, Georgia's absence hurt her.

"My mother isn't available for me to speak to."

"I'm sorry to hear that. You can talk to me if you want to. I'll do my best to be a good stand-in."

Georgia pulled out of the embrace and stared at Mrs. Sheppard for a moment. She wanted to confide in somebody, to talk about her weird mixed-up feelings because holding them inside her for so long had made her feel as though she was going to burst. But what could she say about Christian? He was her secret best friend.

"There's a marine at work," she said in a rush.

"Oh?" Mrs. Sheppard sat down on the couch and patted the cushion beside her. "Sit down and tell me about him."

Georgia nodded and picked up her baby before joining her on the sofa. "I like him. Not like. I like my other patients, but in a different way. He's my friend." She looked up at Mrs. Sheppard helplessly. "I'm not supposed to be friends with my patients."

"Well, maybe not all of them, but I think it's okay if you have a friend, especially if that friend is a handsome marine."

"Oh, Christian's not handsome. He's too huge to be handsome. He's six inches shy of seven feet tall and he even scowls in his sleep, but there's something about him. He's lonely, I think. His parents died. He's got no other family. Only one person comes to visit him. He needs me to be his friend."

"There's nothing wrong with that, Georgia. Why do you seem so upset?"

"I think he might not want me to be his friend anymore. He sent me away last night."

"Oh, honey." She patted Georgia's hand. "That's a man just acting like a man. They have no idea what they need. It's a woman's job to tell them. My Wade was just like that. Didn't know what was wrong with him until I told him. Now, with your *friend,* try to give him a little space. Ignore him a little bit. If I know men, and I do, he'll be calling you back in no time."

Georgia left Mrs. Sheppard's apartment thinking about her advice. She hadn't told her the whole story, but she couldn't have revealed it all to the nice older woman. Especially how she was beginning to feel about Christian. She had embarrassed him, and instead of playing coy she wanted to apologize to him.

Maybe she should give him some space. She knew that every time she was near him their relationship was becoming less of a friendship and more of something she wasn't prepared to handle.

He was going to leave soon. It was just a matter of time before he walked out of her life.

She went to work that night, and instead of following her normal routine she saw Christian early, right in the middle of the rest of her patients. He couldn't keep the surprise off his face, but she ignored it.

"How are you feeling tonight, Lieutenant?"

He blinked at her.

"The physical therapist told me that he worked you hard this morning. You'll probably fall right asleep tonight."

"Georgia."

She could feel his eyes searching her face, but she wouldn't look at him. She still felt guilty about last night. She'd upset him. He was her only friend and she had upset him all because she was too fascinated with him to know when to take a step back. She never knew her place with him. She was always the one crossing the line. She was always the one who couldn't keep her hands to herself. He had been polite about it. He had always been kind to her. He always made her feel safe.

"Can I get you something? Another blanket? Are you hungry?"

"No."

"Stop scowling, Christian." She touched his brow. It was the only touch she would permit herself to have. "You're going to give yourself a headache."

She left after that.

Christian waited until 1:31 a.m. to call Georgia. He was so mad at her he couldn't see straight. How the hell could she walk in and out of his room as though nothing had ever happened? As if he was any other patient?

"What's the matter, Christian? Are you in pain?"

"Come here," he barked at her, as if she was one of his soldiers.

Her eyes widened for a moment, but she obeyed him. He sat up, swinging his legs over the side of the bed to meet her.

"What the hell are you trying to pull?"

"Lie back down, you idiot," she said without heat, but she wouldn't look at him. Just like earlier that evening. That bothered him more than anything else.

"I can take a lot of people not being able to look me in the face, but I don't think I can take it from you."

Her eyes snapped up to his. "I'm sorry, Christian."

Shit. He was one of those men who never fell for women's games. He didn't care about tears or pouty lips or hurt feelings, but all that went out the window when he looked at her. She had the biggest, saddest brown eyes. As though somebody had run over her pet.

He didn't like it. Something inside of him twisted painfully. Where was the little bit of sass she kept so well hidden? Where was the woman who was brave enough to call him names?

He grabbed her by the waist and pulled her close so she settled right between his thighs. He hardened slightly. It never failed. Her nearness always did something to him. It heightened his senses. Being this close to her was almost painful.

He had very little control left when it came to her.

"What happened earlier tonight?"

She blinked at him, then swallowed, as if she was trying to gather courage. "I was giving you some space. I thought you were mad at me."

"I wasn't mad at you until you pulled that little stunt tonight."

"It wasn't a stunt. You sent me away. What was I suppose to think?"

He slid one hand up the back of her shirt, and with his

free hand he cupped her cheek. He never had been smooth with women. He had never known how to talk to them, but Georgia was the exception. She was the only woman, the only person, who understood him the slightest bit, and he had hurt her. He hadn't meant to hurt her. He had sent her away simply because if she stayed he would have done something he might regret.

"You're supposed to think that you drive me absolutely insane with your little kisses and soft touches." He pressed his lips to the crease in her neck and groaned. Her skin was so soft. So different from his. He wanted to place his lips all over her naked body. All over her curvy little behind and on her hips and feet and legs and every place that lips could go. "You have no idea what's going on in this head, Nurse Williams. You have no idea how I really feel about you, because if you did you would be running away. I'm trying very hard to be respectful. To treat you the right way. To keep my hands off you, but you make it very hard for me when you touch me the way you do."

She relaxed into him and shut her eyes. "This feels nice."

He stroked his hand down her back as she snuggled into him. He wondered when the last time anybody had held her was. Thinking back on his life, he had never shared an embrace with a woman like this. Holding somebody so close was more intimate than sex. She trusted him. She wasn't afraid of him when so many women were.

This was new for him, and he didn't understand why out of all the men in the world she'd chosen him to trust. He didn't want to do anything to break that trust.

"It does." He delivered slow, soft kisses to the seam of her neck. She was so soft. She smelled so damned good. She responded to his touch so well that if he died never getting to kiss her anyplace else he would be happy. "Do you have any idea how your lips feel on me, Georgia? I can't describe it, but every time you kiss me I can't go back to sleep because I spend the whole night reliving how they felt on me. And when I do sleep, I dream of you. Of kissing you. Of touching you. It's driving me insane."

"I won't do it anymore," she said in a broken whisper.

"I don't want you to stop." He pulled her closer. "But you're going to have to." He took his lips from her neck and looked up at her. She was so beautiful. Even in her prim scrubs. Even with her hair bound back so tightly. It almost hurt to look at her. "You can't touch me like that anymore."

"Okay," she whispered.

"Don't you know why?" He searched her face for understanding, but all he got was those big sad light brown eyes. "You can't touch a man who's never been touched before. He doesn't know how to handle it."

"I can't be the only one who's touched you before. Who's kissed you. Somebody has to have touched you before."

"Nobody. Not like you anyway. I'm big. I'm ugly. A lot of people are scared of me."

"You're not ugly, Christian. I think you're gorgeous."

Beautiful sweet girl. He could tell by the look in her eyes that she wasn't lying to him. He hoped one day that she would find somebody who would take care of her. He hoped that she would meet somebody worthy of her love. "I like you very much, Georgia Williams." He kissed her cheeks more times than he could count. He wanted to kiss her lips, to taste her, but he knew that if he stepped over that line he would not be able to stop himself. Even touching her now, holding her close, was dangerous. His control was about to snap at any moment.

He had to let her go. But he couldn't give her up completely. Not their friendship. That meant something to him.

That was something he would always think of fondly. She would be the good memory to get him through bad days.

He loosened his hold on her, slightly preparing to release her, but he couldn't force himself to just yet. He needed a few more moments to soak up her sweet warmth. After a few moments she placed her hand on his knee. The touch almost undid him, but he didn't ask her to remove her hand. But then it slid up to his thigh, and in a move that he never expected, she touched his cock.

He looked up at her. It had to be an accident. Sweet little Georgia could never be so bold, but she looked him in the eye and wrapped her fingers around him. Yes, she could be that bold. She was sweet, but there was another side to Georgia that he was forgetting about. One that screamed out to be let free.

"Georgia, what are you doing?"

"Just this time, love." She rested her head on her shoulder as she slid her hand down his shaft. "Show me how to do this for you."

He clamped his hand over hers, prepared to pull it away. It was the right thing to do. He knew he didn't deserve this or her. He had done nothing in his life to earn it.

"Please," she said, seeming to read his mind. "Show me."

He turned his head to look down at her. She looked right in his arms. She felt right with her body nestled into his. "You're absolutely beautiful. Did you know that?"

A slow, stunning smile spread across her face. His heart squeezed. *Mine.* It was a dangerous thought, but he still thought it. Actually, it was more as though he felt it. Shit. He knew he was going to carry her around with him for a long time, but he wasn't prepared to keep her with him for the rest of his life.

He took her hand and slid it back up his cock and down again, squeezing her fingers more firmly around him. Yes, she was his. For tonight. She wanted to do this for him and he would let her. At this point he was powerless to stop her.

She kissed his mouth. He had dreamed about the way her pouty lips would feel on his. But he didn't kiss her back. He didn't taste her mouth or push his tongue past her lips to deepen their connection. Because he knew if he did he wouldn't be able to stop. He knew if he started kissing her he would haul her into this bed and make love to her. And if he made love to her he would never be able to let her go.

She deserved more than him. More than a big, cowardly, wounded soldier.

He loosened his grip on her hand, letting her take over. She was a quick study, giving him long slow strokes that felt so good they were acutely painful. Her touch was everything he could have imagined, but it still wasn't enough. He wanted more of her. He wanted her closer. He slid his hand up her back, under her bra, touching as much bare skin as he could manage.

"Georgia," he breathed.

She moved her hand faster, seeming to know he was close to the edge. He pumped into her grasp, imagining what it would be like to have her all the time. Not having to steal moments in the middle of the night. Imagining what it would be like to know that when he woke up she would always be there.

Those thoughts proved too much. He came. Hard. His seed spilled all over her fingers. She looked up at him as if she wasn't sure what had happened. But then she smiled at him again and stepped away to the sink to get a washcloth. She cleaned them both, and set her full pouty mouth on his one last time.

"Good night, soldier."

Georgia slept soundly that next morning. She hadn't expected to. She expected to be horrified at what she had done with Christian. But she wasn't. She couldn't regret it. She felt close to him when she hadn't felt close to anybody for so long. And it wasn't the type of closeness she felt with her sister. It was more than that, more intense.

He'd wrapped his big arms around her and made her feel safe and beautiful and all the things she had been missing for so long. She didn't feel empty when she was with him. He made her feel powerful and womanly and sexy. He made her want more with him.

That scared her. She shouldn't want what she could never have.

A little sadness settled around her heart. She knew she could never touch him again the way she had last night. They'd talked about it. She had promised. But she was glad she wasn't the only one to feel madness. He felt it, too. It was in his beautiful words and the way his kissed her face and stroked her back.

He thought he was some kind of animal. She could never see him the way he saw himself or the way the rest of the world saw him. He was so gentle with her. He made her want to explore her sexuality. She hadn't realized it was possible because she had never thought she would get over her rape.

It made her feel hopeful. Hopeful that maybe one day she could have a happy life with a man. So when she settled into bed that morning, instead of feeling guilty or shameful like she had been raised to, she dreamed of him and about how good she felt when she was wrapped up in his arms.

When she woke up two hours later she was still exhausted, but as much as she wanted to turn over and go back to sleep she couldn't. Abby was sitting beside her, staring down at her. She was better than any alarm clock on the market.

"Hello again, my love." She picked her up and lifted her over her head in an attempt to wake up her tired muscles.

"You're getting heavy. Now that you've turned one you've packed on the pounds."

Abby frowned at her, apparently not liking Georgia's joke. "Good God, what a face! If you're giving me that look at one, what kind of looks am I going to get when you're sixteen?" Georgia pulled her baby to her chest and held her tightly. Sixteen. Georgia was so tired she didn't know if she was going to make it to see Abby's sixteenth birthday.

The lack of sleep was starting to get to her. Her head ached horribly. Most days she went around with a headache until she forced herself to take some aspirin. Her body was starting to feel the effects, too. She ached all over. But as much as she wanted to get a full night's rest, she couldn't. She needed to spend time with her baby.

When she'd first learned she was pregnant, a counselor at the women's center had brought up adoption. It was an option she had never thought about. But the counselor had told her that some mothers had a hard time coming to terms with how their babies were conceived, that once they were born they had a hard time raising the child of their rapist.

Georgia thought about it then. How would she feel raising a child who looked like Robert? Or acted like him? What if her baby grew up to have some major character defect like the man who made her? It was all terrifying to Georgia, but she'd taken the risk. Because even though the baby was half of him, it was half of her, too. And she knew she couldn't give part of herself away.

She only wished she had some sign that she was doing the right thing for her child. The guilt never seemed to go away. Abby wasn't going to have the life Georgia always thought her children would have. She wasn't going to have a mother and father to love her. She wasn't going to have the best of everything. She didn't even have a mother who could give the best of herself because she spent so much of her time exhausted. But what could she do? If she switched to the day shift she might get some sleep, but she wouldn't get to spend as much time with her daughter.

Georgia worked twelve-hour shifts. Abby would have to spend all day in day care. Even if the separation didn't break Georgia, the cost of that would.

Right now she didn't have a choice. Unless some divine intervention occurred, she was going to have to keep this up until she collapsed.

"You look less blown up, son," General Lee said when he walked into Christian's room the next morning.

Christian smiled, glad for the visit. Since Georgia had left him last night he had spent entirely too much time thinking about her and her touch and her smell and the way she felt pressed against him. Thoughts of her were driving him crazy. He needed a distraction. He needed to turn his thoughts from her. "Thanks. I think."

"Don't mention it." He lowered his big body into the chair beside Christian's bed.

The general, fresh back from his cruise, looked a little different himself. He was very tanned, almost the color of baked bread, and he was wearing blue jeans. Christian found the jeans more surprising than the pink shirt he'd worn before he'd left.

His shirt was still tucked in and his clothes were neatly ironed. But the thing that had changed most about the general was that he looked relaxed. The intensity seemed to have melted from his face, from his entire body. Hell, he looked happy.

"How was your cruise?"

"My wife liked it." He shrugged in typical fashion. "She wants to go on another at Christmas. I agreed to take her."

"Did you like it?"

"Didn't have to pay for a single meal on the boat. I had steak nearly every night. Good steak, too. Not that stuff they served in the chow hall on base. Have you ever had molten-lava cake? Damn thing was like a chocolate volcano. It was good."

"It's okay if you like to cruise, sir. I hear senior citizens often enjoy them."

The general's brow furrowed. "You've become a real smart-ass since you were blown to hell."

"It's your fault. You went all soft on me."

"Soft. I'd still give it to you good in a fight," he retorted, and Christian believed him. "Listen. I have some news for you from your doctor."

"From my doctor? Why isn't he telling me?"

"Because I wanted to, and just because I'm retired doesn't mean I still don't have pull."

Christian sat all the way up, nervous for the first time in a while. A million rapid-fire thoughts ran through his mind. "What is it?"

"You're going to be released in two weeks."

His gaze shot up to the general's. "Oh?" At first he felt elated relief, but then he realized that leaving here meant he would have to return to life, and without the marines, he didn't have one.

"You've been promoted." He stood up and saluted Christian. "Captain Howard, congratulations."

The news sent Christian reeling. Promoted? He thought he was going to be discharged from the marines, not promoted. He didn't deserve it. He'd survived when he shouldn't have. His men had died. His body wasn't what it used to be—he had damaged skin and an arm he could barely move. They were going to let him go back and hold a gun and lead men? It didn't seem real.

"Are you sure?"

"Would I lie to you about something like that? You were damn brave out there and your country appreciates it. The real question is what are you going to do now that you are eligible to go back?"

"I'm going to go back, sir," he said without hesitation. "There is nothing else for me."

"You know there is life outside of the marines." The general shook his head. "I'm not going to go into that with you again. You know how I feel about it. But if you're going to stay in, you don't have to go overseas. You're a born leader. Have you ever thought about training new recruits?"

He hadn't. He hadn't thought about anything except getting cleared to serve again. "It's something I might consider."

The general nodded. "If I haven't told you before, I'm proud of you, of what you did out there. You're the kind of man who would make any father proud."

"I did what I was supposed to," he said, more to himself. The guilt of being one of the few who had survived still gnawed at him. He should have died with the rest of them and for a while after the attack happened, he wished he had. But that had all changed the moment he woke up in this hospital. "My father would have hated that I joined the marines." He thought back to the serious man, who at heart was a gentle giant. "My mother would have lain in front of a bus to stop me. And if that didn't work she would have tried to knock me out."

"Why didn't you go into the family business? Wasn't that in the plans for you since you were a child?"

He had thought about that question from time to time.

There was a place for him, or so he was assured by the man he had chosen to run the company in his father's place. "My mother wanted me to be a doctor. My father never said that he wanted me to run the business, but I think he expected me to come back to it eventually. When they died I was twenty-one. I didn't know anything about running a business. Especially one as big as my father's."

"But you still own the company?"

"I have sixty-five percent of the shares."

"Have you ever thought about running it now?"

"I wouldn't know where to start. I've been a marine for almost eleven years. I don't think I could trade my combat boots for loafers."

"I don't think they make loafers in your size." The general reached up and set his hand on Christian's shoulder. "You're not twenty-one anymore. You've learned a lot. You've led before. I can't imagine leading a company is much harder than leading men into battle."

"It's just a different kind of warfare."

"I'm not suggesting that you take over, but I am telling you that you have options now. You should think really hard before you make a decision."

CHAPTER 10

"Nurse Williams."

Georgia tried to force herself to not flinch when she heard her supervisor's voice. Her head still ached despite the two sets of aspirin she had taken earlier that day and she wasn't sure if she could politely handle much criticism from her boss tonight.

"Yes, ma'am." She turned around, steeling herself for what was to come. The fact that the woman had thought she was sleeping with Dr. Allen still bothered her. She tried to let it go in light of what she had done with Christian. But that wasn't the same.

Nurse Chestnut didn't know what Georgia was doing with Christian, but Georgia knew she wasn't the type of woman her boss thought she was. She'd thought that once she left her father's home, she would be free from that kind of persecution. She had been wrong. And ever since the confrontation with Dr. Allen, Nurse Chestnut had been extrachilly to her. She went out of her way to check on Georgia's work.

"Your review is coming up. I need you to make an appointment to see me so we can sit down and discuss it."

"Of course." It was a meeting that she dreaded, but she knew she did good work. There was nothing much Nurse Chestnut could take exception to.

"I'll need you to come in early because I will not be staying late to conduct reviews."

"Yes, ma'am," she said, even though coming in early was a hardship for her. It was less time she would get to spend with her baby. But she would come anyway because she would not give her supervisor any more ammunition against her. "I'll sign up for a slot that's before I begin my rounds." She turned to leave.

"One more thing, Nurse Williams."

Damn.

"Yes, ma'am?"

"I need you to work a double shift next week."

Everything inside of Georgia rebelled in that moment. There was no way she would go an entire day without seeing her daughter. "I'm sorry, ma'am, but that I can't do that. You know I have a baby at home."

"Lots of other nurses have children at home. They do not seem to have a problem pitching in to help out."

"Well, maybe they don't, ma'am, but they have husbands or families to help them. I am raising my child alone."

"This is your job, Nurse Williams. We are not here to accommodate your poor life choices."

"Excuse me?" Georgia's hands curled into fists. Her father had taught her to speak softly, to never raise her hand in violence to another person. But her father had been wrong about a lot of things. She wanted to knock this woman right on her behind.

"That was uncalled for. Your personal life choices are none

of my concern." Nurse Chestnut studied her, her narrow lips pursed. The disdain on her face was clear, and it had Georgia wondering what she did to deserve this treatment. "Just to be clear, you are telling me that you are not going to work the double."

"No, ma'am. I am not. I have worked more hours than any other nurse on this floor. I cannot work anymore. And if you check my contract you will see I'm only supposed to work three twelve-hour shifts in a row, not four, but I do it because you have so few nurses willing to work the night shift."

"Is the time getting to be too much for you? You are looking a little...stressed. Maybe this unit requires more work than you can handle. A transfer might be in order."

"No, ma'am," Georgia said firmly. "This unit is not too much for me. I have been doing my job well. All my patients are happy and all my paperwork is done on time. You have no grounds for a transfer. And frankly, I do not appreciate you implying so."

Nurse Chestnut let out a small frustrated huff. "Well, I see this is a discussion we should have at your review. Please sign up as soon as possible. The sheet is at the nurses' station."

"I will sign up. And maybe I will bring a union rep with me."

Georgia was still fuming by the time she walked into Christian's room. She was so caught up in her own problems she forgot to greet him.

"I never thought I would say this to a woman, but I'm a little afraid of you right now."

He sat up, swinging his legs over the side of the bed just like he had done last night. She wanted to go to him, to bury her head in his shoulder and squeeze him until all of her irritability seeped out of her. But she couldn't. She'd promised she wouldn't touch him again. And she had to be careful around him now. She couldn't risk her job. Especially when she knew he was only temporary in her life.

"I have a headache," she said truthfully. "But I'm fine. I bought you some pajamas. Your grafts are healed. You can wear real clothes now."

He took the pajamas from her and stared down at the T-shirt and sleep pants in his hands. "You bought these for me?"

"No, I stole them from the store. Of course I bought them for you."

"Why?"

"Because you need them, you ass," she said, exasperated.

He grinned at her. "Sit down, Georgia. I thought you might go all shy on me after last night, but I'm glad to see you still have it in you to call me names."

"I think I'll always have it in me to call you names." She sat down and allowed herself to shut her eyes. She'd thought things would be awkward between them, too. She'd thought that as time passed she would feel wicked about what she had done for him, but it had never come. She would always remember last night with fondness. "Talk to me, honey. You know I can't sit down without falling asleep when I'm this tired. I might not wake up if I do."

"I don't like how exhausted you look. I don't like you working all night."

He sounded possessive. It pleased and annoyed her at the same time. "I don't like tomatoes. There. Now we both have things we don't like."

"What's the matter, Georgia?" he asked quietly. "Something happened to you today."

She opened her eyes to find him studying her with concern. None of her other patients noticed, or if they did they didn't bother to ask what was wrong. He could always read her, and the guilt for taking her anger out on him rose up inside her. "I'm sorry, sugar. My boss is on my case and that, combined with my headache, has turned me into a crank pot."

"Nurse Chestnut." He frowned, his face twisting into an expression some might call ugly. "Want me to beat her up for you?"

She smiled at his joke. He could be funny at times. She wondered why so few people saw that. "I think she could take you in a fight, love. But thank you for asking."

"Thank you for bringing me pajamas." He stroked the soft gray T-shirt in his lap as he looked at her. For a moment she imagined that his fingers were stroking her back. If she ever got married she was going to find a man who liked to give back rubs.

"I'm a little tired of having my ass hang out of these damn gowns."

"I should have bought you some underwear, too. I'm sorry I didn't think about it."

"Don't be sorry. You've done enough for me. I want to give you your money back for these, but I know you won't take it."

"You're right. I won't. It's something I wanted to do for you. It's nothing big." She rose and held out her hand. "Let me help you put them on."

He locked eyes with her and then his gaze fell to her lips. When she offered her help she did it purely as a nurse, but when he looked at her, she remembered what happened when she got near him. Tingles broke out all along her skin.

"You're offering to help me strip down naked and then put your hands all over my body while we try to get these on?"

Heat rushed to her cheeks. "Yes. I don't mind. In fact, it would be my pleasure." She had never seen him fully naked. She dreamed about what it would be like to see all six foot six inches of him without clothes on. To run her hands all over him. To have that big body beside her or even on top of her. But those thoughts would have to stay in her dreams. It couldn't happen in the hospital. It could never happen at all.

"No." He shook his head. "Don't touch me."

"You're no fun," she teased, crossing her arms over her chest. Her nipples had gone hard from the moment he'd looked at her with need in his eyes.

She sat back down, hoping that the slight extra distance between them would turn her thoughts pure. "How was your day? I heard General Lee came to see you."

"Is it news every time he walks into this place?"

"Yes. It's not often that we have two-star generals walk through here, and the fact that he comes to see you makes us think that you must be pretty important."

"The general has been like a father to me. Especially after the attack. A lot of my superiors have a hard time looking at me."

"It's not because of your burns, love. It's because they feel guilty that you have to go through that while they run their wars from behind the scenes."

"Georgia." He took a deep breath. "You are entitled to your opinions about war, but I do not want to argue with you about them."

She nodded, not wanting to upset him, but another soldier had come in that day. His arm had been blown off. The bones in his leg were crushed. It was getting harder and harder for her to see these young men coming in.

"It makes sense that the general likes you. You're both terrifying."

His lips twitched. "I thought you weren't scared of me."

"I'm not. Not in the way you think, at least. But I can see the similarities between you two. He probably sees himself in you. What do you talk about anyway? Where to find extrabig shoes? How to scare the poop out of lower ranking soldiers?"

Christian smiled and Georgia's insides warmed. She loved it when he smiled. It transformed his often grim face. She would like to think he smiled more since he had been here. She hoped he wouldn't stop smiling once he left.

"We usually talk about baking and wallpaper, but today he had some news for me."

"Oh?" She braced herself.

"I'm going to be released in two weeks."

She nodded, knowing that this moment was coming. "That's wonderful for you. I'm sure you're sick of it here."

"I've felt useless for so long. I'm glad to finally be able to do something with myself."

"And what will you do with yourself?" She looked into his beautiful green eyes, wanting so badly to hear the right thing.

"I've been promoted to captain. I'm going back to serve."

Her stomach dropped. She'd known this was going to happen. She'd known that Christian wouldn't feel like himself unless he was in the middle of a war-torn country. But she couldn't take it. She couldn't think about him going to the place where he almost lost his life.

"Congratulations." She stood up, the need to cry coming on hard and fast. She didn't want to do it in front of him. She didn't want him to know that he mattered that much to her.

"Wait." He grabbed her wrist, stopping her flight. "What's wrong?"

"Nothing." She tried to shake him free but it was useless.

"Don't lie to me, Georgia," he said softly. "Tell me."

"This is your news. It's not about me. I have nothing to say."

"I thought you were my friend. I thought if there was anybody in the world who would be straight with me it was you."

"Okay," she snapped. "I think it's stupid for you to go back. You did your time. You almost died for your country. I think you did all you could for the marines."

"That's not true. I can still serve."

"You can and you will, but what's the point? You alone aren't going to stop the war. All you're going to end up doing is dying. And you think it won't matter because you have nobody here to mourn you but that's not true, Christian. I will mourn you. I will cry for you. Why can't you be done now?"

"It's my life."

"No! It's your job. You don't have a life. You use the marines as an excuse not to make a life."

"Who are you to talk?" he said quietly. "What kind of life do you have if some scarred marine is your only real friend? You don't work the night shift for the money. You do it so you can hide from the world, from other people. Your life doesn't have to be like this."

"Don't." She shoved his shoulder. "Don't you dare make assumptions about my life when you have no idea what I went through. What I go through every day just to make sure my daughter is fed. You can turn it around on me if you want, but I didn't choose this life. It happened to me, and I'm determined to make the best of it so that my daughter can have the world. You are not choosing life. You won't be satisfied until they pull you out of the desert in a body bag."

"You don't understand."

"You're right. I don't and I never will." She wrenched her hand from his hold. "I hope you end up happy, Christian. I really do."

"Hello, Miss Georgia," Tobias called to her cheerfully when she walked into his room the next night.

She smiled at the boy even though she knew he couldn't

see her. His good humor was, at times, infectious. She could use some of that good humor today.

The argument she'd had with Christian still rolled around in her mind. It had kept her up all morning. She regretted that they had shared such angry words, but she didn't regret what she'd said. He was just healing. He was just getting the use of his arm back and now he was prepared to go off and risk it all. But as a captain. Ten years of his life wasn't enough time to give. She knew he felt guilty about being one of the few to survive, but when was it going to be enough?

She didn't know why it bothered her so much. She'd known that it was coming. She'd known he was going to go back. She should admire him for his dedication. Instead she was mourning the life he could have had.

All the thinking made her headache worse. The pain from yesterday hadn't gone away. It had intensified, almost to the point where she had a hard time lifting her head. Each noise made it worse. Every beam of light that hit her face was nearly excruciating. Every step she took was a Herculean effort.

Mrs. Sheppard had urged her to call in sick, but Georgia couldn't. She would be off for three days after tonight's shift and she wanted to save her sick time in case Abby grew ill.

"How are you tonight, Tobias?" She rubbed her temples, trying to relieve some of the pressure.

"Better. I can see a little more every day. I can almost see what you look like."

"I hope I don't disappoint you with my looks."

"No. If you look anything like Captain Howard says you do I can't be disappointed."

"Captain Howard?" The mention of Christian's name captured her attention.

"Oh, yeah, he got promoted for bravery. He probably didn't tell you. He barely wanted to talk about it today."

"You talk to Christian?"

"Yes, ma'am. Every day. We've become friends."

"Oh." She didn't know that. But it made sense that he'd befriended Tobias. Tobias was a sweet boy. It would be hard for Christian not to like him. And in a way she was relieved that he didn't sit alone in his room all day. "I'm glad you are his friend, Tobias. He doesn't have many visitors."

"That's because people don't get to know him. I can finally kind of see him now. He's a big son of a bitch but he's a good man."

"He is." She gripped the side of his bed, suddenly feeling a little lightheaded. "He's going to be released soon, I—I hope...." She took a deep breath as her head started to spin.

"Miss Georgia, are you okay?"

"I'm—I'm..." Her legs gave out. She felt herself falling and she smashed her head against the nightstand just before her world went black.

"Miss Georgia!"

Christian sat up when he heard Tobias yell Georgia's name. His heart began to race. His cry wasn't one of excitement but of terror.

"Help me! Somebody help me."

No more thoughts passed through Christian's head after that. He had to get to Georgia. They had argued last night, and while he was angry with her for disagreeing with everything he stood for, he couldn't help but notice how pale she was, how dull her eyes were or the pinched look of pain that never left her face.

"Captain Howard?" He found Tobias hovering over Georgia. "We were just talking and—and she went down. I think she hit her head."

He gently pushed the boy out of the way so he could see

her. "No." His heart stopped. Georgia lay on the ground, her face colorless. She looked lifeless. "Baby, no." He checked her pulse. It was weak but she was still breathing. "Georgia." He lifted her head. "Wake up, honey. You've got to wake up." It was when he felt the sticky warmth touch his hand that he noticed the blood seeping from her hairline.

"Shit."

"Is she all right?" Tobias asked.

"I don't know." He lifted her limp body into his arms and ran into the hallway. It was empty. Not a doctor, not an orderly, not a person in sight.

He didn't know what to do. Too much time was passing. She was getting paler by the second. So he did the only thing he could think to do. He started screaming for help. The patients who were mobile came out into hallway.

"Is that Nurse Williams?" he heard one of them say.

"You," he snapped at the boy nearest to him. "Go find somebody. Now."

"There's an alarm, sir," another soldier said. "It's for codes but I can pull it for you."

"Yes, do that."

"There's an empty room next to mine, sir. Put her in there," another man said.

By the time he had put her in bed, a doctor, two orderlies and a few nurses from other parts of the hospital had arrived.

"What happened?" one of the nurses asked. "Did he throw a tray at her?"

"Get out," he barked at the nurse. Georgia was hurt. If the nurse would rather make comments than help they didn't need her.

"Captain Howard didn't hurt her," Tobias yelled. "She was in my room and she passed out. She's sick. You need to help her."

"Get these patients back into bed," the doctor ordered. "Right now. Georgia—" he touched her face "—can you hear me?"

She didn't respond. She didn't stir and the panic that welled up inside Christian was breath stealing.

"Come on, Captain Howard." The other nurse touched his arm. "Let's get you back to your room. You were a big help tonight."

"I'm not leaving until she wakes up."

The nurse exchanged a worried look with the doctor.

"He can stay," he said, glancing at Christian and undoubtedly realizing there was no way he could be moved. "Come on, Georgia girl, let's find out what's wrong with you."

Six hours later Georgia had five stitches in her head and an IV in her hand and she still hadn't woken up.

Christian tried not to let his worry for her take over. Her color was coming back. The doctor said it was a mixture of exhaustion and dehydration that had caused her to pass out. The bump she'd taken to her head only made matters worse.

As he watched her unmoving body, he was torn between wanting to strangle her and wanting to hold her. He was furious with her for not taking care of herself. She said she had no choice, but there had to be another way. She wouldn't be around to raise her daughter at this rate. Something needed to change.

"Captain Howard." Nurse Chestnut came into the room, followed by Dr. Allen and what looked like two hospital administrators. "Congratulations on your promotion."

"Thank you, ma'am."

"Yes, Captain, we all congratulate you," one of the administrators said before glancing at Georgia. "We also hear that you were instrumental in coming to the aid of Nurse

Williams. We hear practically the entire floor took part in her care."

"Yes." He looked back to Georgia, resisting the urge to touch her. "We had to. It took so long for your staff to get here to help her I wondered if we were going to have to treat her ourselves."

They all exchanged uncomfortable looks.

"Yes, well, the night shift is always sparsely staffed. Nobody expected Nurse Williams to be the one who needed medical attention."

"What exactly was she doing when she bumped her head?" Nurse Chestnut asked, as if Georgia had been up to no good.

"She was doing her job." He looked the woman directly in the eyes. "She was in Lance Corporal Clark's room when she passed out and hit her head."

"I see," Nurse Chestnut said. "And you were the first one to hear his call for help?"

"Yes."

It must have been hearing her boss's voice, but Georgia started to stir a little.

Christian turned toward her.

Georgia sprung up with a gasp. "I'm late for work." She bolted from the bed, ripping the IV from her hand. Christian caught her by the waist just as her feet hit the ground. She was still too weak—her legs crumbled beneath her and he once again had to lift her into his arms.

"Georgia, relax."

She blinked at him. It took a few moments for her eyes to focus. "Christian? What are you doing in my house?"

"I'm not. It's 6:00 a.m.—you're still at work."

"Put her back in bed, Captain Howard," Dr. Allen said. "Her hand is bleeding."

"It hurts." She looked into Christian's eyes. "My head hurts, too. Why are you holding me? What happened?"

He put her back into bed. If there weren't so many damn people in the room he would have tried to soothe her, but he knew that if he let his instincts take over, Georgia's job would be in jeopardy.

"Maybe we should go and let Dr. Allen tend to his patient," one of the other administrators said. "We're glad to see you are awake."

They scurried out of the room before anybody could say anything more to them.

"Let's get you cleaned up again, Georgia," Dr. Allen said.

"Georgia, the hospital insists that you take the next week off," Nurse Chestnut told her. "You'll have to stay here, of course, until the doctor clears you to go home, but we do not expect to see you until you are able to perform your job again."

"I hate to agree with her," Dr. Allen said. "But what you need is rest. You are suffering from dehydration and exhaustion. This is very serious, Georgia. Your body needs to recoup."

She sighed but said nothing.

"We're going to leave you alone to rest now," Nurse Chestnut said when Dr. Allen was finished treating Georgia's hand. "We'll have someone come check on you in a few hours."

She tried to sit up, but Christian prevented her from doing so with a firm hand on her shoulder.

"I don't want to be left alone here."

"You are not to get up, Nurse Williams." Nurse Chestnut frowned at her. "Dr. Allen needs to get back to work and Captain Howard needs to get back to bed."

"Could you sit here with me for a little while, ma'am?"

Nurse Chestnut blanched. "Of course not," she snapped,

but when Christian and Dr. Allen frowned at her she softened her voice. "I have work to do, dear. Maybe Captain Howard would agree to stay with you for a few more minutes."

"I will."

"It's settled. I'll see you when you return to work." She left without another word.

"I'll come check on you in a few hours, Georgia," Dr. Allen told her. He gave Christian a long look before he left the room.

"I thought they were never going to go." She rolled over to face him. "I knew she wasn't going to stay. She'd rather get eaten by fire ants."

"Georgia." He grabbed her face. "Do you realize why you are here? You collapsed from exhaustion. You hit your head. You cannot go on like this anymore. What's going to happen the next time you pass out?"

"Why do you care?" She searched his face for a moment. "You're leaving soon."

He was leaving soon. He was leaving her soon. He didn't think about it at first when General Lee had given him the news, but it was happening. In two weeks he would have to go back to living life without her.

It was too much to think about, so he pressed his lips to hers and kissed her deeply. He needed to touch her, to be close to her, to know she was really okay.

She responded, even though she was still weak. Her hands came up to hold his head in place and she moved her lips beneath his, her tongue touching his. Her kisses were sweet and soft and more sensual than any sick woman should be able to give.

He pulled back before the kiss could go any further. He knew that was a mistake when he looked down at her and saw that her lips were pink and slightly kiss swollen. Plus she looked content and sleepy and it made that thing in his chest squeeze again.

"Will you take my hair down? It's too tight."

"You've got stitches." He lifted his hands to unbind her hair but hesitated for a moment. He had dreamed about taking her hair down, about it lying across his naked chest. He'd never thought he would get to take it down now, especially after she got hurt.

"Go on," she urged him.

He untied her hair band and watched the heavy mass fall past her shoulders and gather on the bed. "It's so long," he muttered. He couldn't stop himself. He buried his fingers in it at the base of her neck and rubbed her scalp.

"That feels good." Her eyes drifted shut again and she turned her face toward him. If he leaned down just a few inches his lips would touch hers.

"Go back to sleep, baby."

"I want to. I'm so tired."

"It's your time to rest."

"Wait." She tried to sit up but Christian grabbed her by her shoulders and eased her back down.

"No getting up, Georgia. Do you understand me?"

"Don't bark at me like I'm one of your soldiers. I have to get home to my baby."

"You can't go home yet. How are you going to take care of a baby when you can't even stand on your feet?"

"It's almost seven. I pick her up at seven."

The panic was clear in her voice, and as much as Christian wanted to strangle her, he admired her, too. He'd never loved anything or anybody this much in his life. She sacrificed it all for her daughter. "I'm going to call your babysitter for you." He picked up the phone. "What's her number?"

"I should do it. She'll be worried if you call."

"Give me the number. And if you don't calm down I'm going to have somebody sedate you."

She glared at him, seeming to have more spirit now that she was sick than she'd had when she was well. "Fine." She rattled off the number.

He pressed a kiss to her forehead as the phone rang.

"Her name is Mrs. Sheppard," she told him, the anxiety never leaving her voice.

"I know."

"Hello?"

"Hello, Mrs. Sheppard. I'm calling from Jericho Medical on behalf of Georgia Williams."

"Oh, my lord. What happened? I told her not to go to work. I knew she was too sick."

"You told her to stay home?" He raised his brows and looked down at Georgia. "She's stubborn. The world is not going to collapse if she takes a damn sick day. Excuse my language, ma'am, but she is suffering from exhaustion and dehydration and has been ordered to rest for the next week. She will not be able to pick up Abby until this afternoon. I don't think she should drive, either. Do you think it would be possible for you to pick her up today?"

"Of course. Of course. Are you her doctor?"

"No, ma'am."

"You wouldn't happen to be the young man she has become friends with?"

He looked down at Georgia's worried face. Had she talked about him to this woman? Did he mean more to her than what he thought? "I might be that man."

"Oh." She lowered her voice. "She needs somebody to take care of her, Christian. She thinks she can do it all on her own but she needs somebody. We all do."

Mrs. Sheppard knew his name. What had Georgia said

about him and why did he feel as though this woman was trying to send him a message? Georgia did need somebody to take care of her, but it couldn't be him. She deserved better.

CHAPTER 11

When Georgia opened her eyes, there was a huge angry-looking man hovering over her, but his fingers were gently stroking her hair, which ruined the effect.

Christian had been there every time she'd opened her eyes today. He was angry with her. He was worried about her, and while she was glad not to be alone while they forced her to stay in this hospital room, she wished he would go away. Because every time she opened her eyes and saw him there it reminded her that he was leaving soon and that she would never have this again.

"Why are you still here?"

"You said you didn't want to be alone."

"I know, but I'm okay now and you should be back in bed. You're not fully healed yet."

He went silent for a moment. His expression was blank, and Georgia knew that was his way of being stubborn.

"Christian…"

"Damn it, Georgia. You scared the shit out of me. You wouldn't wake up. I picked you up off the ground pale and limp and you expect me to go back to my room and forget that it happened? And the thing that gets me the most is that I know that you are going to go back to the same shit that got you here in the first place."

"And now you know what I feel like hearing that you are going back to serve."

"Georgia," he barked at her. "That is different and I will not discuss it with you further."

"I'll be fine." She turned away from him. "I'll make sure I start using my sick days to catch up on some sleep."

"You need to eat better, too, and drink more water."

"Yes, sir." She mock-saluted him.

"Don't be a smart-ass." He touched her shoulder, causing her to turn back over. His gaze was so damn intense on her face. If he felt this strongly about a nurse he met a little over a month ago, then she could only imagine how he would treat his wife or somebody he really loved.

That kind of emotion must be heavenly and suffocating at the same time, but she knew that any woman Christian chose for a wife would be a lucky one.

"Come closer. I need to tell you something."

"What?"

She took his face in her hands and kissed him. He had kissed her mouth for the first time that day, and no matter how much sleep she got or how many fluids they were pumping into her, it had made her feel more alive than she had ever felt before. It took him a moment before he returned her kiss. She knew that every time she touched him he had to restrain himself. She knew how strong he was, how it would take no effort for him at all to overpower her, but he didn't. Looking at him she knew he would never physically hurt her. He was the opposite of what she thought men were.

"Stop it," he said into her mouth.

"Why?" She lifted her lips from his only to drag them to the burned side of his face. He shut his eyes as she kissed the corner of his downturned mouth, where the fire had caused his skin to pucker. It was odd, but she loved his burns. She wouldn't want to see him any other way.

"You promised."

"I lied."

"Georgia."

"What? I've got stitches in my head and an IV in my hand. I should be entitled to some comfort."

"This isn't at night. There are dozens of people walking around the hospital in the morning. Do you really want to get caught with me?"

"No, I'd rather get caught with Sergeant Johansen down the hall, but you're the one that's here."

His lips unwillingly curled into a smile and she took advantage of it and kissed him again. He groaned, and this time gave in immediately. When he kissed her she felt it down to her toes. It made her not want to stop. It made her want to kiss him for hours.

"You're leaving in less than two weeks. I should get to kiss you all I want."

He pulled away slightly, speaking into her lips. "You have no idea how hard it is for me to hold back."

"I do, Christian. I know all about men who lose control. My daughter is the product of one. I appreciate you."

His expression turned pained, and he reached forward to cup her face in his hands. "Why did you pick me? I'm not a man who has made a lot of good decisions in my life."

"You're not as bad as you think, love."

"Excuse me."

They both jumped at the sound. General Lee stood in the door and Christian visibly relaxed.

"General, I didn't expect to see you today." He stood up, partially shielding Georgia from the general's view. They hadn't been doing anything when the man walked in, but just a moment before they had been, and Georgia was mortified. They hadn't even heard the door open.

"No. I wasn't planning to come." He looked around Christian to Georgia. There was no judgment in his eyes, merely curiosity. "I came to talk to you about your plans for the future."

"This is Georgia. She's a nurse here."

"I know. Nice to meet you, ma'am. The whole hospital has been buzzing about you. I'm sorry that you are unwell."

"Thank you, sir. If Christian hadn't come for me it could have been a lot worse."

He nodded. "He's a good man. Son? Would you mind if I spoke to you alone for a few minutes?"

"I'll meet you back at my room."

The general nodded and left the room.

"That was too close, Georgia."

"I know."

"If it had been anybody else…"

"I know. I think you'd better stay in your room for the rest of the day."

He nodded. "Are you going to be okay alone?"

She was alone before he came into her life. She would be alone after he left. She wouldn't be okay, but she would survive. She didn't have any other choice. "Yes." She nodded. "You can go."

Four days into her week off Georgia was feeling more like her normal self. Mrs. Sheppard came after her like an angry mama bear and took care of her for the first two days. She made sure Georgia ate three meals a day plus snacks. She took

Abby while Georgia napped and helped her more than anybody had since her father kicked her out. She wished she could
find a way to repay the older woman, but no object seemed
good enough or big enough to thank her.

Even though her body was recouping and she was enjoying
the extra hours with Abby, Georgia felt a little guilty about
not working. She'd never had a vacation, working well into
her ninth month of pregnancy even after her doctor ordered
her to stop. But she didn't know how to be idle. Her father
had had her and Carolina doing chores the moment they got
up. They had to help with breakfast and do the laundry. He
required them to scrub the bathrooms daily.

I'm teaching you to be proper wives.

But he never said a word to her brothers about being proper
husbands. She'd silently balked at that when she was still living under his control. It felt wrong to her that her brothers
had to do nothing while she and her sister were forced to be
subservient to them.

She wondered how they were now. They weren't bad men.
They'd just believed everything their father said. She hoped
they'd found their own paths. She hoped they'd learned how
to treat a woman.

That made her think about Christian. There had been a
slightly heavy ache in her chest since she'd sent him back to
his room four days ago. She couldn't be missing him already.
She had come to terms with his leaving. She had convinced
herself that he was a pleasant little interlude in her life. That
he was somebody who took away from the monotony of her
life for just a little while.

"Mama?" Abby looked up at Georgia with wide eyes. She
was holding the new baby doll Georgia had gotten her for
her birthday.

"Yes, love?"

Abby stood up and lifted her arms to picked up. It was almost as if she was checking to see that Georgia was still there. Abby was used to being shipped off to Mrs. Sheppard's at this time of night. It was as though her little body had some kind of alarm clock that warned her when it was time for her mother to go away.

"I'm not going anywhere. You have me for three more whole days and nights." She settled Abby in her lap as her daughter snuggled against her breasts. "You're a good girl. You know that? You're better than you should be. If you threw tantrums or acted like a brat sometimes, Mama wouldn't feel so rotten about leaving you. But you don't. You seem to know how hard things are for us. I appreciate you." She kissed her forehead. "I want you to know that and I hope I don't forget to tell you that from time to time."

Abby looked up at her, her little face scrunched in confusion. "You have no idea what I'm rambling on about. Do you, baby?"

"No!"

"Ah, your favorite word." She grinned at her daughter before she picked her up and smothered her face with kisses.

The ringing phone saved Abby from being kissed to death. Placing her daughter on her hip, she answered it.

"Hello?"

"Georgia?" a quiet voice asked. "Is that you?"

All at once Georgia started to tremble all over. Abby touched her face, reminding her that she couldn't fall apart. That this was the voice she had been longing to hear for so long.

"Mama? I'm here."

"My sweetheart," she choked.

Georgia noticed the difference in her voice. Her mother sounded frail, almost broken. For a moment Georgia thought her mind was playing tricks on her and that this woman on the other end of the phone couldn't be her mother. But it was. She knew her mother's voice as well as she knew Abby's face. Her dulcet-toned accent couldn't be replicated.

"Tell me you're happy, Georgia." Her voice came out strangled. Panicked. "Please. I need to know."

Out of all the people who had betrayed her, she wanted to be mad at her mother the most, but she couldn't muster up any anger. Georgia and Carolina may have been indentured servants to the family, but their mother's fate was far worse than theirs. She had lost a child, too. Her firstborn son. She had taken the brunt of her husband's harsh change in behavior. He treated her as if her loss was less than his.

Fiona had always been so delicate, so beautiful. Her soul didn't seem like the kind that could survive living with such an unyielding man. And yet for years, she'd seemed to soldier on.

Little by little, though, she'd stopped laughing. She would put on a show for the parishioners, curling her lips when it seemed appropriate, but the family stopped seeing any real joy come from their mother.

At first their father pretended he didn't notice, but even he couldn't miss that his beautiful wife was slipping away into herself. He said it was her nerves. He blamed it on his daughters for not doing enough of the housework to take the burden off their mother. But that simply wasn't true. And even though Fiona never said a word against her husband, all of her children knew they were loved. She showed them in secret ways. They seemed to be what kept her going, and now they were all gone, grown up with lives of their own. She was left in a house with a bitter man who had never gotten over the death of his son.

Georgia couldn't stomach that. Especially after she had read her sister's letter.

"Come stay with me, Mama. You don't have to be there anymore. Live with me, Mama. I'll take care of you."

"I—I can't."

In the end she always chose her husband. Georgia swore she would never be like that. Abby would always come first. "Please, Mama." She tried one more time, the tears streaming down her cheeks. "Just come see me, then. I miss you."

"He's coming. I have to go. I love you."

She disconnected, and with her daughter in her arms Georgia broke down and sobbed.

Christian was restless. He was tired of being confined to his room, to this hospital. He was tired of spending his days doing nothing. Eating shitty food and waiting for something to happen. He knew he had to go back.

His superiors had finally come down from Washington to officially offer him his promotion to captain and to thank him for his service. They told him he had options now. They said he could be an instructor, like General Lee had suggested, or he could lead his own company in Afghanistan.

He had done a tour there already. It was much different from Iraq. The terrain alone was a major obstacle to overcome. He knew the statistics. This would be his fourth time overseas. He had already been hurt. He might not come back alive. But what was his other option? He didn't see himself in the classroom. He needed to be where the action was. This long stay in the hospital had made that incredibly clear.

He left his bed, tired of seeing the damn thing, and paced around his room. The doctors told him he had another full week there. He wasn't sure why. Parts of his skin were still tender and healing, but his body was ready. His brutally bruised ribs had healed. He didn't have full use of his arm, but he could move it well enough. He was sure it would be fine when he was able to really use it. His physical therapist was surprised at the ferocity with which Christian had approached his workouts for the past week. If he wasn't exhausted and sweaty by the end of them, then he hadn't worked hard enough.

He couldn't wait to go running, to lift weights, to be physical. The day he walked out of this hospital couldn't come soon enough.

"Hello, Christian."

He turned around to face the only person who made him doubt his plans, who made him want to rethink throwing himself back into action.

"Georgia." Something physical happened to him when he saw her. It was similar to the rush he felt when he was returning enemy fire or the first time he parachuted out of a plane. His blood surged, his heart pounded in his chest. His reaction to her was so strong that he knew it wasn't normal. It was maddening. He missed her. Seven days without seeing her, without hearing her sweet Southern accent, without feeling her touch on his ruined skin. He'd thought about her as much as he'd thought about his future this past week, and it confused the hell out of him. "Welcome back."

"Thank you." Her eyes touched his face before they traveled to his nightstand—to the big pink gift bag that sat on top of it. "What's that?"

"Happy birthday." His face burned with embarrassment. He had debated for three days about whether he should acknowledge it. She had only mentioned it to him once. He didn't want her to think he remembered every word that passed her lips, but he did, and in the end he wanted to thank her for making his time at Jericho Medical less miserable.

"Christian." Her eyes welled up with tears.

"None of that," he ordered.

She nodded and tilted her head back to keep the tears from running down her face.

"It's nothing much," he tried to explain. He had General Lee bring a small cake and present for Georgia. He expected the man to question him, to ask about the woman who he'd almost walked in on kissing Christian. He'd never said a word about what he'd witnessed. He'd simply asked what flavor of cake he wanted.

"Come open your present."

She shook her head. "I don't want to."

"Why not?"

"You're making this hard."

She didn't have to elaborate. He knew exactly what she was talking about. He was making their inevitable separation that much harder.

"Open it anyway." He crossed the room and grabbed her hand, which was a mistake, because whatever strange pull that existed between them intensified tenfold. Her small, warm hand felt right tucked into his.

He led her to the chair and let go of her hand as soon as possible so he could give her his gift. "I wasn't sure what to get you, so I got you something I thought you could use."

"A bathrobe." She looked up at him. "Bunny slippers." Her smile lit up the room. "Bubble bath. A book!"

"It's to help you rest." He looked away from her. He hadn't bought a present for anybody since his parents died. Seeing how happy she looked caused a lump to form in his chest. It made him want to press his lips to her smile and drink in some of her happiness. "You need to rest more."

"How did you know I loved art?" She lifted the coffee-table book and gently stroked the glossy pages.

"I didn't. I had to take an elective in college and the only one they had to fit in my schedule was Women in Art Through the Ages. My professor wrote the forward to this book and I thought you might like it."

"I love it," she whispered. "This is the best present I've ever gotten."

"It can't be."

She nodded. "It is. My father wasn't one of those flashy preachers. We only had what we needed, never more. And any extra money we had went directly to the needy. I admired that about him. He believed in what he preached, but he thought most art was scandalous. Unless it was of flowers or fields or Jesus, we weren't allow to see it. When other girls were sneaking off to meet their boyfriends I was sneaking off to go to the library so I could look at art books. Thank you, Christian." She hugged the book to her chest. "I will keep this forever."

He had to clench his hands into fists to keep from pulling her out of that chair and kissing her. They couldn't do that anymore. The last time had been too close of a call. Plus they were friends. This crazy attraction was only because they were stuck in the confines of the hospital. In the real world they might not have given each other another look.

"How are you feeling? You look much better," he said, to take his mind off those thoughts. Her color had returned to the pretty shade of honey it was when they'd first met. Her cheeks were fuller. She was always beautiful, but now that she was well rested he had a hard time tearing his eyes away from her.

"I feel fine. Mrs. Sheppard keeps feeding me. At first I felt bad about her going through all the trouble but she says it makes her happy to have somebody to cook for again. I think she gets lonely, too."

Too? He focused on that word. Georgia was lonely. He knew how it felt to be lonely even though he spent half his time trying to deny what he felt.

"I gained five pounds this week." She blushed adorably.

"You could stand to gain a little more."

"That's what every woman wants to hear from a man. I do believe you are getting smoother, sir." They smiled at each other for a moment. "My week was good and well needed, but tonight was hard. I had to leave Abby with Mrs. Sheppard again after a week of having her to myself. When I handed her over she looked at me as though I had betrayed her. It was almost as hard as having to leave her for the first time."

"What do you dream about, Georgia? If you didn't have this job and all your bills to worry about, what kind of life would you live?"

He had taken her by surprise. She blinked at him. "I don't know. I never thought about it."

"Think about it now."

"I'd marry a rich old man who was too old to bother me. Tell my boss off. Quit my job and spend all day with my baby."

"What else?"

"I would bake again. I haven't had time since I left home but I used to love it. I would teach Abby how."

"What else?"

"I would take my mama away from my father. Maybe send her on a big vacation around the world. She's always wanted to go to Florence, Italy."

"What about for yourself? What would you do that is purely selfish?"

She shut her eyes and thought for a minute. Her pouty lips curled into a dreamy smile. "Lobster. A big two-pound lobster with melted butter, corn on the cob and maybe some steamers. Or scallops and a baked potato with tons of sour cream and butter. And for dessert, blueberry pie with a big scoop of vanilla ice cream."

Out of all the dreams in the world, that was the one she chose for herself. It made him smile. The nearly blissful expression on her face made him harden. She would be a good wife to some man. To him…

That thought was unwelcome. He didn't love her. He wasn't really sure he was capable of such a feeling, but he knew he couldn't go off to war and leave her behind. She would be a distraction. He wouldn't be able to concentrate knowing she was at home waiting for him.

"That sounds almost naughty."

"It is. I had lobster only once in my life. One of the wealthy parishioners invited us to a lobster bake at his beach house. My father said such decadence was sinful, but that lobster was just about the best thing I have ever tasted." She opened her eyes and looked at him. "You're making me want things I can never have."

She could have them. She could be some man's wife. She could spend more time with her baby. She could have lobster again. Her dreams weren't so big. She just had to reach out and take them.

"It's not so bad to dream sometimes, Georgia."

"I guess not." She stood. He did, as well. "Thank you for this, Christian. For everything."

"You didn't have any cake." It was foolish to want to keep her there any longer. As the minutes ticked by he was finding it harder and harder to keep his hands to himself.

"Save it for me." She placed her gift bag on the floor and reached up to hug him. "I should be getting back to work." She wrapped her arms around his middle and rested her head against his chest. He had missed the feel of her against him. "Good God, you're tall."

He sat on his bed so that they were eye to eye, chest to chest. Her neat little body was tucked between his legs. "Is that better?"

"No," she breathed.

He brushed his lips across hers. "I think it is."

She groaned his name. "You're not supposed to do this to me."

"I can't help it." He captured her lips in a kiss, not like the ones they had shared before. There was no sweetness in his kiss. Only need. She responded so quickly, gripping the back of his head, holding his face to hers. Her mouth tasted good. Like mint mixed with tea. He could taste her all night. Thankfully she seemed to let him.

This time, unlike all the other times, he couldn't be respectful. He couldn't control the way his hands wandered her body. He grabbed her behind, cupped the firm flesh in his hands and squeezed. She reacted to it. She kissed him harder, pulled him closer, rubbed her breasts against him. He could feel her hard nipples through the thin material of her scrubs. It was too much. He grasped her breast, rubbing his thumb over the hard little point.

She gasped and looked up at him.

"I'm sorry, Georgia. I'm sorry," he panted. "I lost control."

"No, I liked it. I like the way that feels."

She hesitated for a moment, but then she took his hand and slid it beneath her shirt and placed it on her naked breast. It filled his hand. He rolled her nipple between his fingers, watching the look of ecstasy that crossed her face. His erection pushed against his pants, begging for freedom. She aroused him like no other woman had. He had to be inside of her.

His kissed the column of her throat down to the top of her chest while he stroked her breast.

He had to see her naked. He had to have her beneath him and on top of him and every way he'd imagined since they'd first met. It was too much. She'd finally broken him.

"I need to be with you, Georgia. I need to. I can't stop myself anymore."

"Okay."

"Okay?" He pulled his lips away from her to look into her eyes. He never dreamed she would agree so quickly.

"Yes. But not here."

"No." He removed his hand from her breast. It couldn't be here. He wanted to make love to her in a real bed, in a nice place where they didn't have to leave for hours. "I'm going to Afghanistan soon after I leave here. I have a few days in between. We could spend them together."

She shook her head. "Just once, Christian. We can only be together once."

He nodded, understanding her reasoning. If it was more than once it would be nearly impossible for him to walk away.

He stroked his hands down her back, unable to break their connection for even one moment. "You should say no. I don't deserve you. You shouldn't give me your body."

"Why not?"

"I'm not as good as you think. I've done bad things in my life."

"As a soldier?" She ran her fingers through his hair. "I don't like war, but surely God won't blame you for what you did in the name of your country."

"No, it's worse than that."

"Tell me." She ran her slim fingers along the curve of his mangled ear. She looked so understanding, so patient, so ready to hear his confession.

He swallowed hard. He never shared what he had done with anyone. "It happened when I was stationed in Japan."

He told her the whole story, about Miko, about his friends, about how he didn't do all that he could have to help an innocent girl.

She didn't say anything for a long time after he finished. She'd been raped and ended up pregnant. She should hate him, because in the end he was just as guilty as his friends.

"It doesn't change my mind about you," she finally said.

"How could it not?" He gripped her waist, pulling her closer. "I could have stopped it."

"Maybe. But you were still a kid and you don't know exactly what happened that night. You tried. You did a lot more than some other people might have done and you spent the past eleven years being the best man you could possibly be. You've got to forgive yourself."

But he couldn't. "I wish I could find a way to make up for it."

"You can." She ran her lips along his scarred cheek. "You are going to be the first man to make love to me. You are going to show me how beautiful sex can be."

I am, he thought as he kissed her. He held her face to his and kissed her long and deep. She went slack in his arms, leaning her entire weight on him.

He didn't deserve her, or this chance to be with such a forgiving woman, but he was going to let himself have something good and sweet and pure for just one night. Because after he left her he was going to devote the rest of his life to the marines.

"Nurse Williams! What on earth are you doing?"

They broke apart only to see Georgia's supervisor, Nurse Chestnut, staring at them with a look of disgust on her face.

Georgia kept her expression calm, but dread filled Christian. He knew he had just cost Georgia her job.

CHAPTER 12

Fired on her birthday. Georgia knew as soon as she heard Nurse Chestnut's voice her career at Jericho Medical was over. She didn't say a word to defend herself, because there was nothing she could say. She had been kissing Christian. She had engaged in an inappropriate relationship with a patient. But she didn't regret a single moment of it. She was just sad that her time with him was over.

Her father would have said that getting fired was the least of what she deserved. He would have said it was wicked to offer her body to a man who wasn't her husband. He would have told her she was going to burn in hell.

Maybe what she'd done with Christian was wicked. But she knew she wasn't going to burn in hell for it. It wasn't wrong of her to want to spend one night with a man who made her feel amazing and safe, and treated her kindly and remembered her birthday.

Georgia was never like her sister. Carolina was the sweet one. Her father's favorite daughter. She never spoke out of turn or did anything to anger him. Georgia may not have been the sweet, docile girl her father wanted her to be, but she wasn't a bad person. She always tried to follow his rules, to take the message he preached every Sunday to heart. But that didn't get her anywhere, because in the end he'd accused of her being a wanton, a fallen woman, a whore. All because some man had taken advantage of her.

No, she refused to feel guilty about her relationship with Christian. Instead she felt desperate. She had lost her job. Her prospects for another were slim to none. Who was going to be her reference? She knew how this incident would look to a future employer. As if she was untrustworthy.

She racked her brain for options. She was going to apply for jobs anyway. Maybe she could get her old one back at the hospice center. She wasn't sure what she would do if nobody hired her. There were only two other options. Go on public assistance or take Carolina's offer and move in with her. Both options were unattractive.

She could work. She was a good nurse. She didn't want to take money that she didn't earn. But the thought of going to live with her sister was even worse. She would have to go there in shame. As a failure. Her sister and brother-in-law would have to support her and Abby and she couldn't stomach that, either.

So the pulled out the paper the next morning and started looking for jobs.

It took Christian a day and a half to get released from the hospital, and another half day before he was able to track down where Georgia lived. He couldn't get the image of her face out of his mind. Her boss was berating her, attacking her character, but she kept her head up, and in a move that stunned him and Nurse Chestnut, she'd kissed him softly on the mouth and walked out of his room. He couldn't let it end like that. He'd ruined her career.

The next morning he'd gone to the hospital administrators to explain to them that what had happened between him and Georgia was his fault. And it was. She'd known how magnetic they were when they were near each other. She'd tried to keep her distance but he wouldn't let her. He'd kissed her.

After much discussion and a little bullying, he got the administrators to overturn Nurse Chestnut's decision. Georgia was a good nurse. Her patients loved her. They could find no other fault with her besides a lapse in judgment when dealing with Christian.

In the end they agreed to give her a three-week unpaid suspension, but he knew Georgia couldn't afford to miss any paychecks. He had to fix that.

He had more money than he knew what to do with. He could help her out. He could make her life comfortable. But when he pulled up in front of her apartment building, the thought of giving her money didn't sit right with him. He didn't know what else to do. He was planning to go to Afghanistan in two weeks. After that he might never see her again.

He took a deep breath as he ascended the stairs to her second-floor apartment. The building was dark. The hallways were long and narrow. He didn't like the idea of Georgia walking through them alone at night. But he shook off his troubling thoughts and knocked on her door.

"Coming," she called.

His heart raced as he waited. Would she even want to see him? He wasn't so sure. She hadn't seemed upset with him when she'd left two days ago, but he wondered how she would feel now. Now that she had had time to process what had happened to her.

"Christian," she gasped when she opened the door.

His heart lurched in his chest. He had never seen her out of her scrubs before, but there she was before him in a nearly threadbare white tank top and a pair of jeans that curved to her body nicely. And what a body it was. Large firm breasts, a small waist that he could wrap his hands around and round hips that appealed to a baser need in him. But her body aside, it was her face that nearly knocked the breath out of him. Worry seemed to have etched itself in her eyes. She was exhausted. He couldn't imagine how the past two days had been for her.

"You shouldn't answer the door without looking in your peephole. Strange men could be standing on the other side of your door."

"I never thought I would see you again." She shook her head. "You're not supposed to be released for another five days."

"Do you think after what happened I was going to leave things how they were?"

She shook her head. "I don't know. I tried not to think about you very much." She stepped aside. "Come in."

He entered her tiny apartment. It was one room with an old daybed and a small table in the corner. But besides that there was nothing much except a crib in the corner and a TV. It was very tidy.

She would do any marine proud, but that was the only positive thing he could think about this place. The radiator appeared to be busted. There were cracks in the wall, big splotches where the paint had chipped off. It didn't feel homey or comfortable to him. Christian wasn't a man who was used to comfort, but when he thought of the place she called home he never thought it would look like this.

"Sit with me, Christian," she said, distracting him from

his thoughts. "I just put Abby down for a nap. We'll have to be a little quiet."

He nodded and sat next to her. His thigh brushed hers. The bare skin of her arm brushed his and it brought back memories of how she felt in his arms. It made him remember the aching need he had for her two days ago. It hadn't gone away. That little bit of contact made his blood heat. It brought everything he felt for her right back to the front of his mind.

What the hell was his problem?

He had come here to make things right. He shouldn't be thinking the same thoughts that had gotten him in trouble in the first place.

"If you've come here to apologize, you don't have to. It wasn't your fault and I don't want you going the rest of your life thinking you ruined mine. You didn't ruin it. I'll get another job. I'll find my way."

The hospital hadn't called her yet. For a moment he thought about giving her the news, but he didn't want her to get another job. He didn't want her to come home to this dingy little place. He wanted her to be happy and raise her baby and have some of the things she wished for.

"I didn't come here to apologize, Georgia. I came here to ask you to marry me."

Her gaze shot to his. Her mouth hung open. He'd shocked her. Hell, he had shocked himself. He had never thought about getting married, about having a family again, or a home or roots. It would be crazy to have those things with the kind of life he led. But after hearing the words come out of his mouth, he didn't want to take them back. This was his chance to make up for things.

Miko had crossed his mind a lot over the past eleven years. He wondered what had become of her, and if she lived in poverty or was shunned from her family or if she and her child had any part of a good life. Years later he was faced with another woman, with a child and a hard path to travel.

He could fix things for Georgia. He had the power to make her life good. He couldn't let this chance to make things right slip through his fingers.

"Are you going to go back to war?"

"No." The word came out of his mouth before he even thought about it. He knew he couldn't leave her if there was a chance he was never coming back. She could be a wealthy woman if he died overseas, but he knew Georgia well enough to know that she wouldn't want that. "I could take care of you, Georgia. You wouldn't have to—"

"Yes," she said, surprising him. "Yes, I'll marry you."

She'd said yes before he could explain himself. She didn't want to hear his reasons for marrying her. It wasn't because of love or devotion or any other reason she'd ever dreamed she would get married for.

Christian had proposed to her out of some misplaced sense of guilt. That was the only reason he wanted to marry her. He thought he was going to take care of her, support her. Make her life a little easier. But that wasn't why she was marrying him.

She was marrying him because it would keep him from going back to war. And because she could take care of him, show him what it was like not to be alone in the world. Yes, marrying him would make her life easier, but she didn't want him to think he'd saved her. She could land on her feet without him.

"Did you say yes?" He leaned back in his seat, a slightly dazed expression on his face.

"I did." She studied him silently for a moment, taken aback by how vulnerable he looked in that moment. She could almost see the little boy he once was, and it made her heart squeeze painfully in her chest. Not many could see past his six-foot-six scarred exterior, but she could, and she knew there was a good man beneath it.

She never thought she would see that good man again. Having him next to her in her tiny apartment, in the real world, was surreal to her.

When she'd kissed him goodbye two days ago, she'd thought that would be the last time. She never thought they would be here. She'd never thought she would agree to be his wife.

Their lives were about to change. He was giving up his career. His life as he knew it. He wouldn't have to risk being flown home in a casket. He may not have realized what his staying here meant to her. He was giving up something he loved, and when they were married she would go out of her way to thank him for that, to be a good wife to him. She would make it so that he wouldn't regret not going back to the marines.

"Are you sure you want to marry me?" he asked her, tearing her from her thoughts.

"Do you want to take your proposal back?"

"What?" His gaze shot to hers. "No. I would never do that."

She reached for his hand, twining her fingers through his, looking for a way to relieve the bit of awkwardness that crept up between them.

The touch seemed to startle him. He looked down at their joined hands and then up to her face. "You're going to be my wife."

He stroked his thumb along hers, then turned her hand over so that he could trail his fingers along her palm. She was going to respond to his statement, but tingles broke out on her skin and her tongue couldn't seem to form words.

She might be marrying him for other reasons besides safety. He was the only man she wanted to share her body with. She'd known from the moment he'd touched her breast the other day that no other man could come close to making her feel that way.

Unconsciously her body leaned against his and she tilted her face up to his, seeking to close the distance between them.

"Mama?"

Georgia jumped at the sound of her daughter's voice. Abby was sitting up in her crib staring at her. At Christian her little face scrunched in a frown.

"Did we wake you, love? I'm sorry."

She stood to go get her daughter. Christian followed close at her heels. If he were going to marry her, then that meant he was going to be Abby's father. Not just her husband. It was the only way it could work. The gravity of that thought hit her as she reached her daughter's crib. She stopped in her tracks and looked up at him.

"I love her more than life itself, Christian."

"I know," he said softly.

"If I marry you, I expect you to be her father. I want you to love her and protect her and support her. I know that's a lot to ask, but she comes first in my life. She always will. And if you can't accept that, you can retract your proposal with no guilt."

She searched his face as the weight of it all fell on him. But instead of scaring him, as she expected, his expression grew determined. "You said yes. You're not getting out of marrying me." He set his hands on her shoulders and gently squeezed. "Introduce me to my new daughter."

Her heart flipped over in her chest at his words, but being a parent was easier said than done. She was sure she had made some mistakes when it came to Abby, but she didn't want marrying Christian to be one of them.

"Ma?"

She turned and lifted her daughter from her crib. Christian was a good man. He would treat her right. He would be kind to her baby. If this was going to work she had to trust him.

"Abby, love." She lifted her up to Christian, trying not to think about all the things there were to worry about. "This is your daddy."

"Hello, little one," he said softly.

Abby stared at Christian and then did something Georgia never expected her little girl to do. She gasped, turned away from him and buried her face in Georgia's shoulder.

Christian's face fell. He wasn't a very expressive man, but she could clearly see the hurt on his face.

"My burns…" His face turned to stone. "She's afraid of me."

He took a step away from her, and Georgia could see him mentally shutting down, but she wouldn't allow it. When she looked at him she barely noticed his burns, and if she did it was only because they made him more beautiful to her. "It's not your burns. You're an enormous, perpetually scowling man, honey. And she hasn't been around any men before. That was my fault. I let what happened to me affect how she feels about men."

"She's just a baby. I'm sure she's not that deep."

"If this marriage is going to work, you have to agree that I'm always right."

His lips twitched and she took that as a sign that she should try again. "Abigail. This is your daddy. I want you to say hi."

She lifted her head from her mother's shoulder and turned to look at Christian. She frowned at him. "No Da!"

"Fine." Georgia set her on the floor and wrapped her arms around Christian's solid body. It had only been two days, and yet it felt like a lifetime since she had touched him. But she couldn't forget her daughter was watching them. Georgia knew Abby would only accept Christian if she did.

"Hello, Daddy." She ran her hand up his burned arm. "I like Daddy," she said, not looking at her daughter. "He's big and strong, and he smells really good." She looked up at him. "Why do you smell so good?"

"I finally got to shower using soap I like."

"I like it, too. Bend your head so I can kiss you."

"Okay." He closed his eyes and let her pepper kisses all over his face. "Not that I'm complaining, but what are you doing?"

"If I like you, she'll like you." She looked down at a still-frowning Abby. "Eventually. Won't you, baby?"

"No!"

Georgia sighed. This was not going to be as easy as she hoped.

CHAPTER 13

He was getting married. Christian had to keep repeating that to himself as he stared at Georgia later that day. *Married. Family. Home.* Words that were never in his vocabulary. He had never thought it would happen for him. But it was happening. He had proposed without thinking and changed the course of his life with just a few words.

Now he actually had to take care of her. Giving her the protection of his name wasn't enough. He had to make her happy or it wouldn't erase the misdeeds of his past. It wouldn't make up for Miko. Or his parents. He kept thinking about his mother and how she would have wanted this for him. He missed her. He missed them both, and starting a family of his own made the ache of not having them around more profound. It was probably why he never thought about having a family. A part of him thought he didn't deserve one. He was too selfish to make sure the one that he had was safe. What right did he have to any happiness now?

Georgia's hand cupped his burned cheek. He looked over at her, her big eyes filled with an emotion he couldn't name.

"What is it, sugar? You regretting your decision to marry me already?"

His lips unwilling pulled into a smile. It was her accent. So sweet. So Southern, with just a little touch of proper in it. "I might be. You've got a mean little baby."

"I know." She turned around to look at her daughter, who was sound asleep in the back of his rented car. "You don't know how awful I feel about it."

"Don't." He glanced at Abby. She was a beautiful child and he was about to become her father. More than marrying Georgia, becoming a father scared him. He didn't even want to touch Abby. She was so small, so fragile looking, that he was afraid that he might hurt her if he did. He didn't blame her for being scared of him. He still had a hard time facing the mirror himself. "We should probably get her to bed. It's getting late."

Georgia looked out the car window to her surroundings. They'd agreed they couldn't stay in her tiny apartment. He didn't want to hurt her feelings, but the place was a dump and the more time he spent there the more he hated her father for allowing his daughter and granddaughter to live in near poverty. He wanted to show them the opposite side of life. He needed to make sure they wanted for noting.

So he had taken them to the historic district of Charleston. His parents had bought a home down here his sophomore year of college, when his mother had gotten tired of the long, cold Connecticut winters. He guessed it was his home now, along with everything else his parents had once owned.

He hadn't been back to the house since his parents' deaths. He didn't want to think about going there. It was too hard. Even though it wasn't his childhood home, he knew there would be memories and traces of his parents and pain. So he was taking his soon-to-be wife and daughter to a hotel for a little while.

He knew he had to go back to the place where he was last happy, but he couldn't bring himself to do it just yet.

"We should be putting her to bed. We passed a motel when we got off the interstate. If you turn around I think I can remember how to get there."

"We are staying here, Georgia."

He had parked in front of the Blue House Inn, one of the oldest hotels in the city. From the outside alone it was dazzling with its brick facade and illuminated fountains. But he didn't stare at the building—instead he watched Georgia, who frowned in confusion before turning back to him.

"We can't afford to stay here."

"We can."

"But, Christian…"

"It's okay, Georgia. I promise."

He expected her to ask a dozen more questions, but she didn't. She just stared at him with a worried look on her face. He wanted to reassure her, but he didn't know what to say. The moment he'd asked her to marry him he stopped knowing what to say to her. She hadn't said much to him, either, since they'd left her little apartment. It was as if the gravity of what was about to happen to her had finally hit. They were getting married. And while she knew more about him than anybody on the planet, she still didn't know much about him at all.

"Grab the baby. I'll get the bags."

The inside of the hotel was even more beautiful than the outside. He watched Georgia look up in amazement as they walked through the lobby. It wasn't as ornate as some of the hotels he had stayed at in New York City as a kid, but it had a kind of homey luxurious feel, with its large, curving wood staircase and original fireplaces.

As they approached the front desk, the woman behind it forgot to greet them. She was too busy taking in Christian's face. He thought it was bad in the hospital, where some of the nurses couldn't look him in the eye, but now that he was out of the hospital, he felt more disfigured than ever. The guy at the car rental place and the cashier at the department store had both looked at him in wonder.

He tried to push down the circus-freak feeling that crept up inside him whenever somebody looked at him, but he was having a hard time tonight. His face felt like a mask that he wished he could rip off.

"We need a two-bedroom suite with a crib, if you have one available."

"Of course. Of course." The woman's eyes snapped to her computer screen as she furiously searched for what he asked for.

"He got those burns in Iraq," Georgia said, a thread of ice in her voice. "I don't know who raised you, but my mama taught me it was impolite to stare at people. Now, I'll excuse it if you were staring at him because you find him attractive. I think he's quite gorgeous. I hope that's the reason you were struck stupid when we walked up."

"Yes, ma'am," the young woman whispered. "He's probably the biggest man I've ever seen."

"Oh, he is. Now, did you have any luck finding the room we asked for?"

"Yes, ma'am." She looked up at Christian. This time her eyes connected with his instead of his face. "I just need your information."

Ten minutes later they were on their way up to their room. Christian thought he would be the one fuming. He thought he would be annoyed with Georgia for making a scene in the lobby and part of him was, but when he looked over at her and saw how tight she held her body he realized his little Southern lady was extremely pissed off.

"I can't believe her," she huffed as she bounced her sleepy baby. "We should be getting a discount on this room. I thought people who worked in fancy hotels would be trained better. She didn't even say hello!"

"Ma," Abby whined.

"I'm sorry, baby." She absently handed Abby Christian's way. "Take her. I'm upsetting her."

"Georgia, I…"

He didn't have the chance to protest that he had never held a baby or that he didn't know what he was doing or mention the fact that Abby didn't want to be held by him, because Georgia had placed her daughter in his hands and paced away.

He had to tighten his grip on Abby just so she didn't slip from his hands. At first he was afraid he had hurt her, but she just frowned at him and then rubbed her eye with her tiny little fist. He held her closer just like he had seen Georgia do. Abby rested her head on his shoulder.

"No Da," she said softly as she snuggled into him.

"Oh, hush." He brought his other hand up to rub her back. It was an odd feeling holding something so small. He felt the warmth of her little warm body seep into his, and smelled the sweet scent that all babies seemed to have. It was a foreign feeling, but it wasn't a bad one.

He caught her studying him out of the corner of her eye, her little forehead furrowed. Maybe she wasn't afraid of him. Maybe she just didn't like him. He could deal with that. A lot of people didn't like him.

The elevator stopped and Georgia reached into his pocket for the key card, still muttering something about hospitality. He followed her to their room, and when she opened the door she finally stopped being angry. She was too distracted by her lush surroundings.

"How much does this room cost a night?" She whipped around to face him. "We could probably rent an apartment for a month for this price. We need to go back downstairs and ask for a different room. This is not a room. I don't even see any beds."

"That's because they are in the bedrooms, Georgia," he said softly so that he would not disturb Abby again. "This is what I asked for. We are staying here."

"But...I didn't even hear what you said because I was too busy... Oh." She blinked at him. "You're angry with me, aren't you? I never know when to keep my mouth shut. My father used to say I was never going to be able to keep a husband because I would talk him to death and now I've gone and made you mad and we haven't even gotten married first. I just didn't like the way she looked at you and then this room. You made a decision and I question it. I'm sorry, Christian."

"Georgia, come here," he demanded.

She closed the gap between them, her head hanging in shame. Her father was the biggest asshole on the planet. He hoped never to meet the man because he didn't know what he would do if they were ever in the same room together.

"What did I tell you about not speaking your mind in front of me?"

Her head snapped up to look at him.

"You don't have to keep your mouth shut. I am not the ultimate decision maker. You may give your opinion anytime you wish. But there are two things you should know first. I don't need you to defend me, and you don't have to worry about money anymore because I have more than I know what to do with."

"I know you don't need me to defend you, but I will. I always will, because that's what a wife does for her husband. It's my job to take care of you."

"I think there are some things we need to talk about." Like what exactly her idea of marriage was. He knew they were doing this wrong. Other couples had learned things about each other. They made plans of where and how they were going to live. He didn't even know Georgia's middle name.

She nodded. "We do. I need to get Abby ready for bed. Why don't you go relax and I'll meet you back here."

"No. I want to see how you get her ready for bed."

Her eyes went wide again. "You do?"

"Yeah. I'm going to be her father. I should know how to take care of her."

"Oh. Okay. Well, grab her bag and come with me."

He could tell he had taken her by surprise, but it was important for him to become Abby's father in every way possible because he knew that it meant so much to Georgia.

When Georgia got out of the shower that night Christian was already waiting for her in bed. She nearly smiled at the sight of it because it reminded her of how they had spent every day besides this one, with him waiting for her in bed.

This time, though, they weren't in a hospital but a luxurious hotel suite that probably cost more than she made in a week. And Christian was no longer in his hospital gown or even the pajamas she had bought him. He only wore a pair of boxers. His wide, half-scarred chest was bare.

Tingles ran through her as she made her way to the bed. The attraction to him hadn't faded in this different setting. She was relieved to learn that, because this man was about to be her husband. They had been through a lot together, and yet she had the feeling she was marrying a stranger. There was still so much she didn't know about him. Still so much she was almost afraid to find out.

"Part of me is thinking that I can't stay too long because I have to get back to work."

His lips twitched at her comment. "There's no Nurse Chestnut here." He held out his hand to her. "This bed is big enough for the two of us."

She took his hand and climbed into bed beside him. She couldn't help but to notice how he stared at her. Her nipples tightened as he took her body in. She had never worn so little around a man before, and now she was in bed with one, wearing a nightgown that was so threadbare it was nearly see-through. Her hair was down, too. Christian had seen it down before the day she hit her head, but he hadn't seen it like this. She spent an extra ten minutes in the bathroom brushing it until it shined. She wasn't normally vain, but tonight she wanted to look pretty for him.

This was the first night of the rest of their lives.

"You're nervous." He took one of her hands in both of his. He was always so gentle. She hadn't failed to notice how he'd been with Abby earlier that night. How he'd rubbed her back and settled her onto his massive shoulder even though he knew Abby didn't like him. "Why?"

"No man has ever seen me like this. Or in a bed."

"I can sleep on the couch tonight if you want."

"No," she said quickly. She didn't want to be by herself tonight. She knew she wouldn't be able to sleep knowing he was in the other room. "I want to sleep here with you, but I might get up twenty times tonight to check on Abby. I've never slept more than ten feet away from her."

"That's why I had this brought up when you were in the shower." He pointed to a white baby monitor on her side of the bed.

"You've thought of everything, haven't you?"

"Only the things that would keep you in this bed."

She looked up into his eyes, surprised by his words. "You think I'm skittish?"

"No. I think you're exhausted and I want you to get as much rest as possible." He lifted his hand to run his fingers through her loose hair. "I don't want you collapsing on our wedding day."

Her eyes drifted shut as his fingers touched her scalp. She never knew fingers in her hair could feel so heavenly. "When are we getting married?"

"Soon, but I don't want to do it at city hall. I want a real wedding."

She opened her eyes and looked at him just to see if he were serious. He was.

"My mother would have wanted it that way. I didn't do much in my life that she would have agreed with. I think she would have liked me to have a real wedding."

"Okay," she breathed. How could she say no to that? "Who do we invite? We don't have any family."

"Mrs. Sheppard. Tobias. The general." He shrugged. "Are you sure there isn't anybody in your family you want to come?"

Georgia hesitated. She wanted her mother to be there, to meet Christian and to see her get married, but she knew her father would never allow her to go.

"What about your sister?"

Carolina. She had just been thinking about her, wondering if she could live with her sister and still live with herself. Carolina would come and, more important, Georgia had missed her terribly these past two years.

"I've been mad at her for so long."

Christian leaned in closer, placing his lips just beneath her ear. "Maybe it's time to forgive her. You're starting a new life. It's time to put the past behind you."

"But—"

He set a soft kiss on her skin and she shivered from the contact. "But nothing. What better way to get back at them all than by being happy?"

"I don't want to get back at them."

"Then why won't you invite your sister?"

"I should. I will."

"Good." He pushed her back on the bed and wrapped his arms around her, and for the first time in a long time she felt absolutely safe. "Let's get some sleep. It's been a long day."

"Wait." She was pressed against him and he was warm and hard and he smelled good and he made her want to get closer.

"What?" He opened his eyes.

"Um…" She didn't know how to ask or even what to ask for. She just knew she wanted more of him.

He yawned widely and she immediately felt guilty. This was his first night in a real bed, in a quiet room that was very far from the hospital. He needed to sleep.

"You said we didn't have to worry about money. How? I don't think there has been a time that I haven't been worried about it. I can work."

"No. Have you ever heard of Howard and Helga's?"

"The ice-cream company?"

He yawned again. "My father owned it. I own it. We're going to be fine."

"Christian…" Howard and Helga's was no little ice-cream company. She didn't think there was a person alive who hadn't eaten one of their flavors. It was her even her father's favorite brand. She was marrying a man of means. A millionaire. Something inside of her lurched. She really knew very little about the man she was marrying.

"There's a plant just outside of Charleston. I'll take you there sometime." He pulled her closer, sliding his hand beneath her nightgown to cup her bottom.

She lost her train of thought. His hand felt so good there. It was possessive. As if it was his to hold. After all that had happened to her, she never thought she would like a man to have free rein over her body, but with Christian every touch was right. Every inch of space he invaded she was more than willing to give away.

"Are you okay with this?"

"Yes."

"You'll tell me when you don't like something?"

"Yes."

"Can I kiss you?"

"Yes. I never thought I would see you again," she said, touching his face. "So you may kiss me whenever you want."

He said nothing more, just buried his hand deep into her hair and set his lips on her. It wasn't like their last kiss, which was hot and full of need and nearly uncontrollable. He was holding back. He was giving her just enough to make her crave more. She rubbed her body against his, opened her mouth to give him further access, and while she felt his erection between her legs, he never deepened the kiss. He never touched more than her backside. He just continued to give her the longest, slowest, deepest kiss of her life.

He broke the kiss, dragging his lips across her cheek and down to her throat. He didn't kiss her, though, just rested his lips there. She wanted to urge him on, to beg him not to stop, but sex…lovemaking…was so new to her she didn't know how to begin.

"Your hair is so beautiful," he finally said after long tor-turous moments. "Do you ever wear it down?"

"Only at night. We weren't allowed to wear it down during the day."

"You can do whatever you want now, Georgia. Your life is about to change."

And with those words he kissed her face and drifted off to sleep.

Christian woke up just before 6:00 a.m. He could sleep in all he wanted, but the marine in him always woke him up as the sun rose. He was about to give up that life and become a private citizen. He was about to give up everything he had known for the past ten years. He thought that not knowing how he was going to spend the next years of his life was going to throw him into a panic, and normally it would have, but this morning, unlike every other morning of his life, he woke up with a soft woman wrapped around him.

He looked down at Georgia, who was cuddled around him. Both of her arms were twined around his neck, and her soft thigh rested between his legs. He'd made the mistake of kissing her last night. He knew how responsive she was, how damn good her body felt when it was pressed up against his. He knew how hard it was to control himself when she was around. His lack of control was why they were getting married in the first place. Because of that kiss, the urge to flip her over and make love to her nearly took over. But he knew it wasn't the right time. He knew that they were both tired and that they had just undergone huge life changes.

If he was going to make love to her, he was going to take his time and do it right. Georgia deserved their lovemaking to be special. She deserved everything he had to give.

The sound of baby babble from the monitor distracted him from his thoughts. Georgia was sound asleep. He had seen the exhaustion on her face last night, the little bit of worry that never entirely faded away. He didn't want to wake her. She needed to rest because the next few days were going to be long ones.

He shut off the monitor and tried to ease from beneath her. She held on to him tighter.

"No," she groaned.

"Go back to sleep, baby. I need to get up."

She moaned and rolled over, allowing him to ease out of bed and go to Abby.

She was standing up in her crib when he got there, but as soon as she saw him her placid expression turned into a confused frown.

"Da?"

"Yes. Good morning, Abby." To his own ears he sounded like an ass, but he didn't know how else to greet a baby.

He lifted her from her crib and deposited her on the floor. He wasn't sure what to do with her next, so he sat down beside her.

He thought about calling room service to bring them up some breakfast, but he wasn't sure what one-year-olds ate. Did she even have any teeth? Could babies eat scrambled eggs? What about oatmeal?

She looked up at him with her huge green eyes, seeming to sense his inner turmoil. "Mama?" she seemed to suggest.

"She's sleeping, but you've got me for the moment. We are just going to have to figure this out together. Are you going to let me change your diaper before we eat?"

"No!"

"Good," he sighed. "I didn't want to do it anyway."

"No Da!"

"Yes Da," he countered. "I'm afraid you're going to be stuck with me. I'm going to marry your mother."

He could have sworn she rolled her eyes. She pulled herself

up and walked around to his side. She looked at the burns that ran the length of his arm. Even to him they looked scary, as if part of him had emerged from a horror movie, but Abby didn't seem afraid, only curious.

She touched his arm, running her tiny fingers over the most burned part of his skin. "Ow?" She looked up at him.

"Yes."

She surprised him by climbing in his lap and reaching up to his face. He lifted her to give her better access. She took his face in both her hands. "Ow?"

"Yes, ow."

"Da?"

"Yes."

"No Da!"

Christian sighed again. This whole fatherhood thing wasn't going to be easy. "Come on, you mean little thing. Let's gets some oatmeal."

Georgia woke up in a panic an hour later. At first she didn't know where she was, but then she remembered. She was in a luxurious hotel suite about to marry a man whom she knew next to nothing about.

But he wasn't in bed beside her. She vaguely remembered Christian telling her he had to get up. He must have heard Abby. She shot out of bed at that point. She'd never intended for him to take care of her. She was always the one to pull her baby out of bed in the morning, even when she was working those twelve-hour shifts. And Christian didn't know what he was doing. She should have been up earlier. It was her job to take care of Abby.

But when she opened the door to their bedroom, she spotted Christian and Abby at the table. He was feeding her oatmeal with a determined frown on his face. Abby wasn't exactly being cooperative. She was shaking her head and speaking to Christian in some kind of annoyed baby babble.

"I get it, Abs. You don't like me, but could you stop yelling at me for ten minutes and finish your breakfast?"

"Da! No. No. No!" But she opened her mouth and accepted another spoonful of oatmeal.

Georgia laughed. The sight of a big scowling bare-chested marine with her little angry baby was too much for her.

"Mama!"

"Hi, baby." She kissed her daughter's head and then, because Abby was watching, kissed Christian on the lips. "Good morning, Daddy."

He grabbed the back of her head, causing the kiss to go on longer than she had planned. Her parents had never shown affection in front of them. She had never seen them kiss or hold hands. Nothing more than the occasional touch.

Her mother had once told her that a wife only shows her husband how much she loves him in the privacy of their bedroom. That was before her brother had died, before her parents had changed into shells of themselves. When they were all happy.

She wanted to be happy with Christian. She wanted to be a good wife for him.

"I'm sorry I wasn't up to feed her," she said when he let her go. "I was just so tired. I'll be up tomorrow."

"You don't have to. Sleep as long as you want. I wanted to feed her. I even changed her diaper."

"But—but that's my job."

He shook his head. "Trust me, I'm not going to fight you for the privilege to change her stinky diapers, but it doesn't just have to only be your job. I want her to get used to me." He looked at Abby. "We're going to bond if it kills me."

Abby let out another string of angry baby babble, seemingly arguing the point, to which Christian responded by gently tugging on her ear.

Abby's little mouth dropped open in indignation, which caused Christian to throw his head back and laugh.

"You're going to be my toughest soldier."

He scooped her off the table and stood up. "I'm going to get her dressed and then we are going to go out." He leaned down and kissed Georgia's cheek. "You are going to take my credit card and buy new clothes or whatever else your heart desires."

"But—but…"

"You're not alone anymore, Georgia. You're going to have to learn to trust me."

"I do," she said truthfully, even though she felt her heart sinking. She had asked him to step up and really be Abby's father, but she never expected him to take to it so fast. For so long she'd thought she was the only one who could take care of her baby the right way. But in came Christian, who'd known her child less than twenty-four hours, and yet he seemed to do just fine without her.

Part of her hated him for it. But another part of her felt herself falling in love with him because of it.

CHAPTER 14

"When you asked if you could stop by, Christian, I never thought you would show up with a baby," General Lee said when he opened his front door.

"This is Abby. She's Georgia's daughter. Say hello to the general, Abs."

Abby looked up into the general's unsmiling face and then turned to bury her face in Christian's shoulder. "No!" Then she remembered that she didn't like him and lifted her head. "No Da!"

"Not exactly friendly, is she?"

"She's a mean little thing, but I like her. She's going to be my daughter."

"Oh?" General Lee stepped aside to let him in his home.

"Yes, I'm getting married."

General Lee nodded. "I knew you would do the right thing."

Christian's brain stopped working for a moment. More than his words, the expression on General Lee's face told Christian that the man knew more than he was letting on. "Excuse me?"

"Really, Daniel." An elegant redhead appeared from the hallway. "Ask Captain Howard to sit. Can't you see he is holding a child?"

The general sighed. "Of course I can see that, dear. But the man is as big as a bull, so if he can't survive holding a twenty-pound baby for a few minutes, then the marines as we know them are doomed." He nodded at Christian. "Sit down, boy, before my wife goes off on a tangent. Doesn't think I'm fit for polite company and maybe I'm not, but you are definitely not what I would consider polite company."

The general's wife sighed. "Can you at least introduce me to your friend before you continue complaining about me?"

"Christian, this is my wife, Alma." General Lee grabbed his wife around the waist and kissed her cheek loudly. "The love of my life."

Alma rolled her eyes, but her cheeks were pink, reminding Christian of a schoolgirl. He thought back to the general's story about how they had met. Alma and Daniel might bicker, but the love between them was apparent.

"It's nice to meet you, ma'am."

"And you, as well," she said, approaching. "I've heard so much about you." Her face lit up when she looked at Abby. "Oh, my word, what a gorgeous little girl you have."

Abby smiled beautifully at Mrs. Lee, which proved Georgia's point that Abby was more comfortable around women than around men. He wasn't sure if he wanted to change that about her or not. He just wanted her to like him. "Thank you, Mrs. Lee."

"You're welcome. Now sit. Sit!" She pointed Christian to an easy chair while she and her husband took a seat on the couch. "Can I offer you something? We've got sweet tea, coffee and juice. My husband keeps a couple of bottles of good whiskey in his office."

"No, thank you. We have to get back to her mother soon. She didn't say anything, but I know she was worried about me taking Abby out."

"My Daniel here has never taken our girls out alone. I think he was more afraid of them than Vietnam." She gave her husband an affectionate smile. "Your lady is very lucky. I did overhear you say you were getting married, didn't I?"

"I am, and I would be honored if you would both come as my guests, but I would really like to hear what your husband knows about my upcoming nuptials."

"I don't know anything, son," he said with a straight face. "But I was pretty sure if I sent that rat-faced nurse in on you two, you would end up getting married."

"What? You sent Georgia's boss in that night?"

"I saw you two kissing that day. I saw how she looked at you. God damn it, son. When a woman looks at you like that, big, ugly, half-blown-up son of a bitch you are, you marry her."

"You mean to tell me you ruined a good woman's career just because you thought I would do the right thing? How did you know I would marry her? Or that she would say yes? Do you have any idea what kind of shit storm you caused? I don't know what happened to you since you decided to retire, but you seem to be morphing into some kind of meddling old biddy."

"No!" Abby chimed in, yelling at the general. "Da. No! No! Mama."

"Exactly," he said to the fussing baby as he tousled her curls. "You're right. It all could have gone to hell, but look at you. If I didn't know any better I would think you'd been that baby's father from birth. And I never once heard you say you didn't want to marry her. If I didn't know in my gut that this was the right move for you, I wouldn't have interfered."

Christian didn't know what to say, so he stood up. It was too much for him to process in that moment. "I have to get back to Georgia. I'll call you with the final plans as soon as they are set. It was nice meeting you, Mrs. Lee."

When Christian walked back into their suite, Georgia wasn't there. He was surprised. He didn't miss the expression of panic on her face when he told her he was taking Abby out. He thought for sure she would be waiting there for them when they got back. But the suite was quiet.

Absolute quiet was the one thing he wasn't used to. He had been at war for the past five years. He'd slept around other men. He could barely remember the last time he had a place he called his own, and then he was stuck in the hospital, which was never truly quiet with all the footsteps and beeping machines and other patients around. One grew accustomed to constant noise, and now that it wasn't there it almost felt as if something was missing.

"Mama?" Abby asked him.

"She's not back yet."

Abby sighed and rested her head on his shoulder. "No Da."

"You must be tired. That or you're starting to like me."

She frowned at him, making her feelings clear.

"You want to take a nap? Babies do that, don't they?"

"No!"

"Fine." He sat down on the couch with her. She nestled herself in the crook of his arm and studied his face again for a moment before she shut her eyes.

He took that as a good sign. He let his eyes close as he thought back to the revealing conversation he'd had with General Lee. He was annoyed with the man for messing with his life, with Georgia's. It all could have gone so horribly wrong. It could still go so horribly wrong, but right now he almost felt a little hopeful.

There was a warm sleepy baby in his arms and a beautiful woman who was going to marry him. He was going to have a family. He didn't want to think about the fact that Georgia would have never agreed to marry him if she hadn't lost her job. He didn't want to think that he wouldn't have the kind of marriage his parents had. That neither of them had much of a choice. That there might never be deep love between them.

A pair of soft lips brushed over his burned cheek. Georgia stood before him, her gaze passing over his face. He couldn't read the look in her eyes, but he knew that nobody had ever looked at him that way. Besides the general, she was the only one who could look at his face and not study his burns. He wondered if she was as oblivious to them as she said she was. He didn't know how that could be possible. Even if he couldn't see the burns, he knew that his face was disfigured nearly every moment of the day, except when she looked at him like she was looking at him in that moment.

He gripped the back of her neck and pulled her closer. She blushed just before he kissed her. Sweet girl. Her kiss was shy. But her lips were warm and her mouth moist and he didn't stop wanting to kiss her. She broke away, and her cheeks were red. She pressed her fingers to her lips.

"Why do you look so shy? That's not the first time we've done that."

"Those are the kind of kisses you should only give me when the lights are off and the door is closed."

He grinned at her. If she thought that was the only kind of kiss he would give her when the lights were off she was in for a surprise. "You kissed me first. Kissing me in the daylight could cause potential problems, then. Your touch causes my brain to malfunction. That's why I have to marry you. Maybe you shouldn't touch me at all until we're behind closed doors."

"Oh." She blinked at him. "Okay."

He wasn't sure if she took him seriously, but before he could really think about it he noticed the change in her appearance. Her hair was down, and was inches shorter than the last time he has seen it. It framed her face. Soft bangs made her already beautiful eyes stand out even more.

"You cut your hair."

He pulled her down on the couch next to him so that she wasn't hovering above him and Abby anymore.

"You don't like it?"

"I—I..." Before she had a girlish quality about her. But now he could only see a woman next to him. He more than liked it. He wasn't eloquent enough to describe what it did for her. Lifting his hand, he ran his fingers through the silky strands. "It looks good."

"I know you like to touch it sometimes." She blushed again.

He wasn't sure why she was suddenly so shy with him. She had seen him at his absolute worst. He had to keep reminding himself that this was new to her. To them. They had never spent so much time alone together. Before they had the hospital and the fear of getting caught to check their emotions, but now it was just them in the real world. This would take some getting used to.

"It's usually too hot and heavy to wear down so I thought I would get it cut."

"You did this for me?"

"Yes, but I feel kind of bad. You paid a lot of money for this haircut."

"I don't care how much it costs. Do you like it?"

She nodded. "Thank you for giving me the money."

"Don't thank me, Georgia." He stroked her cheek with the

backs of his fingers. "Some men are afraid that their wives are going to bankrupt them. Mine feels bad for getting a haircut."

"I'm not your wife yet. I think we might need to talk about some things now."

"Mama?"

Abby woke up, rubbing her eyes with her fists. Christian lost his train of thought when he saw how Georgia's eyes filled with love when she looked at her little girl.

"Hello, baby." The smile that broke out on her face could have lit the room.

Abby launched herself out of Christian's arms and into Georgia's. "Mama! No Da!"

"Abby," Georgia groaned. "You need to be nice."

"No." She snuggled into her mother's chest.

"Yes." She kissed her daughter's head. "But it's okay if you like me better. I did go through twenty-seven hours of brutal labor before you were born, before they cut you out of me." She shut her eyes and rubbed her hand slowly down Abby's back. "I missed you like crazy today, baby girl. How did things go with Daddy?"

Christian stared at her. She looked so beautifully peaceful sitting there with her eyes closed and a baby in her arms. She looked natural and homey and right. An image of her with another child came into his mind. A boy this time, with curly blond hair and green eyes. That jolted him. Having a child of his blood had never entered his mind before. It was something that he never thought he wanted.

"We got along. I didn't drop her or lose her once."

Georgia opened her eyes and gave him just a hint of a smile. "I trust you with her, but seeing you walk out the door with my baby was one of the hardest things I've ever done."

"Why?"

"Because it made me realize that I had no other choice to

trust you. It made me realize that my life will never be the same."

He could hear the nervousness in her voice. He didn't blame her for it. He just wondered what he could do to make it better. "I think we need to have that talk now."

"We should, but can we have it on the way to my sister's house?"

CHAPTER 15

She tried to concentrate on the scenery around her as Christian drove them to her sister's home.

It was familiar territory. Memories flooded her. Happy ones. Sad ones. Ones she'd rather forget. It was almost like going home, except it wasn't. Carolina lived in the next town over. In a wealthier area, a place where many of her father's parishioners had come from once upon a time.

They had stopped coming. A lot of people had stopped coming to their church after Abel died. Her father had changed. Instead of preaching of love, happiness and forgiveness, he preached of repentance and of right and wrong. It scared some people away, but it invited others. A more hardened bunch. A group of people who claimed that only God could judge and yet they judged and shamed anybody who wasn't like them. Robert was from one of those families.

He had moved into town just after his sixteenth birthday when his family had returned from Africa. They were missionaries.

We spent our lives trying to convert the heathens and savages, Robert's father would always say.

Georgia's father loved them. He called them the most righteous. The most devoted to God's word. But Georgia found their devotion to be nearly militant. Nearly hateful. They failed to enjoy the beauty of the world around them because they were too focused on judging people who didn't live up the standards they thought everybody should live by. But she'd thought that Robert wasn't like them at first. He was a little more carefree. He always had a smile on his face and a kind word for her.

Her father had approved of him. Robert had planned to go to theological school and become a minister. He'd told her father that he wanted to take over the church when he was ready to retire, that he wanted to learn from him. That had made Abraham Williams a very happy man. None of his own sons had taken an interest in following in his shoes. So he'd invited Robert into the family. He'd trusted his daughters with him. He'd wanted Robert for Carolina. He thought they would get married when Carolina finished her teaching degree.

It didn't work out that way. Robert was never interested in Carolina. He was only interested in Georgia, and what he wanted from her had nothing to do with marriage.

She hadn't realized that Christian had pulled off the road until she felt his hand on her face. "Are you sure you want to do this, Georgia?"

She looked at him—his face held its perpetual scowl but his eyes were worried. "I'm fine."

"No." He took her hand and uncurled it. It was then she realized that her fingernails were biting into her skin. Little red angry imprints marked her palm. "You aren't. What are you thinking about?"

She looked back at Abby, who had fallen asleep. "I try not to think about how I got her. Most days it's easy, but today it's not. My father loved him like a son. He was my brother's best friend. I trusted him and he did that to me."

"You tell me where he is, Georgia, and I'll kill him."

He wasn't joking. And as much as she wanted an end to him, she knew her conscience couldn't rest if he were to die that way. "No." She shook her head. "I'm supposed to be happy. I'm getting married. I'm moving on. I shouldn't let this bother me."

He leaned over and kissed her forehead. "You wouldn't be human if this didn't bother you."

She slid her fingers into his, squeezing his hand. She realized it was the first time she ever really had someone to lean on. It was a nice feeling.

"We can turn around right now," he said into her skin, his soft breath tickling her as he spoke. "We don't have to do this today. You tell me what you want and I'll make it happen."

"We have to go. We can't turn back now."

"Okay." He kissed her face once more before he let her go and pulled back onto the road.

"Talk to me, honey," Georgia said after a few moments of silence. She moved over in the seat as far as she could to get closer to him. She gently rested her fingertips on his burned arm, absently tracing the scars as he drove. He knew they were approaching her sister's house. With each mile they drove Georgia grew paler and paler.

He couldn't imagine what it was like to be in her shoes, to have a baby by a man who hurt you. To go face a family member who had originally deserted you.

His parents were gone and he missed them so much the hollowness in his chest never seemed to go away, but it must have been worse to be her. To have a whole family who threw you away for no reason.

"What do you want to talk about?"

"Our life," she said softly. "Tell me what you want for us."

He swallowed. It was a hard thing to answer. He never thought he would be here, with somebody else to care for. "I was thinking we could get married on Sunday. If that's okay with you. There's a little park with a garden in it my parents used to take walks in. I thought it would be nice to have it there. But if you don't want to," he said quickly, "we can have it someplace else."

"I would like to have your parents there, Christian. There's nothing I would like better."

She understood. He didn't have to explain himself and he was grateful for that because he wasn't sure he had the words. "I have a house in Charleston. It was my parents', but it's empty now. I thought if you liked it, we could live there for a while. I'm not sure about much else, Georgia. Up until a few days ago I thought I would die a marine. I don't know how to be a regular man."

"I don't know how to be a regular woman. I guess we'll have to figure it out together." The GPS directed him to pull onto a road that led them to a neighborhood of large stately homes with rolling manicured lawns. He watched Georgia's eyes grow wide. She hadn't told him much about her childhood, but from what he did know he was sure she hadn't grown up like this. To her father something like lobster was sinful and decadent. Even up to her adulthood, she'd lived in relative poverty.

Her life was about to change. He hoped she was prepared for it. He finally came to a stop in front of a large brick house with brown shutters. She grabbed his hand, squeezing it as if trying to take some strength from it.

"I know this must be her house," she said in a rush. "She told me she always wanted a big brick house. That it was her dream. This must be it. She married a dentist, you know. He would be able to give her a big house like this." She turned to look at him. "What if she's not home? I should have called. I know better than to come over uninvited. I didn't think. Maybe we should come back another time. I don't even see any cars."

The front door opened and a pretty young woman with light brown skin and tawny-colored hair stepped out as Georgia finished saying those words.

"She's home, sweetheart," he said softly. Georgia's eyes swiveled toward the front door. Her face went a little paler, her mouth dropped opened a little.

The woman—her sister—stared at Georgia, her delicate face frowning in confusion, her eyes locking with her sister's through the open car window. A man stepped out behind Carolina. He placed a supportive hand on her back, but just as he opened his mouth to speak she left the front step, running toward the car. It only took Georgia a few moments before she jumped out of the car and ran to her sister. The women smashed into each other, falling to the ground, hugging each other so hard that he couldn't tell where Georgia began and Carolina ended.

There were no words between them, and if there were Christian wasn't able to make them out over the loud sobs. Their tears seemed to be happy tears, and sad tears, and tears that cleansed. It became hard for Christian to watch the women's reunion. It made him uncomfortable. He'd never had a sibling. He was the only child of only children. He never knew the connection of having one. The bond seemed stronger than he could ever imagine.

He turned and looked back at Abby, whose eyes were now

open. She looked out the window and then back to him. "Mama?"

"She's saying hello to her sister."

Abby blinked at him. "No Da?"

"Yes Da."

She sighed.

"Up?" She reached her arms out to him.

"Yes. I'll pick you up."

He stepped out of the car, retrieving Abby before they went to Georgia. She didn't notice him approaching, she was so wrapped up in her sister. But her sister's husband did, and he stared at Christian, his eyes widening as they took him in. There was no greeting. No acknowledging he was a man, or even human. The man just stared at him.

"Captain Christian Howard," he said gruffly, introducing himself.

"Doctor Miles Hammond." The man was soft-spoken, small. Couldn't have been much more than five-seven. "You're a very large man." Dr. Hammond extended his hand. "I used to pray to God and drink my milk and eat all my vegetables when I was a child because I wanted to be big like you. When I was twenty-one and still only this size, I stopped eating my vegetables and drinking my milk and praying to God. Now I eat cheeseburgers and red-velvet cake. It's nice to meet you, sir. I'm Carolina's husband."

"I'm going to marry Georgia. And this is Abby." Christian relaxed a bit. Ever since the explosion, he had been sensitive about his burns. So much so that he forgot that it was his size and build that put people off first.

He stepped forward again, touching Abby's arm gently. Abby buried her face in Christian's neck, seeming afraid. "Hello, little thing," he said very softly. "I'm your uncle. You're going to have a cousin to play with soon."

He looked toward his wife, whose arms were still tightly twined around her sister. The women were quiet now. All their tears seemed to be cried out. They just held each other, as though they were trying to make up for all the years they couldn't.

"Carolina, love." He walked over and placed his hand on her back. "Please get up. I would like to meet your sister."

"My sister," she said in a whisper. "She's here."

Georgia finally looked up, and her eyes went directly to Christian's. He could see the myriad of emotions running through them. This must be so much for her. The proposal and reunion and the knowledge that her life was never going to be the same. He walked over to her and extended his hand, wanting to take away some of the fear in her eyes.

She took his hand and squeezed it, placing his burned skin against her cheek. "Carolina," she finally said. "This is the man I'm going to marry."

"Your house is lovely, Carolina," Georgia said to her sister as they walked hand in hand through the upstairs. They had been together a little more than an hour—the first few minutes Carolina had spent reminiscing about their childhood and about Oakdale and how much it hadn't changed since she had left. It all sounded so idyllic, as if it might be a place that Georgia would like to live if she hadn't grown up there, if she hadn't known what the town and its people could be like. But she pushed that thought away. She was with her little sister. Her young, married, mother-to-be sister. She had missed so much of her life in the past two years. Georgia wanted to enjoy this time.

Carolina was showing her around her large home, excitedly explaining all the little handpicked details as she went. Some things never changed. Carolina had always dragged her along when they were kids. Showing her wildflowers or baby birds. Pointing out anything and everything pretty.

She was glad it was a quality that her sister never lost. Carolina, it seemed, had never lost her innocence. Georgia wasn't so lucky. She had stopped seeing the pure prettiness of the world a long time ago.

That feeling settled in her chest again. The heaviness. She didn't know what was wrong with her. This day was supposed to be beautiful. It was supposed to wash away the past two years of hurt and pain, the feeling of betrayal. But it didn't.

At first she had been so happy to see her sister, to be there, to touch and look at her, but that feeling had worn off as soon as their embrace broke.

When Georgia introduced Carolina to Christian, her sister wouldn't meet his eyes. They had been taught that women were to be submissive, demure, quiet in a man's presence, but Georgia wasn't sure that Carolina wouldn't look at Christian for those reasons.

She stared at him, at the burns on his face. She knew Carolina. She didn't find Christian beautiful like her own husband, who was a small man with boyish features and easy charm. Georgia might have been able to push that feeling under the rug, because she knew that Carolina didn't care for large men, but when she didn't look at Abby at all when Georgia introduced her, when she didn't hug her or touch her or show any of the affection to the niece she claimed that she wanted her baby to be close to, the heaviness settled in her chest and failed to lift.

She tried to shake it off, to tell herself that she was crazy. She had missed her sister. She wanted to know her husband and unborn child. She wanted some sort of family, if not for herself, then for Abby.

"I love it here." She smiled prettily. "Miles is so kind to me.

He lets me do whatever I want with this place. He never gets cross with me when I ask him for things. He says he wants me to be happy. That's why I'm so glad you're back, Georgia. I can be happy now. I can't wait to show you this next room."

Georgia nodded as they stopped before a large guest room, complete with a small crib. "This is your room, Georgia. I figured that you didn't want to sleep away from the baby, so I put a crib in here. I was so sure you were coming back." She hugged her. "I knew Miles thought I was crazy when I asked him to buy another crib, but I was right. You came back to me."

"I'm getting married, Carolina." Georgia blinked at her sister. "That's why I'm here. To ask you to come to my wedding. I'm not going to live with you, honey."

"But, Georgia…" Carolina looked at her, confusion mixed with hurt on her face. "You don't have to marry him anymore. We'll take care of you. You can help me raise my baby."

"I'm marrying Christian. On Sunday. I don't want you to take care of me. I never did. I just wanted my sister back in my life. In our life."

"Is that man making you marry him?" she asked softly. "We can help you get away from him. I know he must frighten you terribly, but Miles can help you get away from him. Maybe one day you can find a nice husband who won't care what happened to you. There must be other men out there. It doesn't have to be him."

Carolina had always been a little flighty, a little timid, too sweet for her own good, but Georgia hadn't thought she would be so judgmental. She'd never thought her sister's words would feel like a hundred slaps to her already sore face.

"He doesn't frighten me. He's not making me marry him. I'm marrying him because I want to."

"I think you're doing it because you didn't have any other

options. I know how proud you are. You don't want to let us take care of you, but there is no shame in letting your family help you and the baby. It's much better than being stuck the rest of your life with some scarred giant that you don't love."

Georgia felt her temper spark. She had never raised her voice to her sister or said an unkind word, but she couldn't take what Carolina was saying. It wasn't fair to Christian. He was too good a man to be spoken of like that. "Letting my family help me? You watched him throw me out with nothing more than the clothes on my back. You sat there quietly while Robert told the family I tried to seduce him. When he told them I had been giving my body to another man. You saw my bruises, you saw the blood on my legs. And you didn't try to help. You didn't try to help me then. You let them choose my rapist over me."

"They wouldn't have believed me. I was just nineteen years old. I don't know why you are so angry."

"You don't know why I'm so angry? You could have said something. Anything. You were my sister, the only person I thought I could turn to. But you were just like the rest of them. You turned your back on me. You wouldn't even look at me as he kicked me out. Now you have the nerve to say that you want to help me? You don't want to help me. You want to treat me like your charity case. Your poor ruined sister. You want to act as though what happened to me was just some unpleasantness that can be brushed under the rug. I cannot forget what happened and you cannot pretend like it didn't. Her name is Abby. She is a product of what happened to me. You won't even say her name. You wouldn't look at her."

"I got the picture you sent. She looks like him. Like Robert. I wasn't expecting that."

"And I wasn't expecting to be raped. I refuse to have you

treat her like some little second-class bastard child because she makes you feel uncomfortable."

"But, Georgia, it's not—"

"Christian may be a scarred giant, but he has shown me more kindness and respect in the past few months than I have gotten in years from my own family. I'm not marrying him because I have to. I'm marrying him because I want to, because he's there for me and is sweet to me. I'm marrying him because he deserves a good wife. And I deserve someone who is going to love my daughter like his own and not look at her and see her ugly beginnings, but see her for the lovely, smart girl she is."

Georgia turned around to step away from her sister, from her backward thinking, and Christian was standing there. With Abby in his arms and Miles at his side. Both men looked horrified, and she couldn't blame them. She was horrified herself.

"Mama?" Abby called to her.

She went to Abby, to Christian, to her small family. She took Abby from Christian and squeezed her, needing to feel her, needing comfort from the only person who ever loved her unconditionally. And then when just Abby wasn't enough, she took Christian's arm and wrapped it around her shoulders. She needed to feel his weight and warmth and solidness before she fell apart. He kissed her forehead and then darted a look at Carolina. He must have heard some of their argument, how much she didn't want to know, but she knew she was done here at her sister's house. "Can you take me home, sugar? Please."

"Of course." And without another word they left Carolina and all her judgments behind.

"What do you think we should do after we get married?" Georgia asked him later that evening. They were back in their hotel suite sitting side by side on the couch. A sleepy Abby sat on Christian's lap, her head resting against his stomach.

Georgia had been quiet since they'd left her sister's house. They all had, even Abby, but Georgia seemed completely lost in thought. He wanted to peer into her mind, to see what she was thinking, but he was afraid he already knew. He had heard most of the argument between her and her sister. The part where Carolina said that Georgia was marrying him because she had no other options, the part where she'd said that by marrying him she would forever be stuck with a big scarred giant.

Georgia had defended him. She said all the things that he had expected her to say, and that should have made him feel better, or right, or something other than what he was feeling.

But Carolina was right. Georgia didn't have much of a choice. She *had* to marry him. She *was* going to be stuck with a big scarred giant. She had lost her job. She had no money, nowhere to go.

She thought she'd lost her job.

He never told her about the suspension, that it was just going to be three weeks without pay. He had meant to. He had gone there to tell her, but when he saw her, when he saw how she lived, he knew he couldn't leave her like that. He knew he would regret it for the rest of his life.

Now he realized that he had to tell her about her other options. She could go back to the life she had even if it killed him to let her go.

She didn't love him. Out of all the kind things she said about him, the one thing she hadn't mentioned was love. He didn't expect her to love him. He probably should never expect it. It was impossible to ask, but for some reason when he was watching her argue with her sister he wanted to hear the words roll off her tongue.

I'm marrying him because I'm in love with him.

But they didn't come, and he felt hollow because of their absence.

"You know the hospital overturned your termination," he said, not wanting to admit it. "It's just a suspension without pay. You could go back to work in a few weeks if you wanted."

"What?" She turned to look at him fully, her eyes going a little wide at his admission.

"I talked to them after they fired you. I told them that it was my fault—that I was the one kissing you. They overturned your termination. You could go back, Georgia. You could be a nurse again. You have options."

"No." She frowned, her nose scrunching as she processed his words. "I don't want to go back there."

"If you did you wouldn't have to marry me."

"But I want to marry you," she said without a beat of hesitation or second thought. "I want to be a good wife to you." She rested her head on his shoulder and reached for her daughter's small hand. "Do you want to back out?" she asked so softly that he barely heard her. "You don't have to marry *me*. It's a lot to ask of you."

It wasn't a lot to ask. Spending the rest of his life with a beautiful, soft woman would be no hardship for him. He didn't deserve her. "I wouldn't have asked you to marry me if I didn't want to be your husband."

"I'm so sorry I made you go there, Christian. I wasted your time."

"You didn't. I like Miles. While you and your sister were upstairs we sat in his den and talked. He was in the navy. Every firstborn male in his family has been in the navy. He wants to continue the tradition with his son. He asked me if I wanted my son to go into the marines. I said no. I wouldn't want my child going through what I went through, and then I realized that I wanted a son. That's what I want to do after we get married, Georgia. When you're ready, I would like to have another child. I'm the last Howard. My parents were only children. They were older when they had me. I want to carry the name on. My father was a good man. He wasn't like me. He was a gentle giant. He was love. I want to pass part of him on to my son. So my day wasn't wasted. You shouldn't be sorry."

"When I asked you what you wanted to do after we got married, I meant where should we take our guests to eat. But I'm okay with that, too. I would like to give you a son. I want Abby to have a sibling, to know that kind of love."

"If you married me, you would be stuck with a big scarred giant. You don't have to defend me. I know what I am."

"Yes. I know who you are, too. You're the best friend I've ever had, and it's my job as a wife to defend you. And I will defend you. There are no *ifs,* Christian. Only *whens.* I will marry you on Sunday. I will be a good wife to you."

"But what about your sister?"

"Sometimes I hate my father so much for what he did to me, but I can almost excuse it. He broke when my brother was killed. Both of my parents did."

"Your brother was killed?"

"Didn't I tell you? I have three brothers. Abel was the eldest. He was my parents' joy. But he started dating a married woman and was murdered by her husband. They were never the same after that. My father blamed the woman. He didn't blame Abel, who should have known better, or the man who killed him, but the woman. He said that she led him into temptation because she wasn't raised right. She wasn't raised in God's image. He vowed to raise his daughters in God's image. I knew what was going to happen when he found out

I was pregnant. I knew, but I didn't expect Carolina to be silent about it. I'm the most angry with her. We were so close. I thought she would have stood by my side."

"I don't think she knew how." He lifted his hand and trailed his fingers through her loose hair. "I think you need to be angry, Georgia. You have been dealing with so much these past two years that you haven't had time to be. It's okay to be mad. It's okay to if you need more time, but I don't think your sister's a bad person. I just don't think she knew how to help you then."

"I didn't want her help. I just wanted her to look at me before I left. I wanted that one sign that she loved me. She wouldn't look at Abby today. She avoided her when we were there and it all came back to me. I don't want Abby to go through life feeling as if she's some unfortunate mistake I'm stuck with in her own family. I want her to feel nothing but love."

"She will." Christian brushed his hands over Abby's curls.

Abby looked at him, rubbing her eyes with her chubby fists. "No Da."

"Yes Da," Georgia said.

She cupped Christian's face in her hands and kissed his eyelids and the bridge of his nose, his chin and then his mouth. In his life he had experienced deep kisses, and soul-sucking kisses and hot, hard, passionate kisses, but when Georgia kissed him like this he could honestly say that this kind of kiss was his favorite.

He brushed her hands away from his face and pressed his mouth to hers, needing to feel more. Her kiss was warm and sweet and shy and soothing. If he ever had any doubts about marrying her, these kisses banished those thoughts.

She was blushing when he pulled away.

"You should only kiss me like that in our bedroom."

He smiled at her. "I don't think I can contain myself. You make me want to kiss you." He stood up. "I'm going to put this one to bed. Why don't you take a bath and get comfortable?"

"Oh, I can do it." She stood up and put her hand on his shoulder. "You've done enough today, Christian. I can do it."

"I haven't done anything today. I want you to relax."

She looked at him for a moment, a little anxiety sweeping across her face. "It's my job to put her to bed. It's my job to take care of her."

"Then what's my job?"

"To provide." She seemed surprised that the words had come from her mouth.

He might have been surprised, too, if he hadn't known how she was raised. Georgia's father had taught them some very antiquated lessons on the roles of men and women. Another man might be glad that his future wife wanted to serve. But Christian had grown up with August Howard, who read to him at night and made him breakfast in the morning. His father was very much a part of his life, and the more time he spent with Abby the more he realized that.

"I can't believe I said that. I've gone through so much alone. I've provided for her and loved her by myself for so long." She locked eyes with him. "I'm not marrying you just so you can provide for us. I'm marrying you because I want you to be my family."

"I know, Georgia."

"I want to put her to bed. I would like to put her to bed every night, because I used to work the night shift and I didn't get to do it. Mrs. Sheppard did, and I swore if I ever got the chance to stop working the night shift, I would always be the one to put my baby to bed."

That he understood, and handed Abby back to her mother.

"You take the nights. I'll get her ready in the mornings. Is that okay with you?"

She nodded. "I didn't expect you to be like this with her. My father never made us a meal or put us to bed. He never did anything with us."

"I'm not your father, Georgia."

"I know." She grabbed his arm and pulled him toward her to kiss his cheek. "I'm grateful for that, honey. You don't know how grateful I am."

CHAPTER 16

Georgia lay beside her daughter in the other bedroom, just holding her close and smelling her clean scent. She hadn't slept with her daughter that day. It was the first time since she was born. When she was working she used to snatch a few hours of sleep in the morning with Abby by her side, even after she was fired, before Christian came. She used to spend time with Abby like this, studying her while she slept, marveling at her perfect little features. And while she had done so, she had hoped she could find a way to spend more time with Abby. *Prayed* was a more fitting word. If she believed in God, she would say that she prayed for time with her daughter.

But she stopped believing in God the day her father threw her out. But maybe that wasn't true. When she looked at Abby, when she thought about Christian, she had to believe there was a God. She just was mad at Him for a little while.

Her prayers had been answered. She wasn't going to have to work anymore or struggle. She wasn't going to be alone. In just a few more days she was going to be Christian's wife.

She thought some kind of peace would come over her with

that knowledge, but it didn't. Instead she was terrified of the change and worried she wouldn't make him happy, and excited that she was going to be able to spend her life with a man who made her feel so many things.

She had to go to him now. He was waiting for her in the bedroom they were sharing. She had stalled a little. Taking a bath with Abby, spending an extralong time dressing her, reading to her from the only storybook they owned. Being alone in a bed with Christian, feeling his large, heavy, warm body against hers, wasn't comfortable. It made her feel hot and odd and tingly. It made her want to be closer to him.

Sex.

She kept thinking about it. Thoughts of it and him had snuck into her mind so many times that day, so many times since she had met him.

She had never had sex before. Or made love. She had only been used.

It would be her first time with Christian, and she was so nervous about it she couldn't concentrate on anything else that evening.

It would be nice.

It had to be nice, because it was with Christian.

She kissed her daughter's sleeping face and placed her in the crib.

It felt so different being with him outside of the hospital, outside of her stress and her worries and her fear of getting caught. It was odd for her to see him as healthy. It was surreal to watch him be so gentle with her baby and amazing how her baby seemed to feel so safe in his arms even though she was pretending she wanted nothing to do with him.

Georgia couldn't pretend.

He was lying in the bed shirtless when she walked into the room. His hair was damp from the shower. He was mindlessly flipping through the channels, his muscular body totally relaxed. *Man* was the only word that came to mind when she thought about him. One of her father's old sermons came to mind.

A real man works hard.

A real man takes care of his family.

A real man loves his wife.

A real man doesn't complain. He just does what a man is supposed to do.

She wondered what her father would think of Christian. It wouldn't matter to her. She would never change her mind about him anyway.

He sat up when he noticed her standing there, giving her an almost bashful smile. "I didn't expect you to show up until after midnight. You finished your rounds early."

"You're still the last patient I like to see." Her eyes went to the scars on his arms and torso. They were still angry, but so much a part of him that she didn't see them sometimes. But then she remembered how he got them and how they came to know each other. "Do you feel okay, sugar? You just got out of the hospital and early, too. You seem so strong, but I worry about you."

"Come here," he said softly.

She obeyed and he reached for her, wrapping her in his large body. "You smell like Abby. Did you enjoy your bath time with her?"

"Yes. Are you feeling okay?" She gently touched his scarred wrist. "Do you still hurt?"

"My skin feels tender in some places and really tight in others, and I'm more tired than I've ever been, but I'm fine, Georgia. Much better than I was."

"Would you tell me if you weren't?"

"No." He placed his large hand on her thigh and his lips on her neck. "Can I touch you?"

"Yes," she said, feeling breathless. "I like this. I like when you touch me. I'm not used to it. I kind of want to jump from my skin, but I like it."

He slid his hand beneath her nightgown, running his fingers along the back of her thigh, his lips leaving slow, soft kisses along her neck. "You make me feel good, Georgia." He was so gentle with her.

This was going to be nice. It had to be nice, because it was going to be with Christian.

His hand brushed over her belly and then up her torso to the underside of her breast. She let out a moan, but then stifled it, biting her lip, trying to control some of the wild feelings that were racing through her. But then the pads of his fingers stroked her nipple, and she jumped at the sensation.

"It's okay," he soothed. "Trust me."

She did. He was the only person she had truly trusted in a very long time.

His hand cupped her breast; he squeezed her a little, lifted her as if to test the weight. He did this all while he looked at her with those intensely green eyes.

She couldn't meet his eyes. She felt shy around him, especially now because what he was doing to her felt wickedly good. She began to feel the warmth grow between her legs, that subtle mysterious throb, the dampness. And then he rolled her onto her back, his big body coming over hers. He kissed her, slid his tongue between her lips and kissed her. She didn't know how to kiss him back when he kissed her like this, so she gripped his face and held him to her, and he delivered the slowest, deepest kiss of her life.

He lifted his mouth from hers and looked down at her for a long moment. She didn't want this to stop. She missed his mouth. She wanted to feel that connection with him. She slid her hand down his hard stomach, down into his boxers to hold him in her hand again. She would never forget that night, how it made her feel, how powerful she felt giving him such pleasure.

"I think we should wait." He grabbed her hand, sliding his thick fingers between hers.

She blinked at him. "Wait?"

"Till we're married."

"We don't have to." She didn't want to. She was ready for this, ready for him, ready to put her past behind her and only look toward the future.

"I know. I don't want to wait, but I think when we make love it should be as man and wife."

"Okay." It was all she could say. It was what he wanted.

Christian walked into Abby's temporary bedroom the next morning, finding her standing up. She looked at him for a long moment, assessing him, almost as if she wasn't sure what to make of him. He didn't blame her. One day she was living just with her mother, spending so much of her time with a babysitter, the next day she was faced with him, a big ugly man who was supposed to be her father.

"Good morning, BB."

"No Da. Up." She lifted her arms to him and he smiled to himself. He had never thought much about children before, especially babies, but this kid had a big personality. She was going to be a handful when she got older. He found himself looking forward to it.

Life without the military seemed empty to him, but with Georgia and Abby, there were possibilities. He could have another purpose in life. Georgia's words came back to him.

She wanted Abby to be loved for who she was, not thought of by how she was made. He could do that.

He could show her how a father was supposed to treat a daughter and how a man was supposed to treat his wife.

"Up? Is that all I'm good for in this relationship?" He lifted her from the crib and kissed her forehead.

She scrunched her little face, frowning ferociously at him.

"I don't care if you don't like it. I'm going to do it again." He kissed one cheek and then the other, causing her to sigh and drop her head on his shoulder. "That's right. Get used to it. I'm not going anywhere."

He took her out into the small dining area. "Oatmeal again this morning, BB? Or maybe cream of wheat for breakfast? What do one-year-olds like to eat?"

"She likes fruit and yogurt for breakfast sometimes. She loves Cheerios, too."

He turned around to face Georgia. Her hair was messy, her cheek was marked with the lines of a pillow and she wore the primmest nightgown he had ever seen. But she was still the most beautiful woman he had ever known.

"You're up."

"Yes. It's hard to stay asleep when you leave the bed. It feels cold without you."

Sunday, he reminded himself. They would make love on Sunday, just a few days away. He had made himself stop last night. He hadn't wanted to. He'd wanted to drive himself into Georgia until the world no longer existed, but he remembered that she was still innocent in a way. She wasn't used to being touched by a man, loved by one, and it was evident last night when she'd jumped at his touch and looked away from him as if she was too embarrassed to meet his eyes. He had to do it right. He had to make her comfortable with him; he had to make their first time together mean something.

"I'll buy you a bull mastiff after we get married. You won't feel that way anymore."

She grinned at him. "Can I join you two this morning? I promise I'll be quiet."

"I don't know, BB? What do you think?"

"Mama. Eat."

"It's a yes. I think I could go for a thick stack of French toast. What about you, Georgia? I haven't had really good food since I got hurt. I think we deserve to pig out this morning."

"And bacon. And maybe a couple of eggs."

"Get dressed. I know the perfect place."

He hadn't been back to his parents' old neighborhood since he'd left for the marines. It had been twelve years, and then he was reeling too much from the loss of them to take much note of the surroundings, but now that he was here with Georgia things were different. He could see the beauty of the area, the lush greenery, the eye-catching colorful houses. The history. Charleston was a beautiful city. But it was a place he never wanted to come to.

He had been so mad at his parents when they'd first moved here. They had sold his childhood home. On breaks from college, instead of going back to Connecticut, where he had grown up, he came here. To the balmy South, where it didn't even snow, where none of his friends were.

"That was just about the best food I've ever had in my life, Christian," Georgia said to him as they walked through White Point Garden, a park just a few blocks from his parents' home. "How did you find it?"

"My parents' house is in this neighborhood. My father and I ate here every Sunday morning. That place almost made up for them moving me away from all my friends when I was eighteen."

"You're from Connecticut, right?"

"Yes, my father grew up in Westport, but I grew up in a big old rambling farmhouse in Litchfield. One winter when I was seventeen we got six feet of snow in just a few hours. My mother, who had fibromyalgia, was tired of being there and so isolated. She thought the warmer weather would help her and it did. They loved it here, but I was so pissed at them for moving. I failed to see how much happier they both were living here."

"We could go back to Connecticut if you want, Christian," she said softly. "I won't mind. There is nothing left for me here in South Carolina."

They could go back, but for some reason he didn't want to. He knew she was estranged from her family, but it seemed wrong to take her so far away. There was hope for Georgia and her sister. There was love there. He couldn't take her away from that.

"I think this is a good neighborhood for Abby." He looked down at the little girl in her stroller. "There's a playground not far from here. We could walk to it from my parents' house if we lived there. I want to show it to you."

She nodded. "I want to see it."

The closer they got to his parents' house, the quieter Christian became. Georgia wished she knew what to say to him, but there was nothing adequate she could think of. She knew he was alone in the world—maybe it was one of the things that had attracted her to him in the first place—but it wasn't until now that she realized how hard going through life with no family at all must be. Her family was gone from her life, not dead. If she wanted to, she could see their faces again, but Christian couldn't.

She would have to give him children. Just seeing how he

was with Abby made her realize that Christian was a man who needed to fill up his life with children, with family. It would make him happy.

"Do you have any grandparents?" she asked as they turned down a quiet, tree-lined residential street with pastel-colored houses.

"My father's mother passed away when I was ten. My grandfather died when I was sixteen. I never knew my mother's parents. She left home when she was sixteen."

"Do you ever think about finding them?"

"No. They never thought about finding her. Who lets their sixteen-year-old just walk away from them? And what was so bad about them that my mother had to walk away?"

"Did you ever ask her?"

"No. I was so young and selfish when they died. I didn't think about not having any other family until I had none. I wished I could have known more about them before they died. It's one of my biggest regrets."

He stopped in front of a large white house with black shutters and a wraparound porch with two oak rocking chairs.

There was a garden, which was neglected and overgrown, but there were flowers. Hydrangeas and sunflowers and rhododendrons. Her mother used to garden. Georgia and Carolina would help her weed. She had grown vegetables there, too. Tomatoes and cucumbers, bell peppers. Till this day Georgia still craved fried green tomatoes that came from her mother's garden. She wondered if she could grow some, if there was space beneath all the greenery to have her own little vegetable garden.

"I know it's a little shabby and needs to be updated, but it's a good house. My parents had it redone about fifteen years ago."

She nodded absently and took Abby out of her stroller. She walked up the driveway to the porch. She could place hanging baskets there. Begonias or maybe petunias. They could paint the porch, too, give it a fresh coat of white paint. The flowers would look so pretty against it. It was a large enough space for Abby to play on. They could sit out here in the evenings and watch her play. Maybe they could get a swing. It would be nice to have dessert outside, or maybe breakfast in the mornings. A little café table would fit nicely in the corner.

"Georgia." Christian placed his hands on her shoulders. She turned and looked up at him. He looked concerned; a line of worry was creased into his forehead. "I know it's not the nicest place on the block—"

"It's the best house I've ever seen," she said, unable to peel her eyes from it. "I can't believe you lived here."

That was all he needed to hear to let the weight ease from his chest. He thought he would feel more pain seeing his home again after so long. He thought grief would overtake him, but it didn't. He was more concerned about what Georgia thought of this place.

She hadn't said anything when they first saw it. It had been neglected, terribly so. He hired a local guy to come a couple of times a year to make sure the house hadn't fallen down. Just the bare minimum to keep the neighbors from complaining. The paint was peeling in spots on the porch and his mother's little garden was so thick and overgrown that he could barely see through it.

The inside wasn't much better. Most of his parents' personal things were gone, in a storage unit that he had never been to. The remaining furniture was covered in dust cloths and the curtains were so bleached by the sun that it was impossible to tell what color they were originally.

He didn't feel his parents here like he'd thought he would. He almost thought it would feel as though their ghosts were walking around this place. But it didn't. This place felt more like a vacation home to him, a place where he had some pleasant memories, but it had never truly felt like home.

"Why didn't your parents sleep in this bedroom?" Georgia touched his cheek, pulling him out of his thoughts.

"My mother had problem with her joints, the stairs were too much for her, so they turned the den into their bedroom. I slept here."

"Did you?" She gave him a soft smile. "I can just imagine you in this big bedroom, in one of those large four-poster beds with one of those pretty girls from the College of Charleston."

"I've never had a girl in this bedroom. There were women before you, but I've never had a girlfriend. Or been in a real relationship. I'm an ugly son of a bitch and I'm not very nice." His eyes passed over her. She was so pretty. So sweet and small, the opposite of everything he ever was. "Are you sure you want to be married to me?"

She closed the gap between them and rested her head on his chest. "It hurts me when you try to get rid of me."

"I'm not trying to get rid of you. I'm letting you know how I am."

"You're a lot better than you think you are. There have been a lot of soldiers since I worked at Jericho. You're the only one I've ever lost my head over, and my job."

"There's something about you, Georgia." He kissed her forehead. "You make me want a whole new life."

"I can see us here. I can see the future. I want to live in it now."

"Okay." He pressed his mouth to hers and she opened for him. She was learning. Her kisses were still shy, still innocent, but there was something erotic about them. He couldn't wait to have all of her. He couldn't wait to explore her fully. He couldn't wait to have her as his wife. "Let's go get our marriage license. Then we can start making plans to move here."

"That sounds like a very good idea."

CHAPTER 17

After spending the next two days with Christian, Georgia fully understood why he was a commanding officer. He simply got things done. There were workers at their house repairing the kitchen and painters in Abby's room and movers delivering furniture. He told her didn't want to start their new life as a married couple in a hotel room. He wanted to start it in their home, and he did everything he could to make that happen.

They would officially start their life together tomorrow. But to Georgia, it felt as if it had started already. He took care of her and Abby as if nothing else mattered in the world. He was going to be a good husband. She had always thought her father was a good husband. And maybe he was. He was harsh with his daughters, cold and unyielding, but Pastor Williams was a man who loved his wife. Or at least Georgia thought he did.

Her mother, Fiona, was always a very delicate woman. A daughter of a preacher, too, she never raised her voice or spoke her opinion. She was meek. She told her daughters that their jobs as wives would be to honor and obey their husbands, to look after their homes and children, to treat their men like kings. Carolina had always soaked up those lessons, but they had never sat well with Georgia.

Obey your husband.

Why didn't the husband ever have to obey his wife? But even with that rule, her parents' marriage seemed to be solid. Even after Abel had died and father turned bitter. Sometimes she would see them sitting at the kitchen table together at night when they thought they were alone. Her father would hold her mother's hand, and he would look at her with... tenderness. It was the only way she could describe it. He looked like a man who loved his wife. He would speak to Fiona softly. He treated her as though she was fragile. He made his daughters do all the cooking and cleaning, anything and everything to make sure his wife didn't have to.

Georgia wondered who was doing that now. The cooking and the cleaning. The washing and the ironing. The polishing of her father's shoes. Carolina was gone. Her brothers... She didn't know what had happened to them. Who was taking care of Mama?

She'd thought about her mother a lot these past few days as the wedding got closer. She thought about the phone call they'd shared a few weeks ago. Her mother had sounded so unhappy. She'd sounded as though she was breaking. And while she felt sorry for her mother, while she wanted to take her away from her world, she was angry at her, too.

Fiona wasn't strong enough. She was never strong enough. She never stood up to her husband. She never made her feelings known. She never spoke a word against him even though she knew he was wrong. She just let things happen. Nothing could make Georgia send away her baby. No one.

"What's the matter, sweetheart?" Christian asked her with a kiss to her forehead.

She looked up at him, at this good man who had been placed in her path, and she felt foolish. Bitterness kept rising in her chest these past few days. Before, when she was working and so overtired, she couldn't think straight. She didn't have time to dwell on her family, but the past few days since Christian had taken so much weight off her shoulders, she was able to do so, and the more she thought about them, the angrier she felt.

But she shouldn't allow her past to haunt her. She had a good man in her life. She needed to make sure he was happy.

"Nothing." They were alone in their bedroom now. Christian had just put Abby in her crib for a nap.

Georgia reached for him, needing to feel his big body wrapped around her, needing those nasty thoughts to dissolve. She wanted to feel his skin and his lips. She wanted to feel his weight on top of her. He had barely touched her since he'd told her he wanted to wait and it bothered her. She slept in bed with him every night and smelled his skin and was surrounded by his warmth and she wanted more. Her breasts ached when she was around him; her nipples turned to hard little points whenever she brushed against him. And that throb between her legs had grown almost painful.

There was a time in her life when she'd never thought sex would interest her. She'd never thought her body would crave to be with a man, but Christian had come along and he'd changed all of that for her.

"Will you lie down with me for a little while?"

"No." He stroked his hand down her back, sending a rush of tingles along her skin. "Everything is all set for tomorrow, Georgia. The justice of the peace is coming. I called the restaurant to reserve a back room. I got my dress uniform out of storage. There's only one thing left."

She looked up at him. "I need a dress."

"Yes."

"I'm no good at buying clothes. I don't know where to begin."

"You're beautiful." He kissed her forehead again. "You'll look beautiful in anything, but I called for help. Picking out a wedding dress is something you shouldn't do alone."

She frowned at him. "You're not coming with me?"

"No. I don't want to see you in your dress until you're walking down the aisle toward me. I called your sister. She's downstairs."

"But…" She was speechless and angry and hurt and… relieved. Mrs. Sheppard and her daughter were going to be at her wedding, and they were her friends, but when she was a little girl she had never imagined getting married without her sister by her side.

"Talk to her. I know you're mad, but she wants you in her life and I think you should be. I don't have a family—losing mine made me realize how important they were to me. But you can have yours back, or at least a piece of them. Please take this chance, Georgia."

She looked up at him, knowing she didn't deserve him, afraid she wasn't going to be enough to keep him happy.

"I don't know whether to smack you or kiss you."

"Go with the second." He gave her a small smile before he pressed his mouth to hers. She felt a little burst of heat when his lips met hers and she immediately wanted more. She reached for his face, to pull him closer and kiss him until the world drifted away, but he stopped her and pushed her hands toward her sides. "Not now."

She felt a little stung by his rejection, but she knew they

would be man and wife tomorrow. She knew in a few hours she could show him all her appreciation and affection. She would give her body to him.

"She's in the lobby. I called for a car. Have lunch. Talk to her. Miles and I will watch BB."

Georgia nodded, nervous to see her sister again after their fight. "You're good man, you know." She lifted his scarred hand and kissed it. "The best one I know."

She left the room and their hotel suite without looking back. Miles was in the hallway walking toward her. He was carrying a box of pizza and what looked like beer in glass bottles. "Hello, Georgia."

"Hello, Dr. Hammond."

"I'm Miles to you and you know it. We're family." He frowned for a moment. "I'm sorry about Carolina the other day. I love her more than anything in the world, but sometimes I feel as if she's been raised in a bubble. I blame Oakdale. The town is run by your father's church, and it was bad before you left, Georgia." He shook his head. "In the time you've been away, it's gotten worse. Your father is a miserable man who preaches hellfire and brimstone, and your mother is at the point where she's going to break. I want to get Carolina away from there. I don't want to raise our baby in an environment of hate, but she doesn't want to leave your mother. I've been offered a partnership in a practice here. I'm going to take it. Now that you are in Charleston it will be better for us. You'll be good for her. She needs you."

"Carolina doesn't know you're going to move here yet?"

"No. I'm going to tell her after you are married. I really like Christian. He'll make you a fine husband. If you were my sister, I would pick a man like him for you."

"Thank you, Miles. I appreciate that."

"She needs you, Georgia. You're her anchor. Please forgive her."

Carolina was sitting in the lobby when Georgia got off the elevator. She looked so much like their mother, like a lady. She wore a blue sundress printed with tiny flowers and a cardigan to cover her shoulders. Every hair on her head was in place and her hands were neatly folded in her lap.

They were so different. Georgia had never mastered being ladylike, or docile. She never was as serene as her sister.

"Hello, sister."

Carolina's face lit up for a moment when she saw her, but then she sobered for a moment. "I've been a terrible person." She stood, her pretty eyes filling with tears. "I hate myself. I was stupid and wrong and bad."

"Oh, Carolina." Georgia reached for her sister. "Shut up."

"No. I'm sorry. Did I ever tell you I was sorry? I'm so sorry. I am. I know if it were the other way around, that you would have been there for me. You would have left with me. But you are so much stronger than I am. I knew you would be fine. In the back of my mind I knew it. You don't understand how hard it was after you left. Daddy had him over for dinner. He apologized to him over you. But the boys couldn't stomach that. Especially Eli. Robert was supposed to be his best friend. I don't know if he believed that Robert forced you, but he didn't believe Robert was telling the truth. They stopped talking. He told Robert not to come around anymore and he and Daddy got into a big fight over it. Eli stopped going to church. He moved away and he and Daddy barely talk anymore. And then Gideon left for the army. He barely comes home, even when he's on leave. He sends Mama letters to our house. Josiah is still in Oakdale. He feels real bad about what happened to you, Georgia. He believes you. He wants to make amends, Georgia. He told me that just yesterday. He's got a little girl now. I didn't tell you that. But he has a little girl. She's six months old. He got married to Lacey Matthews and he told me that he couldn't do what Daddy did. He couldn't choose some stranger over his daughter. He's been so different since he had the baby. I—"

Georgia put her hand up to stop her sister's endless words. It was too much to take. It was too much to hear in that moment. "Let's find me a dress. We've got the rest of our lives to talk."

"You mean that? You're not mad at me anymore? I'm so relieved. You don't know how mad Miles was with me after you left. He said he thought I was raised better than to judge Christian by the way he looks. I was and I'm sorry. He's a good man, Georgia. He called me and asked me to come, and he's rented that big black car for us today to take us around. I was wrong about him. I'm sorry. If you like him and Miles likes him, then he must be a good man."

"He is, honey. And I forgive you. Let's go."

"You nervous, son?"

Christian looked over at General Lee, who was standing by his side as best man, glad he was there. If he couldn't have his father with him then the general was the next best thing. "No. Do you think I should be?"

"She's a lovely girl. She'll be good for you. I heard that you haven't officially resigned yet. You aren't thinking of re-enlisting?"

"They offered me Afghanistan, but I can't go overseas and leave Georgia and Abby behind. It would feel wrong."

"Lots of soldiers do it."

"Yeah, but I can't. If I died she would be pissed at me."

"There's a base not too far from here. You could be an instructor. I already put in a good word for you."

"I'm leaving," he said even though he had failed to take the final steps. "Once a marine, always a marine, but I'm not going to be on active duty anymore."

"What are you going to do? Have you decided?"

"I'm going to learn about my company. I'm going to be involved." How? He didn't know yet.

The music started playing and thoughts of his future work drifted from his mind. Georgia walked down the aisle with Tobias. The young boy was giving her away. It was Georgia's idea. She said he was her favorite patient.

Tobias was beaming as he used his cane to guide them. His still-wounded eyes were covered in sunglasses, but the smile on his face was incredible. He was honored to be there and Georgia was happy to have him.

She smiled up at him, and laughed when he whispered something in her ear.

Christian almost lost his breath looking at her. She was happy. He was afraid today she wouldn't be. Her sister was there but the rest of her family wasn't. Their wedding was simple and small. He wasn't sure it was what she wanted, but looking at her in her pretty white dress as she came toward him, he knew this was the right wedding for them.

Tobias stopped before him. "You're a lucky man, sir. I wanted to be the one who married her."

"Sorry, kid. Find yourself another nurse."

Tobias handed Georgia to him, that big smile still on his face. "Good luck. I'm happy for you."

Tobias's mother led him back to his seat, leaving Georgia with Christian. She smiled up at him. "Hello, Jarhead. You look so handsome in your uniform."

"Hello, Nurse Williams. You're too beautiful in your dress."

The justice of the peace cleared his throat. This was it. It was their time to get married.

CHAPTER 18

"Are you all right, Georgia?" Christian asked her as she stared out of the bedroom window of their new home.

She was a married lady now. Her wedding had been beautiful and intimate. It wasn't what she'd dreamed of when she was a little girl. She hadn't been married in her father's church. There weren't a hundred people there. But her sister had been there. And the general and his wife. And Tobias had given her away. Mrs. Sheppard had cried and gushed over her. Abby had been there. It was the perfect day, and she realized that somehow she and Christian had managed to cobble together a little family. That the people at her wedding were the people she could depend on if she needed something. She wasn't alone anymore.

"Yes. I'm more than all right. I'm happy."

"I'm glad to hear that, Mrs. Howard." Christian wrapped his arms around her waist. He smelled good, like soap and shampoo. It wasn't the same scent she was used to when they'd spent all those weeks together in the hospital. There was no medicated salve, no sterile hospital smells. No people around.

They were truly alone. For the first time. She was his wife. When she walked into his room that first night she never thought she would end up here. She never thought they would end up married.

"Did I ever thank you for calling my sister?"

"No." He lifted the hair off her neck and kissed her. "But you don't have to thank me. It was nice to have her and Miles there."

"And the general, too. He's a funny man. He used to terrify me, but he's a big puppy dog, isn't he?"

"Yeah." His lips trailed slowly down from the base of her hair to the top on her back, and it was as though somebody had turned the heat up inside her. She felt warm everywhere. "He's been very good to me."

"I think he liked Tobias," she said as his lips brushed her shoulder and his hands stroked down the bare skin of her arms. She broke out in gooseflesh. "I—I've never seen Tobias so happy. He told me his vision is a little better. He can make out shapes now."

"I'm happy for him." He turned her around and pressed her back against the window. "What you're wearing is very beautiful." He fingered the thin strap of her silk nightie.

"Thank you." She darted a glance at him. His chest was bare. He only wore a pair of boxers. She had seen him like this every night since he had come for her, but it was still her favorite way to see him. "I like what you're wearing, too. My sister said that I needed something pretty to wear on my wedding night. I didn't know what you would like so I got this."

"It's perfect."

He slid one strap off her shoulder, revealing her breast. She nearly gasped at the exposure. He had touched her before. He had been closer to her than any other man, but he had never seen her naked. He kissed her cheek as his hand slid down the exposed skin of her chest to cup her breast. She sucked in a breath and her knees went weak. She was glad her back was pressed against the window. She needed the support. The way he touched her made her want to slide right down to the floor.

"Wasn't it nice of my sister to take Abby for the night?" He slid the other strap off, causing her nightie to fall to her waist. Her nipples grew even harder. She swallowed. "Carolina was trying really hard today with her. She held her all throughout dinner."

"I noticed." He stepped forward and tugged the nightgown all the way down, exposing her. She wasn't wearing any panties. She figured she didn't need to tonight. But now there was nothing to cover her and Christian took his time looking.

She felt self-conscious. She wasn't thin like her sister. Her belly had never gone flat after she'd had her baby. Her thighs touched. She was far from perfect, and yet he looked and looked and looked. All without saying a word.

"She said she would take her whenever we wanted some time alone. Miles told me that he wanted to move here. That'll be nice. You would have another friend in the area."

Christian grabbed her by the waist and pulled her into a hug. Her nipples scraped his chest and the throb between her legs had grown painful. "Are you nervous?"

"My heart is about to burst from my chest and fly all around this room."

He cupped her face in his large hands and gave her a slow kiss, his tongue sweeping inside her mouth. It was as if he was tasting her, savoring her. These were the kind of kisses she'd craved the past few days, the ones that made her mind melt and her legs turn to jelly, the ones that made her forget the world.

"I won't hurt you," he said into her mouth. "I would die before I did."

"I know. This is my first time, Christian." She pulled her mouth from his. "I've never given myself to a man. I want to do this right. I want to make you happy."

"You will." He scooped her off her feet and took her to their bed. He had gotten a large four-poster bed, just like she had teased him about the day she'd first seen the house. The room was lovely, the walls a light sage-green, the furniture picked out by them together. When they'd walked in tonight it was the first time she had seen everything all put together, but she barely noticed because she knew that this was coming. That they would truly join and become husband and wife tonight.

He set her down gently and knelt between her legs. She could see his erection straining in his boxers. He was ready to make love, and so was she. The wetness had formed between her legs as soon as he'd walked in the room But Christian liked to kiss. He liked to touch and take his time. She appreciated that, but right now the anticipation was killing her.

"Please come to me." She reached out for him and he took her hand, but he did not close the distance between him.

"I've imagined this," he said, his voice coming out choked. "When I was in the hospital and in pain I imagined you in bed like this. It kept me from going insane." He leaned forward and kissed her heartbeat. "I don't know if you know this, but you kept me alive in there."

"I didn't."

"You gave me something to look forward to. I think I would have given up if you weren't there."

"Christian." Her eyes filled with tears. She loved him. All along she had been feeling herself slip into love with him, but now she was all the way there. And it rocked her world. "Please come here. Please. I need to feel you."

This time he came. He settled his heavy body on top of

hers and she let out a ragged sigh of relief. She touched him. She ran her hands over his back, and down his arms. She ran her fingers through his thick hair and kissed his shoulders, his neck, every piece of him she could reach. She felt wicked and wanton and helpless, almost. She just wanted more of him.

"Oh, God," he whispered. "You're so sweet." He cupped her breast, stroking her nipple with his thumb, and he kissed her. It wasn't slow and sweet like the last one. It was harder and hotter and wilder. She didn't know how to keep up with him. So she let herself be kissed. She closed her eyes and melted back in the pillows while his tongue invaded her mouth and his hand stroked her breast.

She felt more than she thought was possible. It was like little fireworks going off inside her. It felt too good. She felt guilty, as though she didn't deserve this. And then he started to rub against her.

His cloth-covered erection stroked between her legs, and it was as if lightning streaked through her. She cried out into his mouth. He noticed. He lifted his mouth from hers and looked down at her. She felt her cheeks burn. She was embarrassed. Embarrassed that she had let herself get so out of control.

He said nothing. Just kissed her lips as he lifted his body from hers to take off his boxers. He settled back between her legs and this time she felt his flesh, so long and hot and hard against her. She hadn't seen him yet. She had never seen her husband entirely nude and she wanted to, but he didn't give her the opportunity. "I can't wait anymore, Georgia. I need you."

He sealed his mouth to hers as he guided himself slowly inside her. He was large, very large. His thickness stretched her, but it wasn't painful or even uncomfortable. She was ready for him, so wet she felt it on her thighs.

He growled a little, pushing in deeper, his invasion not

complete, and just when she thought it was enough, that she could take no more of him, he moved out and back into her. It took a few moments for her to grow accustomed to the motion, but it was a nice feeling. His slow stroking and soft kisses. His warm body. Their closeness.

She was married to him. His wife. She had never been happier.

"Georgia…" He sounded as though he was in pain. "You feel too good. I can't hold on much longer."

"Don't hold on, love. I don't want you to."

He moved faster inside her and that place between her legs where she throbbed for him seemed to grow tighter.

"Georgia. Please," he begged her. "Please."

She wasn't sure what he was asking for, so she kissed him, this time with everything she had. She swept her tongue into his mouth, causing him to groan, and she felt that power again. The power she'd felt the first time she'd given him pleasure. She wrapped her legs around him and squeezed tightly. He cursed and shook, and then she felt it, a hot wetness surging inside of her.

He collapsed on top of her, his entire weight pinning her to the bed. She'd never thought she would like to be held down, unable to move, but with Christian she felt safe. With Christian she felt cherished.

She'd once thought that sex was ugly. That it was used to hurt, but Christian made it beautiful. Tears slipped from her eyes. He noticed immediately and threw himself off her.

"Georgia, did I hurt you? I'm so sorry." He touched her face. "I didn't mean to."

"No, you didn't hurt me, you dumb man. You loved me." She reached for him, not wanting their separation for even a minute. "Thank you." She kissed him. "Thank you."

★ ★ ★

He couldn't make her orgasm. The thought pounded in Christian's mind all night as his wife slept in his arms.

On their wedding night, and he hadn't done the job. He had gone too fast. He didn't kiss her all over like he'd wanted to, hadn't touched her enough. He'd wanted to take her breasts in his mouth and suckle. He had wanted to lick her skin and taste between her legs. He'd wanted to give her pleasure tonight. But he'd failed. He had failed at the one thing he was supposed to do.

She didn't seem to mind. She was happy, in fact, even smiling in her sleep. He blamed that smile of hers and those lips and the way her soft body had accepted him. She was no skilled seductress—her kisses and touches were almost innocent—but she turned him on to the point he shook with need.

She stirred in his arms, and then he felt her hand on his thigh and then wrap around his cock. "Can I touch you here?" she asked in a sleepy voice. He went rock hard instantly.

"You're awake."

"Yes." She took her hand from him and turned on the light. "I'm awake because you're awake. I know when you're sleeping by the way your body feels around me. Can I touch you?"

"Of course you can. You don't have to ask."

She looked a little bashful. "Can I see you, too?"

"Yes."

She pulled the blanket down to reveal his throbbing hard-on. "I have to ask. I've never been with a man before. I don't want to do the wrong thing." She straddled his legs and took him in her hand. "It's very big." She frowned down at him. "I've seen others in the hospital, but never one like this." She cupped his sack in her hand and squeezed it gently. "You don't mind that I'm doing this, do you?"

He swallowed hard. "No, ma'am. Not at all."

"You would tell me if you didn't like something I did, right?"

"I would." He looked into her eyes. "Would you tell me if I did something you didn't like?"

"Yes." She nodded. "You haven't done anything I don't like yet, except not lie down with me."

"I wanted to wait until we were married. I had a hard enough time controlling myself around you those five nights. You think I would have lasted during the day?"

She smiled happily at him as her warm, smooth hands continued to explore him. "I like touching you, especially like this. I can see all of you. I feel as if I'm all powerful." She stroked up his length and rubbed the head of his cock with her thumb. He hissed out a breath. "This part is the most sensitive?"

"Yes."

"What would happen if I kissed it?" He jumped in her hand and she looked up at him, surprised. "I heard men like it when women put it in their mouths."

"They do."

"I don't know much about sex," she said apologetically. "We were homeschooled. We weren't allowed to watch television. I feel silly not knowing about it because I'm a nurse. I went to college, but I only know about sex in the most basic of terms, and from what I've pieced together these past few years."

"I'll teach you."

She nodded as she stroked him a little harder, her hand developing a delicious rhythm that was driving him insane. "Would you like me to put my mouth on you?"

Oh. Hell. Yes.

He shook his head, knowing he wouldn't be able to last

two seconds if she wrapped that sweet mouth around him. He was already so close, so fast. "This feels good, sweetheart."

"I like touching you here. I liked the way you feel inside me, too. It was nice."

"Then put me back inside you. We'll both feel good."

She frowned at him. "We can do it like this? With me on top?"

"Yes. Just lift yourself up and slide down on me."

She thought about it for a moment, her face scrunched adorably, all while she moved her soft hand up and down his shaft.

"Please, Georgia. I'm so close. I want to feel you around me again."

Seeming unsure of herself, she lifted her body and guided him inside. He hissed. She was warm and wet and tight. And he was her first lover. Her only lover. He was her husband. He wanted to please her. He wanted to make her feel as good as she made him feel.

"Come here." He sat up so that their chests were touching, so that he could wrap his arms around her and keep her as close as possible. He guided her hips, moving her on him. Her eyes shot to his.

"I want to close my eyes and just feel this, but I want to look at you, too. I don't want to miss anything."

He would have laughed at her statement if he had been able to. She was so innocently sweet. "Close your eyes," he panted. "Just feel. We have a lifetime together."

She kissed him, her eyes drifting shut, her body relaxing as he thrust into her. He was so close, but she wasn't. He wanted to make her come. He wanted to feel her orgasm around him. "Tell me how to make you feel good, Georgia. I want to."

Her eyes popped open. "You are making me feel good."

He moved his hand to her breast, stroking her hard nipple with his thumb. "Tell me what you like."

"I like being with you." Her eyes drifted shut again. "I like everything you do."

That wasn't what he meant, but she was too sheltered to pick up on his meaning. He was going to have to show her, to explore her, to take great care in learning her body with her. She squeezed herself on him, contracting her muscles with every push. He didn't know how she learned to do it, but it felt too good. He couldn't last much longer if she was going to keep doing that, and he didn't have it in him to ask her to stop.

"You're perfect," she said into his damaged ear, and then followed it up by pulling his lobe between her teeth.

He exploded then. It was her words, the way she felt around him, her being in his world that made him lose control. He collapsed back on the bed. She fell with him, but she didn't remove herself from him. She lay there for long moments, her legs spread across him, her hands stroking down his sides, her lips leaving tiny sweet little kisses on his chest.

She hadn't finished. Again. He owed it to her. He rolled her over and slid out of her; for a moment her curvy little nude body distracted him. She reached up toward him, sliding her hand along his cheek. He looked into her face. She was smiling. Her eyes were sleepy. Her expression was satisfied. "Let's sleep now, sugar." She wrapped her arms around him. "You wore me out."

CHAPTER 19

Georgia looked over at her husband the next day as they drove to her sister's hotel. There was something off with him. He was quiet. Distracted. At times he seemed almost disappointed. And she wasn't sure why. She was feeling quite blissful. She had made love for the first time last night. More than once and it was beautiful. She felt like his wife.

They had made love this morning. Christian took his time. He touched her all over and kissed her in places she never thought to be kissed. The soles of her feet and the insides of her elbows. The underside of her chin. It was long and leisurely and she thought that making love with him was the closest to heaven she would ever get.

But he went quiet after the last time. After he asked her if she liked it, asked her if there was anything more that he could do to please her.

He had pleased her. She couldn't think of anything else. She told him how happy he made her, that there wasn't anything else. He went quiet then. He'd said hardly anything over breakfast. He'd said nothing since they got in the car and she wondered what had happened. She wondered if she had done something to displease him. She racked her mind but could think of nothing.

He pulled the car to a stop in front of Carolina and Miles's hotel, but as he went to step out she stopped him with a hand on his arm.

He looked at her for a moment, his beautiful green eyes searching her face. "What is it, Georgia?"

"I miss my baby, but I'm glad we had last night and this morning. I know it's silly to hope things never change. But if I can go to bed and wake up every day like I did today, I would be an extremely happy woman."

He leaned over, took her chin between his fingers and gave her a long kiss. "You don't lie."

His statement confused her, but it was a statement. He wasn't asking her. "No." She should her head. "I don't lie."

He kissed her swiftly and got out of the car, walking around to her side to help her out. Something was wrong and she was too afraid to ask him what was bothering him.

They rode the elevator up to Carolina's room and as they got closer, she grew more excited to see her baby. Abby had spent many nights without her in the care of Mrs. Sheppard, but this was the first time Abby had stayed with somebody she didn't know. Georgia knew her, she knew Carolina so well, but she hadn't seen her in two years. Her sister had always been good with children. She had taught preschool Sunday school, she had gone to college to become a teacher, but the thought of her sister taking care of her child worried her more than she wanted to admit. When the elevator stopped she walked a little more quickly than she should have. But then she forced herself to slow down, not wanting her husband to see how anxious she was.

She really was glad they had last night together. If Abby had been there, Georgia might not have felt so free.

She knocked on the door. Miles answered. He was smiling and holding a babbling Abby in his arms. "We weren't expecting you this early. It's not even eleven yet."

"I missed my girl." She took Abby from him and squeezed her. "How was your night, little one?"

"I could ask you the same question." Carolina appeared from behind her husband. "I know you probably stayed up all night worrying, but we were fine, weren't we, doll baby?" She stroked Abby's cheek with the back of her fingers for a moment.

Georgia felt her husband's broad body press against her back. He touched Abby's head, causing her to look up at him.

"Da!" She nearly jumped from Georgia's arms trying to reach for him.

"My girl." Christian's face lit up. He smiled like she had never seen him smile and if she were a stranger, if she had never seen him before, she would think he was one of the most handsome men in the world at that moment. "How are you, BB?" He took Abby from her, kissed her cheeks and protectively tucked her into his side.

Abby babbled happily and Georgia was torn between being happy that her husband and daughter got along so well and a little hurt that her daughter wasn't as happy to see her.

She was going to choose to be happy, even though she was stung, because Christian needed Abby's love. And he deserved it.

"What do you want for dinner tonight?" Georgia asked Christian two weeks later.

Christian looked up from the hole he was spackling to see his wife standing in the doorway of the den. Sometimes he marveled over the fact that she was married to him. She looked so pretty, so Southern and ladylike with her hair down and in the simple new dress he made her buy for herself this week. Such a contrast to himself—he was covered in paint and plaster and dust from working around the house this morning. He could have hired someone to do the work for him but he had been feeling useless these past two weeks.

He wasn't sure how to be a husband, but he knew his job was to take care of his wife. He had money. He could buy her whatever she wanted, but buying things wouldn't please Georgia. He knew more than anything she wanted a nice home. He wanted to give it to her. He wanted to put his hands on it, his mark. He was no longer in the service. He wouldn't die for his country, but this house could be his legacy. His gift to her.

It didn't feel like enough, though. He wanted to do more for her but she wouldn't let him. She cooked for him three times a day, whatever he wanted. She cleaned the house and made the bed. She ironed his clothes. She took care of Abby and worked in the garden. She let him make love to her every night as many times as he wanted. She even asked him if she could spend money.

She was doing too much. He married her so that he could take care of her. He owed that to her for making him want to live. And he owed his parents for not coming when they needed him, and Miko for not saving her and the men who died in his unit because he was too far from the blast to die with them. He owed all of them and wanted to show everyone he was a decent man.

"Don't cook." He put down the spackling paste and plopped himself on the old sofa they had found in one of the bedrooms. "You've been working in the garden all day. Let's go out tonight."

"Oh." Her eyes narrowed a bit. "Are you sure? I just went grocery shopping. We don't have to spend any more money."

He should have been in heaven. He should have been elated that he had a sweet wife who always deferred to him and lived to make him happy. But he wasn't in heaven. Georgia was being a good wife. But he wasn't sure that they were having a good marriage.

Maybe it was him. Maybe his idea of marriage was skewed. His mother had been anything but docile. She had been loud. She cursed like a sailor. She had heated debates with his father on politics and religion and morals. And she didn't clean toilets.

His parents' marriage was never quiet. It was never predictable. His parents had loved hard. He was almost glad that they had died together, because he couldn't picture one without the other. He didn't think either would have survived without the other. They had married out of love. And he and Georgia... It seemed their marriage was based on guilt and convenience.

"Going out to dinner after you've gone grocery shopping isn't going to bankrupt us. You've cooked every night since we've been married, even on the weekends. It's okay for you not to."

"But it's my job."

"It's not your job!" he snapped. He hadn't meant to raise his voice, but it was a phrase that she said often, as though marriage to him was a chore and not something she really wanted to do. "I'm sorry, but it's not your job to cook. I can cook, too, and clean and help with Abby. We are partners."

"But I'm not working anymore and you paid off all my medical bills and debt. You got me a new car. I need to contribute, and I do it by taking care of you."

He shook his head, not wanting to argue. What had happened to his night nurse? The one with a little sass under her sweet exterior, the one who debated him about war and pain and right and wrong. Two weeks of marriage and he felt as though that woman had been replaced by...by...a servant.

The intense connection they'd had seemed to be fading. Sex had changed things between them. He loved being with her. He loved the way she smelled and sighed and felt, but when he was making love to her there was no connection, no participation from her. She let herself be loved, but she never lost herself, or lost control or screamed out in passion. She was holding back from him. He hated that. He hated that she never had an orgasm with him. He hated that he couldn't connect to her. He needed that. He craved that.

It was what was missing.

"Come here and kiss me."

"What?" She was surprised by his request and he surprised himself, but he needed to feel her in that moment.

"Come here and kiss me."

She crossed the room, looking unsure of herself, but she didn't question him. She knelt between his legs. Knelt on the floor and reached up to him, as if she was his submissive. He wasn't a marine anymore. He wasn't a commander. If he wanted subordinates he would have stayed in. He yanked her into his lap, her legs spread across his so that they were eye to eye, so that he could see her every expression. "Kiss me, Georgia."

She looked at his lips and licked her own.

"Kiss me."

She finally did. She set her lips to his mouth and kissed him sweetly, but he didn't want sweetness from her. He wanted hot and hard and passionate.

Was it wrong to want that from her? He had felt it before. When he was still in the hospital. He had felt her passion and it had brought him back from death. Where had it gone?

"Kiss me harder."

Her cheeks burned and she tried again. Her mouth opened over his. She used her tongue, shyly, unsure of herself. He gripped her face, silently urging her to try harder. She deepened their kiss and it suddenly became wetter, became hotter. He reached under her dress, needing to mold his hand around her lush behind. As she shifted forward, his cock twitched and she jumped a little, breaking the kiss and looking him in the eye.

"Where's Abby?"

"She's sleeping. I just put her in her crib."

They were alone. And newly married. And he wanted her. "Take your clothes off."

"Take my clothes off? Now?" She looked around the unfinished den with the smell of plaster and the paint peeling from the walls. "Here?"

"Yes. Now and here." He would want her anywhere, anytime. That was what got them into trouble in the first place. "Unless you don't want to."

She nodded, setting her hands on his shoulders. "I want to make love if you want to make love."

"No." He shook his head. "It's okay if you don't want to. You don't have to. Tell me no."

"I want to," she whispered. "I want you."

"Good. Take your clothes off and kiss me."

Georgia wasn't sure what was going through Christian's mind. But she didn't question him any further. She had begun to feel aroused the moment he'd tugged her into his lap. There was something about kissing him and him not kissing her back, him taking the passive role, that sent a rush of heat through her. She almost cried out when he grabbed her behind, but she held back, embarrassed for him to know how much he made her want to lose control.

They had made love every night and sometimes in the morning, but for some reason this time was different. It felt different... She couldn't name it, but she knew that pleasant warm dampness she usually felt was nowhere to be found. Her underwear was soaked. She was horrified by it. Part of her wanted to scurry off his lap before he noticed. But a bigger part of her wanted to stay and be with him, feel more of him. He wanted her to take off all of her clothes, with no cover of darkness or blankets or the safety of their bedroom.

She could say no or demand that they go upstairs, but she didn't. She didn't think her legs were strong enough to carry her.

His thumbs stroked her lower back as he waited for her to undress. She had never undressed in front of him before. She always had done so in the bathroom, and when they made love he was always the one who pulled off her nightgowns. But now it seemed he would be no help.

She took a breath before she pulled her dress over her head. His eyes greedily ate her up even though there was nothing sexy about her. She wore a plain white bra and panties. Nothing exotic. Nothing erotic. Nothing she could think of to cause him to look at her like that. She had thought, in that secret part in the back of her mind, that he was getting bored of home life, of her. He was a man used to war and foreign terrain and danger. But when he looked at her with all that rawness in his eyes, she thought, maybe foolishly, that she could satisfy him.

And she would try to satisfy him. Or she would die trying.

"You're so pretty." He cupped her breast in his hand and ran his thumb over the top of her cleavage. "I love to look at you."

"Do you?" She unhooked her bra. Slowly. She felt a little

surge of power when his eyes followed her every movement. She slid the bra down her shoulders and off her arms, but she held it to her chest, teasing him. Not letting him see all of her. "Sometimes I wonder about who you would have married if you had your choice. Would you have picked somebody tall? And blond? Somebody with unfreckled skin and no baggage?" She let the bra slip, revealing all of herself to him, but instead of his eyes going to her breasts, they stayed on her face. His body went rock hard, so tense that she knew she had done something wrong.

"If I had a choice? I would have picked a preacher's daughter with reddish hair and pretty brown skin. I would have picked the woman whose touch and attention was the only thing I had to look forward to when I was so hurt in the hospital. I would pick a woman with the baggage because she's the strongest person I have ever met. If I had my choice, Georgia, I would pick you. I did pick you. I married you because I knew my life without you would be shit."

She stared at him for a moment as his words sunk in. It was as though something inside of her snapped, because she lost all control of herself. She smashed her mouth to his, kissing him hard. He responded. He opened his mouth to her, let her slide her tongue along his. He let her control the kiss. All he did was hold her.

But it wasn't enough. She wanted more of him. She wanted to be so close to him that she felt as though she was inside him. That was what she loved most about their lovemaking—the closeness. How she felt so safe with him. But she didn't feel safe now; she felt dangerous.

"Touch me," she ordered him.

He slid his hands up her bare back. "Where? Tell me where."

"Here." She couldn't bring herself to say the word so she

showed him. She moved his large hand to her breast and brushed her nipple with the tips of his fingers.

"You like that?"

She nodded, and he studied her face to see if she was sure. He pulled her nipple between his fingers, gently tugging. The heat built between her legs. She throbbed and found herself moving against his hardness to search out some relief. The contact felt good, so good that she moved against him again, unable to stop herself.

He shocked her by pulling one of her nipples into his mouth while he tugged on the other with his thick fingers. She gasped. They had made love every night since they were married, but she could honestly say it had never once felt like this. This wasn't slow or sweet. It was need. She felt needy, as though she was discovering something new. Something she hadn't even known she had missed.

"I want to try something with you, Georgia." Christian set his eyes on hers. "I don't want you to be embarrassed because it's something husbands and wives do all the time."

She nodded, not knowing what it was. She trusted him. There wasn't anything in the world she wouldn't let him do.

He lifted her off his lap and laid her back on the couch. She missed his warmth, his hardness, the protection his big body provided her with. He removed her panties and tossed them on the floor, and then he looked at her. He looked at her between her legs. He spread her open and looked there. Sometimes his fingers would brush there before he came inside of her, but this was the first time he had really looked at her. Her face burned.

"Don't." He gazed up at her. "Don't be embarrassed." He lowered his mouth to the inside of her thigh and lightly nipped her sensitive skin. She jumped. She liked that feeling, too. It surprised her.

"Do that again."

He grinned and lightly bit her other thigh. She moaned. She shut her eyes and a thousand new sensations flooded her, and before she had time to process even one he licked her. Inside of her, one long slow lick. Her hips moved. Involuntarily.

"That's right, sweetheart. Move for me." His lips brushed against her as he spoke. Little fireworks went off. She bit her lip trying to hold in her cry. But it didn't work, because he licked her again in that same moment. He licked her where she throbbed, in that place where she needed relief.

She didn't know that this was possible, that being kissed there would feel so...so...otherworldly.

"Christian." She called out his name and he gripped her thighs, pulling her closer to his mouth, and the long licks turned to hot, openmouthed kisses and the pressure, that feeling she always felt when they made love, started to build uncontrollably. All the thoughts fled from her mind. She just moved against him.

An explosion—she didn't know what else to call it—struck her. Her toes curled into the couch as wave after wave of intense feeling rolled through her. She didn't even have the chance to process what was going on inside of her.

Christian freed himself from his shorts and pumped inside of her at a frantic rate. The way his hard body felt on top of hers, the way his clothes felt against her naked body, was too much. Another wave of painful pleasure struck her and Christian fell apart. He finished with a little roar and collapsed on top of her. She wrapped her arms around him and held him close, kissing his shoulder a half dozen times.

"Christian?"

"Yes, love?"

"What happened to me?"

He looked in to her eyes and softly said, "You just had your first orgasm."

"No. I've had one before. With you." She frowned as she thought about it. "Haven't I?"

"No, baby. I know. I can tell."

"Really? I couldn't, but I liked that, too."

He smiled at her and kissed her cheek. "Georgia. You're too sweet for me."

"Christian! Look at this! It's a tiny little house just like the one near the park." Georgia picked up the miniature and peered inside. "And there is tiny little furniture in there. Even a toilet! This is just about one of the sweetest things I've ever seen."

"We've got to get you out of the house more." Christian grinned at her. They were strolling through the Charleston City Market, a vast marketplace filled with food and art and beautiful things Georgia had never imagined people could own.

She looked up at him and smiled. "I'm sorry. You must be embarrassed to be seen with me. I know I'm doing more than my fair share of exclaiming but I've never seen...so many things in one place. Well, that's not true, my brother once took me to the town dump. There were many things there, too. Many stinky, dirty things. But I've never seen so many beautiful things in one place. There was a museum near Jericho. I used to take Abby there to look at the art, but it was so tiny compared to this place and we couldn't touch anything. Here they let you pick things up!"

Christian surprised her by leaning down and kissing her square on the mouth, and in public, too. Her cheeks burned. "You did that to shut me up, didn't you? I'm babbling. I know.

But I'm so happy today. You must be ready to toss me from a roof by now."

"No roof tossing." He took the miniature house from her hands and handed it to the vendor. "We'll take it."

"Oh, no! I didn't mean for you to buy it. I don't need it. I just think it's really nice."

"You barely looked at the jewelry. Clothes didn't interest you, but this tiny little house made your face light up. If it has that power then I want you to have it."

"It's silly, I know, but I never thought there could be a place like this. I rarely left Oakdale as a child, and if I did it was for church functions. When I was older, I was only allowed to go to school. And then I worked at Jericho. I thought I was learning so much about the world then, but I never really saw anything so different. There was the park and the little museum. There was the mommy-and-me story time at the library, but I never got to experience much else. I didn't realize how much there was to see until now."

"I've seen so much," he said in a low voice. "I've been inside of a palace in Iraq and been in an underwater hotel. I've been to parts of the world I never even knew existed until I landed there, and I didn't appreciate any of it until right this very moment."

She looked at Christian. He seemed a little lost. Lost in his thoughts. Lost somewhere in the past.

"I would like to take you to see some of those places. Have you ever wanted to go to Europe?"

"I've dreamed about going to Disney World. I couldn't even imagine Europe."

"I've never been there, either." He smiled again, but this time there was a little sadness behind it. "That's a place we can experience together for the first time."

She studied him for a moment. She had been worried about

him lately. He was keeping himself busy. Renovating their house alone took up most of his time. And they did things together. They took Abby to the park and window-shopped on weekends. Sometimes they would just go for long walks around Charleston. Georgia was happy. She got to spend her days with her baby and her nights beside her husband. She got to weed her garden and cook the recipes she had been dreaming about trying for years. This life was good. It was better than she ever thought she would have, but something was missing.

Something was wrong with Christian. She was worried that this peaceful life wasn't enough, but she was afraid to ask him. She was scared she would hear that this was a life that he had never wanted.

The vendor handed Georgia back her newly wrapped little house, breaking her from her thoughts. "Thank you, sir." She looked at her husband. "Thank you, Christian. I know just where I'll put this."

They walked to the next little shop. This one was filled with sweet grass baskets of all shapes and sizes. "You think we should get BB a dollhouse?" Christian looked down at Abby, who was sitting quietly in her stroller, taking it all in. "I know she's a little young for Barbie, but we could get her a little one."

"I think you have bought her a new toy every day this week. You don't have to do that. She loves you anyway."

"I know. I just want her to have things from me."

"Since she doesn't have your blood?" She wasn't sure why she asked him that. He loved Abby. He never gave Georgia a reason to think he was disappointed with how he'd become her father. But something was wrong and she needed to know what it was.

His eyes snapped to hers. "I didn't mean it that way. You

know it doesn't matter to me. She's my girl. She doesn't have to have my blood for that."

"I'm going to give you a child," she told him. "As soon as I can." She wasn't positive yet, but there might be one on the way now. They had been married a month. They had made love every night and every night she prayed. Prayed for Christian and for Abby and for herself. She prayed about her future family and for the life she only dreamed could exist.

She loved her baby, her Abby, more than anything else in the world, but finding out she was pregnant this time would be a joy. Her pregnancy would be a joy. No being sick with worry. No wondering how she was going to support them. It would be so different from the last time. Her baby would be made from love this time. Her baby would have a father who was a good man. Her baby would be born inside of a union. The way she'd always hoped her children would be.

"Are you sure you want a baby so soon after Abby?"

"Yes." She nodded. "She's a year old, and I'll have you to help me. Plus we haven't done anything to prevent it."

"No," he said absently.

A child darted toward them. He couldn't have been more than four or five.

"Jeffery! Jeffery, stop!" A frantic woman chased after him. Christian reached out an arm and lifted the child off his feet, stopping his mad dash away from his mother.

"Hey there, kid. You shouldn't run from your mother."

The boy looked up at him and Georgia saw it the moment it happened. The moment little Jeffery took Christian in. Fear crossed his face. He struggled against Christian and cried out for help just as his mother reached him.

"Jeffery. What has gotten into you?"

The boy buried his face in his mother's shirt and sobbed something. "That man is a monster."

Georgia had hoped Christian hadn't heard what the boy had said, but the moment she looked up at him she knew he had.

She had seen many emotions cross Christian's face in the time she had known him, but she had never seen him hurt. Not like this.

"He fought in a war," Georgia blurted out.

"Georgia," he warned, but she ignored him.

She went around Jeffery's mother to her back so that she could see the little boy's face. "He fought in Iraq in a war. He was in an explosion. That's why his face is like that. It's burned. He's not a monster. He's a hero."

"Georgia, enough!"

"It's not enough! He needs to understand." She looked back to the boy. "His name is Captain Howard. He is a hero and he is my husband and we have a baby right there." She pointed at Abby and Jeffery's eyes followed. "He is not a monster."

"I'm so sorry," Jeffery's mother said. She was near tears. "I—I… Thank you for your service."

She turned away, but there was a little crowd there. Staring at them, at Christian, who even without his scars was a sight to behold.

"Let's go." His words were clipped. She knew she had done something that he didn't like, but she felt she hadn't done a thing wrong.

"Christian—"

"You don't have to defend me all the fucking time," he said in a furious whisper. "I know what I look like. I scared him. He's just a kid. What else was he supposed to think?"

"I'm sorry you are upset, but I'm not sorry for what I did."

He was not a monster. He was a hero. And she loved him. Those were three irrevocable facts.

She loved him. And she would never stop defending him.

CHAPTER 20

"Da?" Abby toddled into the kitchen alone. He looked down at the little girl—at his daughter—and smiled. He was happy for the break. He had been reading some of the financial papers from his father's company.

He had sent for them a week ago, but he kept putting off looking at them. The house still needed to be worked on. They were turning his parents' former bedroom back into a den, into a playroom for Abby and a sitting room for Georgia. But it was almost done. Another coat of paint, some bookshelves, some new furniture and it would be complete.

There were other projects to be done. The back porch needed to be replaced, new windows needed to be installed, but the papers from his father's beloved business haunted him. He wasn't sure why when being in the house, living here with his family, didn't.

Maybe because there was so much of his father's expectations in those papers. He had minored in business in college even though he'd told himself he was going to be an engineer. But he knew in the back of his mind that one day the family business would be his. When he joined the marines he felt he had let his peace-loving, gentle father down.

He had led men into war zones. He had learned Arabic. He could survive for days on no food and little water, but he didn't think he could run his father's business. He was afraid of screwing it up, of doing the wrong thing and letting his father down again.

But he knew he had to do something. He was restless. He had worked every day of his life up until he'd gotten hurt. And now he just did nothing. Nothing that really mattered.

He could go back. He could lead a unit. He could be useful again.

Georgia didn't need him. She'd survived alone a long time before she met him.

She would be fine if he went back. Her sister was moving to Charleston soon. The general lived nearby. She wouldn't be alone.

"Da!"

He looked at Abby again and held out his hand to her. He had been thinking about going back. He made no plans to do so, but he could. He was still on medical leave. He was still Captain Howard.

"Da, Da, Da, Da, Da," she babbled as she waddled across the kitchen toward him. She placed her tiny hand on his leg. "Up?"

But he was Da, too, and this little girl did something to him that he didn't understand.

"Up? You want up? I think that's all you want from me sometimes." He scooped her up and held her close. Her head dropped to his shoulder. "Are you tired? Do you need a nap?"

"No!" She looked at him and frowned and he could see Georgia in her features. "Out."

"You want to go to the park? I'll take you. Let's go ask Mama."

"No Ma!"

"She's mad at me." Georgia appeared in the kitchen doorway. "I didn't think a one-year-old could hold a grudge, but she can."

"You mad at Mama?" Abby frowned at Georgia, causing him to laugh. "What did you do to my daughter, woman?"

"Your daughter? Well, *your daughter* got into the diaper cream. Had it smeared all in her hair. I took it away and gave her a bath and now she's annoyed with me. When *your daughter* is sixteen and raising hell, I hope that you remember that she's yours and handle it."

"She's only my daughter when she's good. And she's always good for me." He kissed Abby's face. "There must be something wrong with you."

"You think so?"

She crossed the room to them and took Christian's face in her hands and kissed him. He shut his eyes and let himself be kissed by her.

A week had passed since they had made love in the den. He'd changed the way he made love to her. It was hotter, more passionate, but he still couldn't bring her to climax while he was inside of her. With his fingers and his mouth, yes, but not while he was inside of her. It shouldn't bother him, but it did. He was her husband. He wanted to feel her orgasm while he was inside of her. It made him feel like a failure when he didn't.

"Are you happy, Christian?"

Georgia's question surprised him. Nobody had ever asked him that before, and if they did he would have said no. He had been alone for so long. He wasn't alone now. He had Georgia. He had Abby. He had a beautiful wife who would bend over backward to please him. He had the love of a little girl who called him Daddy and came to him when she needed him.

How could he not be happy? "Sometimes I think about them," he admitted to her for the first time.

"Who...your parents?"

"Yes, them, too. They would have liked you and Abby, but I'm talking about my men. Only three of us survived. I think about all the men who died that day when I didn't."

She passed her eyes over his face, zeroing in on his scars. "You lived because you were supposed to, because God wanted you to."

"Why me and not them?" It was a question he had found himself asking a lot lately. Now that he had Georgia and Abby. Now that he had a home to go to every night and all the comforts he could stand. "There were better men than me. Nicer men. More honorable men. Why did they die?"

"I don't know, sugar." She sighed and brushed her lips against his forehead. "I'm glad you didn't die. I was really mad at God for a long time. I used to think why me and not somebody else, but then I met you. And you became my friend when I had nobody else. And you took my daughter in and loved her like your own. I needed to meet you, honey. Abby needs you. And if you're thinking about leaving me here alone to raise this baby while you go off to fight some damn war, you're not going to have to worry about getting blown up. I'm going to beat you up. I don't care if you're seven feet tall. I'm going to climb up there and kick your behind."

He laughed at her bravado and pulled her face up to kiss her. "I missed the sassy girl I met in the hospital. I hate that you feel grateful to me," he admitted to her. "I hate that you go out of your way to try to please me. I just want you to be you."

"I am being me. I'm being your wife. I'm taking care of you, dummy."

"This is not how my mother took care of my father. In fact, my father took care of her. I can take care of you, but you won't let me. You don't let me help you around here."

She shook her head. "You do help out. You do too much for a man who not a month ago was laid up in a hospital. You want to do everything. You want to fight a war and take care of a wife and daughter and fix this house all by yourself. You say you want to be partners, but you don't. You have this crazy need to serve. Serve me and Abby and your country all at the same time. You won't let anybody do anything for you. It's as if you feel as though you don't deserve to be loved."

Maybe he didn't.

"It's my job to take care of you. I got you fired. It's my job to raise Abby because you're my wife. It was my job to get my men out of there safely because I was their leader, and I failed at that. I failed to get my parents from the airport that day and they died because of it. I failed to protect Miko from my friends and she ended up pregnant and alone."

"It's not your fault that your parents died. It's not your fault that a bomb hit your unit. It's not your fault your friends did that to that girl. Don't you know you couldn't control any of that? It's as if you keep trying to redeem yourself. You don't need to redeem yourself. You need to—"

"No Da! No Ma!"

Georgia turned away from him, walked to the kitchen counter and rested her hands on the surface.

"We shouldn't argue in front of her. I'm sorry."

"Yeah, me, too. I'm going to talk her to the park. We'll be back later."

Georgia peered out the window for the fifth time since Christian and Abby left. They had been gone for over an hour, and while she trusted Christian with Abby, she was worried. He'd been angry when he'd left. With her. With the world. With God.

She couldn't blame him. She had been there. Half the time she still was there. But she had Abby to keep her grounded, to keep her going. And now Christian had her, too. It was hard for her to give half her child away. It was hard for her every time Abby reached for Christian instead of her. It was hard for her to let Christian feed and dress her in the mornings, but she had stepped aside because he needed her love.

He was thinking about going back. He hadn't said anything directly to her, but she knew he wanted to go.

Part of her thought that the right thing to do was to let him go, but it wasn't. She knew he was restless. She knew he was used to working, but he needed a family. He was running from it, from her. Christian was wounded, but not just physically. He needed to be loved, because for so long nobody had. Nobody told him that he was good, that he was needed.

She cooked and cleaned and cared for him because that was what she did. She was a mother and a nurse. She had chosen a career that would allow her to care for others. She had grown up the oldest girl in her family. All she did was care for her family, and she hadn't hated one moment of that part of her life. Caring for them made her happy. Caring for Christian made her happy.

The phone rang, causing her to jump. She left the window, rushing to answer it, thinking it might be her husband. They'd had their first fight as a married couple. And it had gone unfinished. He had left seething, and while she was upset with him for thinking his life was less worthy than others, she didn't want them to stop talking.

"Hello?"

"Georgia."

The phone slipped from her hand and bounced on the kitchen counter. She recognized the voice. She knew it like she knew her own, and yet hearing it was a shock to her. She never thought she would hear it again. She never wanted to hear it again. But there he was, calling her after she made a new life despite him. He had tried to take her dignity away, but she had never let it go completely. She wouldn't shy away from him now. She had no reason to.

"Hello, Father."

"Is your mother there?"

"What? Is Mama gone?"

"Don't play dumb with me, Georgia. Is your mother at your house?"

"No, sir." Her stomach turned over. Sweat started to form on her palms. "She's not here."

"Don't lie to me again, girl. Is she there? You let me speak to her right this moment!"

"I'm not a liar." She kept her voice low, calm, even though she wanted to rage at him. "I never was a liar. You just choose to believe a stranger over me. Mama is not here, but if she was, I wouldn't let her go back to you."

"I've been nothing but a good husband to her. She's got no right to leave me."

"You can be a good husband by being a good father, and you were not a good father to me."

"You've got them all turning against me. My sons won't talk to me. None of my children will come to my church all because of your lie. Why have you done this to me? I provided you with a good home. I taught you God's word. I followed it myself. You have forsaken me and you have turned a good man into a suspect with your deceit."

"He raped me!" She screamed it at him. She had never

raised her voice to him before. She had never dared to, but she couldn't take the accusation. Not now. Not after all this time.

"He was a good boy. He was like my son. He wouldn't have done that to me."

"He's not Abel. He's not a replacement for Abel. He hurt me."

The phone was snatched out of her hand. Christian was there. He was there with Abby and a ferocious look was on his face. "This is Georgia's husband. I don't give a shit if you claim to be a man of God—if you call here again and upset my wife I will track you down and kill you. You understand me?"

He hung up the phone and slammed it on the counter so hard that it broke.

She was shaking. Violently. She hated herself for doing it. She hated that her father had the power to unravel her. Christian grabbed her and wrapped her in his body so tightly that he nearly crushed her. But it was what she needed in that moment. She wasn't alone anymore. Because of him she wasn't alone anymore.

That night Christian waited in bed for Georgia to come out of the bathroom. It was their nightly ritual. Each night he would wait for her, his arms folded behind his head as she bathed and got ready for bed. He wished this ritual would end. He wished that she wouldn't hide her body from him, that she would dress and undress in front of him. But he guessed that was just part of her upbringing.

Her life had been so sheltered with her overbearing father and timid mother. He was glad he was in the house when the phone rang. He had just gotten back from his trip to the park with Abby. He was putting Abby in her crib for her nap when he heard Georgia scream.

He raped me.

Those words played over and over in his head all evening. His wife had been raped. He'd known this for a long time, but the reminder of it today triggered something inside of him. That man. That weak son of a bitch was still walking around. Free. Unpunished. Undeserving of life. He had cost Georgia. Her family. Her security. Her trust in people.

In an odd way, the man who had hurt her had brought them together. If it hadn't been for him, if it hadn't been for the bomb that had killed Christian's unit, they wouldn't be together now.

It was funny how the thought of ending the life of the man who'd hurt Georgia planted itself in his head and wouldn't go out. He had told her he would kill for her before, but today he could imagine doing it. Beating the man till he couldn't move, and then going after her father.

He'd had the nerve to call her. To call their house. He'd had the nerve to be demanding. To upset Georgia. He hadn't protected her. That was a father's job. To protect his children.

He thought about Abby. About how she turned to him when she was scared or needed something. He may not feel as though he was contributing enough to the world, but he was enough for Abby.

Georgia was his wife, and friend and lover, but he would move mountains for Abby. He had been thinking about going back. He had been thinking about it all day, but then he thought about Abby. How he would miss her growing up. How he wouldn't be able to protect her if he was thousands of miles away.

How could he serve his country and his daughter the way he wanted to? He had to give his all. He couldn't do either halfway.

The phone rang, breaking him from his thoughts. He was glad for the interruption. He'd always been troubled by his thoughts after having left the marines. Before he got here in his life, he could turn off such thinking and focus on his job, his next mission, but since then, nothing he did seemed to stop the flood.

"Hello?"

"Captain Howard?" He heard Tobias's unsure voice.

"I think you should call me Christian now."

"I like calling you captain. Oh, Captain, my captain, and all that shit."

He grinned at Tobias's statement, glad he had called. He hadn't realized how much he actually missed the kid. "Suit yourself. How are you?"

"I'm going crazy, sir. I hate to ask you this, but do you think you could come and get me so we could hang out? My Mama… I love her, but the woman is treating me as if I'm a baby. She even checks on me when I'm in the bathroom. I swear she would wipe my bottom if I let her."

"I didn't need to hear that."

"I'm sorry," he sighed. "I need some man time. My dad took off when I was seven, so it's just me and my mama and my grandmama and my sister."

He was going to ask Tobias where the friends his age were. Where were the men he served with? But he stopped himself. Nobody understood a wounded soldier like another wounded soldier. "We could go fishing. There's a place not too far from here. We could go for a couple of days. How's Thursday? I'll ask the general, too."

"Sounds awesome! I can't wait to get out of here. I need to get out of here, sir. You don't know how much."

"I do, son. I'll see you soon."

"Thank you, sir. Good night."

They disconnected just as Georgia walked out of the bathroom. Her hair was still damp and she had a jar of her lightly scented lotion in hand. "Who was calling?"

"Tobias."

She sat on the side of the bed and began to lotion her limbs. He just watched her for a moment. She had never done so in front of him before. "Oh. I'm glad he called. How is his vision?"

"I didn't ask."

"Of course you didn't ask. You're such men."

"I'm going to take him fishing on Thursday for a couple of days if that's okay with you."

"Of course it's okay. He looks up to you. I think it's good that you spend time with him."

"I like him, Georgia." He reached for her as soon as she put the top back on her jar. "I want to help him. He says his mother is treating him like a baby. He needs his own job and his own place. He needs to learn how to live with his blindness and not have his family treat him like a victim because of it."

"Were the men in your unit young like Tobias?"

"Some of them were." He nodded. "The youngest was twenty. He was a computer whiz, recruited right out of high school. Four of them were under twenty-five."

"You liked those young men the best, didn't you? You liked to shape them. You liked to teach them how to be men."

He didn't answer immediately, but it was true. He liked the younger ones the best. He saw the potential in them. He saw what they could be. He wanted to make sure that none of the men in his unit were like his so-called friends. He only wanted men of character, and if they had none, he tried his hardest to build it in them. "The general looked out for me when I was young. I had nobody else."

"I think you could still help those young men. The ones

like Tobias. The ones who don't have a place after the war. I don't know how, but I think you could do something."

His parents had done so much charity work when he was a child through their company. They campaigned for paying a living wage to employees, and growing food without chemicals and preservatives. But after they died, that work went away. It ended up being their legacy.

He couldn't do what they did, but he could have his own legacy. It wouldn't be charity. It would just be giving back to the people who gave for their country.

He just didn't know what or how he could do it.

He kissed Georgia's forehead and she burrowed into him, seeking warmth or comfort, he wasn't sure which. "How are you feeling?" Her face was paler than usual. Her mouth slightly downturned. There was a slight heaviness that seemed to hang over her. "I want to talk about you."

"Carolina thinks that Mama went to Florida to stay with her sister. I believe that she did. Mama always loved Florida. Said she wanted to move there when Daddy retired. But I'm still worried. I just can't believe she would leave Daddy, especially now, after all this time. She called me. Did I tell you that? It happened when I was sick. But she called me to ask if I was happy."

"What did you tell her?"

"I couldn't say that I was. I just told her to come live with me, that I could take care of her."

"*You* take care of *her*? She should have taken care of you. She's your mother. She shouldn't have let your father do that to you."

"I know. But she's my mother, and even though she hurt me, I still wish I could have her in my life."

"What about your father? Could you forgive him?"

"After the rape, I told my father that I didn't want to be

around Robert anymore. I didn't tell him what happened. I was too afraid to, but I told him that Robert bothered me. My father told me I was being foolish. He invited him over for dinner that night. He made him sit next to me in church on Sunday. He said Robert was like family, that I needed to get over our quarrel. Robert taunted me. He would look at me as if he could see through my clothes and smile at me. As if he was triumphant. I wanted to die then, Christian. I thought about dying, about ending it all, and then I found out I was pregnant."

"Stop." He put his fingers over her lips when she started to get upset.

"Tell me where he is, Georgia. I'll find him for you. I'll make him pay for what he did to you."

"Christian…"

"Tell me where to find him. Is he still in Oakdale? I'll go tomorrow."

"No," she said firmly.

"Your father, then. I'll make him realize what he's done."

"If he hadn't kicked me out, I wouldn't be married to you."

"Exactly."

She frowned at him. "I should thank him." She lifted her lips to his. "I will thank him. My life is better than it ever would have been." She shut her eyes and buried her face into his chest. He felt her gratitude again and it made him uncomfortable.

He wanted her love. He wanted to hear her say the words. He didn't want her gratitude. He didn't deserve it.

"Will you make love to me slowly tonight?" she asked. "Just like on our wedding night?"

"You don't come when we have sex that way."

"What?" She blinked at him.

He wished he hadn't blurted out those words. But it was

the truth and it had been gnawing at him for weeks. "You don't have an orgasm when I'm inside you, when we make love like that." He felt as though he failed to arouse her.

"Oh." Disappointment crossed her face. "I like the kissing and the touching and the closeness. I like the other way, too, but I don't need that tonight. I just need you to hold me."

"We don't have to have sex for me to do that, Georgia." He wrapped his arms around her and held her as close as he could manage. "We can sleep tonight." He kissed her forehead. "We can sleep just like this."

CHAPTER 21

Georgia pressed a kiss to the smooth side of Christian's face the next morning. He stirred but he didn't open his eyes. So she kissed him again. On his other cheek. Then his chin. She moved her lips down his neck to his chest.

He hadn't made love to her last night. It was the first time since they were married. She knew that every couple didn't make love every night, but she had grown used to it. She had come to expect it. She missed it.

She should have kept her mouth shut. He had misunderstood what she meant. She didn't want to just be held. She wanted the slow, detailed attention he gave to every part of her body. The deep kisses. The soft touches. He said that she didn't come when they made love that way. That she didn't have an orgasm when he was inside of her.

It clearly bothered him. But she wasn't exactly sure why. He made her feel good. He excited her. He made her want more of him. Maybe the fault lay with her. Maybe she was doing something wrong. She was still so new to sex. So new to sharing her body with someone else. She had been afraid of sex for so long. Afraid of men. It was as if she was coming into herself. Every time she was with him she learned more about her body, about what she liked.

She kissed his nipple, then opened her mouth over it, licking him like he so often did to her.

"Georgia," he groaned. He rolled her over, settling his large body on top of hers. She sighed in relief. This was what she had wanted last night. His hardness between her legs. His breath on her skin. "I thought I was dreaming about you."

"I'm here in the flesh, sugar."

He cupped her face in his hands and kissed her, sweeping his tongue into her mouth, making the world melt away. "Good morning, beautiful." He lifted himself off her before he got out of bed. "I'm going to head into my father's company office today. I want to see BB before I go."

He left her alone. In bed. Wanting him. Without even looking back.

When was the last time he had laid eyes on this building? Ten years? Twelve? Christian wondered as he sat in the car and stared up at the large building that housed Howard and Helga's headquarters. He wasn't sure how long it had been since he had been there, but the last time he had come was without his father. Prior to that, he had never been to the office without his father. He used to drag Christian here every summer when he was a boy. To tour the plant. To visit the workers. To impart some knowledge to him about the company.

Before his parents moved South, there used to be a corporate office in Connecticut, the place his father went to daily, but he called this place the heart of the company. He had such pride in it, and after he died, Christian couldn't bring himself to visit again.

He had come once after their deaths to settle some things

with the vice president of the company. To officially turn the reins over, but he'd never made it inside the building that day. His body wouldn't allow him to do so.

So he kept in contact over the years by phone. Contracts, documents and important papers had been mailed to him. Nearly everything that needed to be handled could be handled without him actually having to set foot in the building. But now it was time. It was past time.

It was so much harder than being in his parents' old house. The house was just a place where his parents rested their heads, but this company was their heart.

Every flavor of ice cream made there had been created by his father; every product was named by him. Christian remembered his father coming home and talking for hours about this place, and he could never see what was so magical about it. He never understood why his father had such a love for something so trivial. And then he'd died. And then the people who worked with him came to his funeral. Hundreds of people it seemed. They had all stopped to speak to Christian. They'd all told him what his father had done to touch their lives.

Big things, like college semesters paid for and homes saved from foreclosure. And small things like corny bad jokes that brightened moods and a shoulder to lean on and a kind word when needed.

Hearing so much about his father made it real that he was gone. And Christian knew he could never replace a man who had done so much for the world. He could never leave the same impact.

Coming here, he knew he would see his father's pictures on the walls and the pain would come back. The hole in his chest, that emptiness, would seem bigger. He knew if he walked inside it would be like losing him all over again.

A soft hand covered his, bringing him back to reality, to the present.

He looked over to Georgia, who said nothing, just lifted his hand to her lips and kissed it. She'd asked him if she could go with him this morning. If she could spend the day with him. Even after he'd failed to make love to her this morning. He had wanted to. He should have but he didn't. Sometimes it seemed as if she only made love to him because she felt it was her duty. He wanted to show her that she didn't always have to, that sometimes they could just sleep. But she had looked so disappointed he was worried that he had made a misstep with her. He was afraid he had no idea what to do with his wife.

He leaned over and kissed her cheek. Glad she was there. Glad he didn't have to walk in the building alone. "Let's go inside."

"I'm so glad the general and Alma could take Abby on such short notice." She linked her fingers with his once they left the car. "The general may look like a bulldog but he really is just a teddy bear. Did you see the silly faces he was making for Abby when we were leaving? I hope one of his daughters has a baby soon, because that man was born to be a grandpa."

He liked the sound of Georgia's voice, the feel of her hand in his as they walked through the front doors. She made it easier for him to walk in. "Did you have a grandpa? I haven't heard you talk much about your grandparents."

She nodded. "My mother's parents were missionaries in South America. I rarely saw them growing up. They passed away when I younger. I don't remember much about them. But my father's parents were there more. I was close to my grandfather. He was a preacher, too, but not like my father. He was so happy. Always. He was the kind of man who made everybody want to be happy. He talked to anyone and everyone. Couldn't walk down the street without stopping four or five times. My grandmother was his opposite. She was a woman of few words. She didn't smile very often, never hugged us. She wasn't any of the things one would expect a grandmother to be." She frowned thoughtfully. "I used to wonder how a man like my grandfather ended up with a woman like her, but they worked well together. And when he died, my grandmother… She just fell apart. It broke my heart." She looked up at him, into his eyes. "She loved him so much, Christian. Even though she never said it, the love was there and it was a big love."

He nodded, trying not to read anything into her words. He had married a woman he knew hadn't loved him. He thought about that sometimes. A lot, actually. She was sweet and kind and loving, all the things he wanted in a wife. But he wondered how this marriage might have been different if she was in love with him.

They got into the elevator, riding up to the fourth floor, to the offices. To where his father used to spend his days.

"It was my grandmother who helped me when my father threw me out. She was living in a rest home then, and I went to her because I didn't know where else to go. She gave me money—a thousand dollars—and the name of a woman who could house me until I figured some things out. I don't know what I would have done if she hadn't been there. I would have been lost."

"What happened to her?" he asked her.

"She passed away. Six months ago now. I wanted to go to her funeral to pay my respects. But I didn't. I couldn't. I couldn't bring myself to face them. My family. Sometimes I think I can't forgive myself for that."

"You should, Georgia. After what they did to you, who could blame you?"

"I'll forgive myself when you forgive yourself," she said softly.

He looked down at her for a moment, amazed that she could read him so well. He should have gone to the airport that day. He should have picked up his parents. They would still be here if he had.

"Christian?" His father's friend and VP, Cliff Chin, walked up to them as soon as they stepped out of the elevators. Cliff had known him his entire life. His family used to spend the summer with theirs. Cliff and his father were best friends. The man openly studied Christian, taking in the differences in him since the last time he saw him. His ruined face. His damaged arm. He couldn't hide the pity in his eyes. It turned Christian's stomach. "I guess I should call you Lieutenant Howard."

"Captain Howard," Georgia said. "He was promoted for bravery."

Cliff's eyes went to Georgia. He was surprised to see her there.

"Captain." He extended his hand. "It's so good to see you. I thought I never would again."

"It's time. This is my wife, Georgia. Georgia, this is Cliff. He runs the company."

"It's nice to meet you, sir."

"Likewise. I didn't know you had gotten married, son."

"It just happened recently. A month ago."

"I would have come to your wedding. I would have come to see you in the hospital. Damn it, boy! If I had known you were in South Carolina I would have been there for you."

"I'm not a boy, Cliff."

"You are to me. You were the last time I saw you at your parents' funeral. We would have been there for you if you let us, but you shut us out. This company was your father's life. We were his family, too. We would have helped you. If you hadn't run away we would have been there."

"I didn't run away, and I sure as hell didn't come here for this."

"No. I'm sure you didn't. But since your father isn't here I'm the one who's left to take the piss out of you. You were stupid and selfish."

"I know! I know I should have picked them up from the airport."

"No." His eyes hardened. "Not that at all. That was an accident! You couldn't have prevented it. You were stupid for turning your back on the people who loved you. You were selfish for taking on the pain alone. We loved you, and if you would have taken my calls or bothered to see us in the past twelve years you would have known that."

"What is all this racket out here?" Mara Smith, his father's longtime assistant, appeared. "Christian? Is that you?"

She rushed toward him, all five feet of her. "Get down here this minute!"

He bent, like he had ever since his height shot up. He had known her forever, too. She used to watch him when his parents were in meetings. Mara still smelled the same. Like Chanel No. 5 and peppermints. She even looked the same. It wasn't until that very moment that he realized how much he had missed her.

She studied him, too, sadness creeping into her expression. She touched his face. His burns. His deformed ear. The chin that didn't look like his father's anymore. She burst out crying. "What have you done to yourself? Why did you have to go?"

The guilt came again. Maybe it had never left him, but it was a different kind of guilt. A different kind of loss.

He'd had a family this whole time and he'd thrown them away. He'd withdrawn from them because he'd thought they would hate him.

CHAPTER 22

"Mama?" Abby came up to Georgia as she weeded in the garden.

"Yes, my love?" She slipped off her gloves and lifted Abby into her lap. Abby wrapped her tiny arms around her neck and squeezed. A sweet giggle escaped her as Georgia squeezed her back. "Are you happy, baby?"

Abby babbled something and then pulled away, toddling off to study a newly planted patch of daisies.

Georgia looked at her baby in her brand-new dress and little pink sandals that Christian had dressed her in this morning. Abby was happy. Georgia had never thought she'd been unhappy in their old life. But maybe she had been. Maybe Abby didn't know what happiness really was.

She had her mama all day now. All of her mama. Not the overtired, always worrying woman who took care of her. And she had her daddy, too, now. Her daddy, who took her to the park and fed her breakfast and spoiled her silly. She had a daddy who loved her. Georgia saw the difference in Abby. Her baby was much happier than she had ever been.

She heard the screen door shut behind her and she looked up to see Christian make his way toward her. Her heart lifted slightly at the sight of her husband. She was with him most of the day. They ate together and slept together. Sometimes they just sat together quietly, and every time she was near him she felt those butterflies in her belly.

But when she looked at him, especially these past few days, she knew he wasn't happy. After that tense meeting at his father's company Christian seemed to slip further away from her. Even at night in bed, where she used to feel the closest to him. He hadn't made love to her in days. He hadn't even tried, and he seemed oblivious to her attempts to bring him closer to her. She was losing him. She could feel him slipping through her fingers and she didn't know how to stop it.

She rose to her feet, brushing herself off as he approached her. She didn't wait for him to speak before she reached for him and settled her lips on his. He wrapped his arms around and kissed her back, before he buried his face in her neck.

He wants to go back.

He hadn't told her, but she knew. She could feel it and it scared the hell out of her. She could ask him to stay. She could demand it and he probably would stay. But she knew he would be miserable if she asked that of him. She should just let him go, but she knew that wasn't going to fix whatever it was he was going through. He wouldn't be any happier ten thousand miles away from his family. He would be doing what he always did. Running away from those who loved him. Running away from his misguided guilt. She couldn't let him do that.

"Talk to me, Christian."

"I'm going to go get Tobias soon for our fishing trip. Is there anything I can bring back for you?"

"Just yourself," she said, feeling disappointed. She looked up into his face. He was sad. She could feel it; his heaviness weighed her down. Maybe it was this place. She loved this house and her garden and Charleston, but maybe it was too much for him; maybe the memories were overwhelming.

She couldn't blame him for being uncomfortable here. She hadn't been back to Oakdale since she'd first left. She hadn't visited her grandmother's grave. How could she expect him to face his past when she wasn't willing to do so herself?

"I was thinking maybe we could go away for a few days, if that's okay with you? Somewhere fun. I've never been on a vacation before. We could call it our honeymoon."

"Of course." He absently brushed a kiss across her forehead. "Wherever you want to go."

"I don't know where I want to go. But you've been so many places. Maybe you should pick. Take me to where you felt the happiest."

He frowned at her for a moment. They had talked about this briefly the day they'd gone to the city market. The same day the little boy had called him a monster and wept in fear. He hadn't been the same since that day. She knew he was sensitive about his battle scars. She knew he looked drastically different than he had before the blast, but he was beautiful. She loved his face.

"If I were to take you where I was the happiest then we wouldn't have to go anywhere. Because I'm here with you right now."

She smiled up at him even though her heart didn't feel her smile. "I wish I could believe you."

"You should. I'm glad I have you and Abby."

"But you don't just have us, you know."

"I know. The general is there for me and his wife. We have your sister and her husband."

"And we have the people at Howard and Helga's. Mara gave me her phone number. She doesn't live far away and she wants us to bring the baby for brunch. She wants to get to know you again."

"Georgia…"

"What?" She shook her head. "And then there's Mr. Chin. He loves you, Christian. I can tell just by the way he looks at you."

"I don't want to talk about this." He pulled away from her.

"Why not? Why is it so wrong to talk about your past, about the people who loved you? Who still love you after all this time?"

His face grew dark. His eyes shuttered. She was going to lose him. He was shutting down on her. "My military service was not a mistake. It's something I'll never regret, and I refuse to let Cliff make me feel that way."

"Of course it wasn't a mistake. How could it be? If it hadn't been for the marines you would have never been blown up and you would have never met me. And we both know I'm the best thing that ever happened to you."

He was taken aback by her words, but he grinned at her. A real smile. One she hadn't seen for weeks. She could sunbathe in the warmth of that smile. She hugged him close, not wanting to lose that moment. Not wanting him to slip back into his shell.

Abby screamed out and immediately they jumped apart. She was sitting on the grass not three feet behind them, but she was crying. Her tiny face twisted in pain. Christian rushed to her before Georgia even had the chance to move.

"What happened, baby?" Abby held up her hand. There was a bumblebee squished in her palm. "Damn it, Georgia. She's been stung."

"My poor baby." Georgia reached for Abby, but Christian didn't let her go.

"It's swelling. Just let me take care of this. She shouldn't be out here if there are going to be so many bees around." He walked away from her, back into the house. With her baby. Leaving her to feel as if she'd failed her own child.

She stood there for a moment. Almost stunned that he'd scolded her.

"Hello, neighbor." She turned at the sound of a man's voice. She forced herself to smile even though it was the last thing she felt like doing.

She had never seen this man before. He reminded her of her brother Gideon, only older. He was slender and tall, with skin the color of baked bread. Handsome. He wore a suit with no tie. The top few buttons of his shirt was open.

"Oh. Hello." She walked to the fence where he was standing. He held a briefcase. "I'm Georgia."

"Tim." He extended his hand. "I've been away for the past six weeks on business. The kid who mows my grass told me he saw a beautiful woman working in the garden. I almost didn't believe him. This house has been vacant for the five years I've lived here. I was starting to think I was never going to get a neighbor. I hope you like it here."

"I do. Everybody here is very nice," she said, not really sure what else to say. Conversation with the opposite sex was never something that came easily. She blamed her father, who was so busy keeping her away from boys her own age she felt like a misfit. The only man she was ever easy around was her husband. It was ironic because he seemed to be the only person who wouldn't talk to her.

"Where are you from? You don't seem like a Charleston girl."

"I'm from Oakdale originally."

"Oakdale, South Carolina?"

"Yes, sir."

"I know Oakdale. Had a friend from college who lived there. His father was a pastor. You know an Abel Williams?"

She nodded as a ball settled in her stomach. "He was my brother."

"Ah." He looked uncomfortable for a moment. "I forgot that he passed away. This is one of those moments where I wish I could go back in time and change the direction of this conversation."

He paused for a moment, then continued, "I should have complimented you on the color of your eyes, or have told you that the dusting of freckles across your face is probably one of the sweetest things I've ever seen, but I can't do that just now, because it would make me sound like a world-class creep and quite insensitive to boot. So I'll save those compliments for another day and just apologize. I'm sorry, Miss Georgia, about your brother. He was a good man."

"That's all right. I understand," Georgia said.

"I would like to make it up to you by being neighborly and offering to make you dinner, but since I don't cook and am not sure how to turn my oven on, I would offer to order you dinner from any of the fine takeout establishments in the area. And we could enjoy our fine takeout on my porch over wine and talk about how you're liking Charleston."

"That would be very nice," she said, feeling very flattered. "But would it be okay if my husband and daughter tagged along?" She lifted her hand to show Tim the small gold band on her finger.

Tim's eyes widened, but he wasn't staring at her hand, he was looking behind her. At Christian. She felt his presence, the warmth his big body exuded, even before she turned around. She hadn't heard him come out. She hadn't heard his footsteps behind her.

"I'm guessing that's him."

"Yes."

His face was hard, nasty almost. He seemed bigger than he was, as though his wide body was taking up much more space. He looked ready to kill. When he looked like that she understood why people were afraid of him, why his men never dared to disobey him. Even she would think he was frightening. But she knew him. This wasn't him.

"Hi, neighbor. I'm Tim." Tim didn't look afraid, and for some reason Georgia respected him for that. He just calmly extended his hand to her husband.

"Christian." He ignored the handshake. "Stay the hell away from my wife."

"Christian!"

"Listen—" Tim raised his hands in surrender "—I had no idea she was married. I would have never asked her out if I did."

"You didn't bother to ask her if she was married, either. Just stay on your side of the fence and away from my wife."

"Gotcha." He shook his head and turned away.

"I'm so sorry, Tim," she called after him. And as soon as he entered his house she turned to her husband. "I cannot believe you just behaved like that. He's our neighbor. We are going to live next door to him for a very long time and you just went out of your way to be the rudest, meanest, most insufferable person on the planet. I've never been so embarrassed in my life."

"You were embarrassed? Embarrassed that your monster husband showed up and stopped your flirtation with the pretty-boy neighbor?"

Georgia froze. The hairs on the back of her neck rose. "What did you just say to me?"

"You were flirting with him!"

"What is wrong with you? I told him I was married. I

wasn't flirting. I don't even know how, and even if I was, even if I was the world's biggest flirt, you should trust me, Christian. You should know that I would never go out with another man, let alone think about it. You should know me well enough by now."

"Know you? I know if you really had your choice you never would have married me. I know you would rather be with a pretty boy like him. Someone not so damn ruined. You only married me because it was convenient for you. I'm not keeping you here, Georgia. You can go. If you find somebody else to make you happy, you can go."

Her hand cracked across his face. She had never hit another soul in her life, but she hit him as hard as she could manage.

"Ruined? You are ruined, but it has nothing to do with your scars and everything to do with who you are inside. I'm not leaving you. I never will, but it wouldn't be a bad thing if I didn't have to see you for a while."

She walked away from him this time. Into the house, right to her sleepy baby. For the first time since she'd married him, she couldn't stand to be in his presence.

CHAPTER 23

"We haven't caught a damn thing," Tobias complained.

"Nope," the general agreed. They all sat in the boat Christian had rented on Capshaw Lake, a little man-made lake not far from Tobias's home. "Two days of fishing, not a single bite."

"I can't see his face, but I bet Captain Howard scared all the fish away. I bet he's been looking real mean these past couple of days."

"One big nasty-looking son of a bitch," the general said, not taking his eyes off the lake.

"He ain't even talking. Sometimes I don't know if he's even sitting there. I know he must be there because a man his size can't jump out of a boat and swim to shore without making a lot of noise."

Christian snapped out of his daze and looked at his friends. "Shut up," he said without heat. "I thought you wanted this. The quiet." He looked around the secluded lake. There wasn't another boat in sight. It was why he'd chosen this lake. Tobias needed to get away from the women in his life. "I thought all the female attention was driving you crazy. This is what happens when you hang out with men. You don't get a lot of useless words."

"Yes, son," the general said to Christian. "But there's a difference in being quiet and being downright moody. What's crawled up your ass and died?"

"I would say it's women problems, but I have a hard time believing that, because somebody married to a lady as sweet as Miss Georgia can't have no women problems," Tobias said.

"I screwed up with her," he admitted. He had replayed their argument over and over in his mind. It was his fault. He had started it. He had accused her of something he knew she wasn't capable of, but he had been feeling angry. He'd been angry all week at himself and Georgia and the marines and his parents and the world. And when he'd heard that man flirting with Georgia, when he'd seen her smile at him and speak to him it had all boiled over. "I shouldn't have married her."

"What?"

"Are you insane?"

The general and Tobias spoke at the same moment.

"I'm having a hard time adjusting to civilian life."

"No shit, sir. We all are. I can't see. The general's got no one to boss around and you have no one to lead. It's hard. I think about the blast where I lost my eyesight. I think about it a lot, and not because it was the last day I saw things, but because I survived it when my friend Davey didn't. You lost almost all your men. Of course you're fucked up. It would be fucked up if you weren't fucked up a little. It takes time. Everybody knows that."

"I'm thinking about going back."

"No." Tobias shook his head. "You can think about it, but you can't do that to her. Lord knows why Miss Georgia picked you out of all the other men who would have married her. There was that doctor at the hospital who had a thing for her. She could have married him, or me, anyone she wanted, but she married you. And she gave you her baby and you can't walk out on her, either. My daddy walked out on me, sir. And if you go back, if you choose to go overseas, it'll be as if you're walking out on her even if you think the cause is good. She'll be pissed at you, and you'll deserve it. Miss Georgia don't got a lot of people in her life to love her, and when you married her you signed up for that job. You can't leave her, because trying to find your place in a world you never really fit in is hard. You've got to figure your shit out. You've got to try to harder. Going back is easy. Staying is the hard part. Letting that woman love you when you hate yourself is the hard part. You're the bravest man I know, sir, but if you walk out on Miss Georgia, I don't think I would feel the same way about you."

Tobias's words were effective. Guilt had been his constant companion for years. He hadn't known a life without the feeling, but Tobias's words made him feel a new kind of guilt, a much deeper one. He couldn't change the past.

But he could shape his future.

He had a good thing. He had Georgia and he was pushing her away, just like he did with Cliff and his parents' friends. He had been alone for so long when he didn't have to be. He didn't know how to handle love anymore. He never thought he deserved it.

He looked at the general. "You got anything to add to that, sir?"

"Nope." He took a beer out of the cooler, opened it and took a long swig. "Said it better than I ever could."

"Yeah. I've just been scolded by somebody who's not even

old enough to drink." He reached over and squeezed Tobias's shoulder. "Thank you, kid. I owe you one."

Christian had cut their fishing trip short by a day but nobody blamed him. He hadn't spoken to Georgia since he left. Two days and no contact with his wife. He was shit and he knew it. He had some making up to do, but he didn't know how to make things up to her, or to anybody.

His parents were gone and he couldn't change that, but he could stop blaming himself for something he had no control over. Miko had ended up in bad way, but he couldn't change that, either. He wasn't sure what had happened that night, but it wasn't good to live his life trying to make up for a sin he didn't commit.

But he could make up for avoiding everyone at Howard and Helga's, avoiding the people who would have stood by him, the people who reminded him so much of his parents. It wasn't a bad thing to be reminded of them.

The staff didn't hate him for what had happened. He hadn't realized it, but that was what he was afraid of. He was afraid they would judge him as being responsible for his parents' deaths.

Christian dialed Cliff's home number as he neared home. He had always kept it with him, even though he had never planned to call it. Maybe in the back of his mind he knew that this day would come. Maybe he always knew Cliff would be there if he really needed him.

"Hello?"

"It's Christian."

There was a long silence, so long that Christian was afraid the man had hung up. "Betty wants to see that baby of yours. When are you going to bring your sorry ass over here for dinner?"

Christian exhaled. "Soon. I just need to talk to my wife. I'm sorry," he said quietly.

"I am, too. I should have tried harder with you, but you're stubborn as hell. You got that from both of your parents. But you got your heart from your father. He would be proud of you. We are proud of you. You're a hero."

He said nothing to that. He didn't feel very heroic; he was just trying to make up for a life of being selfish. "I need your help, Cliff. I want to start up something for the guys like me."

"I'm not sure if there are many heirs to ice-cream companies out there, Christian, but I'll see what I can do."

He smiled. It had been too long since he had heard one of Cliff's bad jokes. "I wanted to start up an organization for former military. Something that can offer counseling and jobs and help, but I don't know where to begin."

"I was in Vietnam. Did you know that? When we came back people hated us for doing what we had to do. It was the hardest time in my life. I know what it's like to feel lost. I will help you. I will do whatever I can."

"Thank you. I'll come to the office in a few days. I have to settle some things at home first."

"Sounds good. I look forward to seeing you."

He disconnected as he pulled into the driveway. The side door flew open as soon as he put the car in Park. Georgia rushed out. His sweet little wife didn't look so sweet anymore. Her hair was loose and wild. Her eyes were full of fire.

He deserved everything she had to throw at him. He had so much making up to do.

He stepped out of the car and she ran to him. Jumping into his arms, she burst into tears.

"Oh, honey. I'm so sorry," he said.

"Where were you? I was out of my mind with worry. I thought the worst. I—" She stopped herself and shook her head.

"God, Georgia. What the hell was going through your mind?"

"I—I didn't know where you were. You didn't answer your phone. You didn't call me. It's been two days. You left us for two days."

"I went fishing with Tobias. I told you that. I told you we would be gone all weekend. There was no service. We were in the woods."

She jumped down from his arms and came at him swinging. "You asshole. You big, stupid, self-centered jackass. You went off fishing with your damn friends after that huge fight we had. I thought you'd left me. I thought you'd reenlisted. I thought we were done."

"I'm sorry." He caught her hands but she broke free.

"You're damn right you're sorry. I love you." She poked him in the chest. "I'm in love with you. I love the way you look and the way you make me feel. You're my best friend. That's why I married you. I fell in love with you the moment I saw you in that hospital. I love you more than you love yourself. I wish I could say your scars don't matter, but they do. They make up who you are now and that's who I love. I can't believe you would think otherwise."

"I'm sorry." He grabbed her and hauled her into his chest. "I'm sorry." She wrapped her legs around him and he held her like that for a long time. He kissed her hair and her cheeks and her nose and every piece of skin he could reach. "I can't explain to you what's been going on in my mind, but I'm not going to give you up, Georgia. I need you. The only time I've felt anything near happy in the past twelve years is when I'm with you and Abby. I'm here forever."

"I love you," she said to him right before she pressed her lips to his. "I love you."

He believed her. He had been fighting it, but he believed her. He didn't deserve her. "I've got something for you."

"I know." She took her lips from his and slid them down his throat. "I can feel it. Take me upstairs right now and let me show you how much I missed you."

"Georgia!" He threw his head back and laughed. "I like it when you talk to me like that and call me an asshole and try to beat me up. Although you hit hard. My jaw is still sore from where you smacked me."

"I'm sorry." Her eyes filled with tears again. "I was so mad at you."

"I know." He reached his hand into his pocket and pulled out a simple diamond ring. "And you have every right to be, but I want you to wear this. I don't want anybody thinking you're single."

She looked at the ring and then up at him. "You were an ass."

"I know."

"You should apologize."

"I will."

"I've never had something so nice before."

"Get used to it. You're my wife. You can have anything you want."

"I just want you to be happy. When you aren't, I feel as if I'm failing as a wife."

"I'm totally fucked up, Georgia."

"I am, too, and you're okay with that and that's why I love you."

He pressed his lips to her forehead as he slid the ring on her finger. "I'm going to work on it. I promise."

A car pulled up behind Christian's, causing Christian to step away from his wife to see who their visitors were. An older withered-looking man stepped out of the driver's side.

He was accompanied by three younger men who he had never seen before. Carolina was the last to get out, and then it dawned on him who these people were.

Georgia's family had come back.

CHAPTER 24

They were all there. All her remaining siblings. She studied her brothers. Eli was the oldest. They were eight years apart. Not very close, but not very distant, either. He looked older, more distinguished. The hair at his temples was gray, even though he was in his early thirties.

Then there was Josiah. They were just four years apart. He looked exactly the same. Maybe a little more mature. He had always been kind to her, looked out for her. He was the quietest of them all and had tried to be close to their father after Abel died.

Gideon was the baby. He had crossed over from boyhood into manhood, but he still had his baby face. He had soft, smooth brown skin and curly eyelashes she used to be jealous of. She knew she shouldn't have favorites, but she did. She had changed his diapers. She had been a second mama to him. He loved her, too, but he'd been just as silent. Just as absent as the rest of them the day her father had thrown her out.

Christian grabbed her hand and placed her behind him. It was almost an absentminded move. He was protecting her, but right now she didn't think he could protect her from what was about to come.

Carolina came rushing toward Georgia and wrapped her arms around her. "I'm so sorry about this. I told them not to barge in on you. I tried, but they never listen to me."

"It's okay, honey." She patted her sister's back, knowing how the men in her family were.

She finally looked at her father. It had been so long since she had seen him. He didn't look the same. He looked terrible. His hair had gone a ghastly white instead of the rich black she remembered. He had lost so much weight, his skin drooped. His eyes were glassy. He looked sick. He looked like some of the cancer patients she'd once had.

A little worry seeped into her, but she turned it off. He loved her rapist more than he had ever loved her and he'd gone out of his way to prove that to her.

"I'll send them away right now, Georgia," her husband said. "You let me know what you want me to do."

She took his hand and locked her fingers with his. It was past time she faced them. But she was glad he was here. She didn't think she could do it without him. "I'll hear them out."

"Georgia." Eli stepped forward. "Your eyes are red. Are you okay?" He looked at Christian, and as if he had given a signal Josiah and Eli stepped up beside them. The three of them were acting like some kind of protective trio. "You can come with us if you need to."

She laughed, some kind of crazy hysterical laughter bubbling up inside her. "My husband was away for a few days and I missed him. Were you going to protect me from him? Why start now? Where were you two years ago?"

"Georgia," Josiah began but he stopped and looked thoroughly ashamed. "There are no words for what we let him do to you."

"Which him?" Christian asked. "Your father or the friend you let rape her?"

"Listen here," her father boomed. "I'm not going to let some stranger get involved in a family matter."

"He's not a stranger," Georgia snapped, talking back to her father freely. As a child it was something she'd never had the freedom to do. "He's my husband. Captain Christian Howard. He's a marine, Daddy. I've done good for myself, even though you called me a whore and seductress. I married a good man even though you said no good man would have me."

Her father sneered at her. At her home behind her. "You're no child of God. Look at you. Your skin is exposed. You're wearing pants that show off your body. You're a heathen and I was right about you."

"Get off my property."

"No, Georgia. Wait." Gideon stepped forward and reached for her hand. "I believed you. I heard you crying the night it happened. I know you didn't lie. I know you wouldn't. I just didn't know what to do about it. I didn't think he would throw you out. I should have stopped him, but I was too shocked and now I'm ashamed. I'm sorry."

"I am, too," Eli said. "I should have gone after you long ago. It was Carolina that made us see the way. We want you back in our lives."

"It's not that simple. I can't forget."

"And we're not expecting you to forgive. We came here today to show him that he was wrong about you. He thinks Mama is here. I called her sister. She hasn't heard from her. We're worried, Georgia."

A lead ball settled in her stomach. "Mama's not at her sister's?"

"No. You haven't heard from her?"

"No. I haven't. Have any of you? Have you called the police? She's missing. You can't just wait around here. You have to find her."

"I want to search the house!" Abraham said. "I don't believe her. She's hiding her. She's hiding my wife."

Christian charged her father, but Georgia grabbed the back of his shirt and wrapped her arms around his middle, using all of her strength to keep him in his place.

"Don't hurt him," she begged. "Please."

"He's got no right coming here and demanding anything. I want them gone, Georgia. I want them all gone."

"They'll go. But let them search the house. He'll never give up until he sees she's not here."

Christian looked at her for a long moment. "Are you sure?"

"I am. Let them see. Then they can go."

Georgia led them all into the house, and Christian had never been so proud of her. She held her head up high in spite of the situation. He wasn't sure he could have handled it the same way. In fact, he knew he couldn't have.

Abraham Williams turned to his sons. "Gideon. Josiah," he barked. "You search downstairs. Eli and I will search up."

It was as though he was conducting a search for an escaped prisoner. And maybe he was. Christian was starting to get a real clear image of what it was like to grow up in Pastor Williams's house. It wasn't a house filled with love. It was a wonder how he could have produced a daughter like Georgia, who was so full of love. She loved him, she told him; she was in love with him. Hearing that, knowing of her love, made him feel as if he could do anything, survive anything.

Right now he felt as though he could kill for her. Her father, all three of her brothers. How easy it was for them to come back now. Now that he was there. Now that she was married and didn't need them anymore. Where had they been two years ago? Two months ago? Anything could have happened to their sister. If she wasn't so strong, so many bad things could have happened to her.

Abraham rushed his frail body up the stairs, Eli close behind. At least Eli had the good sense to look contrite. He looked at Christian with an apology in his eyes, but Christian ignored the look and followed the men upstairs. He didn't take the same direction as they did once they reached the top. He went to his daughter's room. To the other girl he had been missing so much for the past two days.

She popped her little head up at soon as his footsteps hit her floor. Her eyes widened in recognition.

"Da!" She stood, reaching for him.

How could he go back? Even when life was hard here, even when his problems seemed insurmountable, there was no way he could go back. Because she was one of the best parts of life. He scooped her out of her crib and she grabbed his face, giving him one of those wet baby kisses that made his heart thud in his chest.

"She missed you." Georgia came up behind him and slid her hand up his back. "Every morning she asked for you, looking at me as if I wasn't supposed to be there dressing her."

"I missed her, too." He kissed her hair. "Who knew the best part of my day would be dressing a baby girl?"

"Is she in here?" They heard Abraham's voice, then his footsteps as he rushed into the bedroom.

He froze once he saw Abby.

"Father," Eli asked softly. "What is it?"

Abraham ignored his son and walked closer to Abby. His glassy eyes took in all her features.

"Shit," Eli swore. "Shit. I'm going to kill him."

Christian knew what was going through their minds. Abby

looked so much like her birth father. He had never seen the man, but their reactions confirmed it.

Abraham reached for Abby, his bony hand touching her cheek. "He lied to me," he wheezed out. His breathing had become heavy. Sweat formed on his brow. "He lied."

His hand went to his chest, a tortured look crossed his face and he fell to the floor.

"Daddy," Georgia screamed. She reached for him, trying to stop his fall, but she couldn't. So she knelt beside him, looking at her brother. "Find me some aspirin. Call 911. Go now!"

Carolina, Josiah and Gideon dashed into the room, but they froze when they saw their father on the floor. He looked like death. He should be dead, but Georgia, as though it was the most natural thing in the world, began CPR. The nurse in her took over and she looked like an angel trying to save the devil's life.

"She should just let him die," he heard Gideon say. "He doesn't deserve to live after what he has done to us."

Christian agreed, but Georgia didn't. She didn't stop trying to save the old man's life.

CHAPTER 25

Where was Mama? Georgia stared out of the window as she sat in the waiting room with her siblings. Miles had come to be with Carolina, who was weeping in his arms. Gideon was sitting red eyed, as if he was holding back tears. Her other brothers were sitting stoically together, waiting for word from the doctor.

Georgia felt surprisingly blank. Maybe that wasn't true. She was worried, but about her mother. She was so sure she had gone to her sister's house. She'd said that she hoped to live there one day, on the ocean. It was her dream. Maybe she was there. Maybe her sister had lied to all of them because Mama needed a break.

However, there was a chance she hadn't gone there, and it worried her. Where could she have gone? Her mother had never lived on her own. She had never taken care of herself. Georgia wondered if her fragile mother could.

A pair of lips brushed the back of her neck, and Georgia turned into her husband's embrace. She had missed him to the point of pain these past two days. She knew he was going through a lot himself, that transitioning to civilian life was hard, but he was still there for her. Like a rock. He'd never wavered today when she needed him.

"How are you feeling, sweetheart?"

"I love you," she told him.

"I don't deserve you." He rested his hand on her cheek and she snuggled into his chest. "You saved his life. You are better than me. You were better than what he deserved. I would have let him die."

"You wouldn't have. You're noble. You wouldn't have let him go without helping."

"I'm glad you think better of me than I think of myself."

"I always will. I think God made you just for me, Christian Howard. I was born to love you."

He said nothing to that, but an odd look crossed his face. She knew it was hard for him to be loved. It was as though he didn't trust it, he didn't trust love.

He cupped her face in his hand and tilted her head back, pressing three slow, soft kisses to her mouth. "I called Alma. She said BB is fine and that they would be happy to keep her overnight if we need her to."

"We need to get them something. They are so kind to us. I'm happy to have them."

"What about them?" He motioned with his head, toward her siblings. "What are you going to do about them?"

"Love them. Let them back in. It won't be easy, will it?"

"No, love."

"But I have to. I have to do it for my soul to rest."

"Mrs. Howard?" The doctor approached them, his face serious but unreadable, and she was brought back to the present. Her father had suffered a massive heart attack. He should have died.

"Yes?" She faced the doctor, suddenly feeling her knees go weak.

"He's stable now, but we are going to have to keep him for a while. He's going to need surgery. You can go in to see him, but only two at a time. He's very weak."

"I understand."

"You saved his life. You should be very proud."

She shook her head. "I'm a nurse. I didn't do anything so special."

Christian didn't agree with her. She grabbed his hand, locking her fingers with his. "Come in with me. I want to see him and then go get my baby."

They walked into his room and Georgia could barely see her father in the hospital bed. It was such a contrast to her memories of Christian in his bed. Her husband seemed bigger than life to her. Her father seemed as if he was shrinking away from it. His complexion had a yellowish tint, and his skin seemed to hang on his bones. He looked like an old man. She had never thought of him as old, but now she couldn't deny that he was. He looked almost unrecognizable as the man she had grown up with.

"Daddy?"

He opened his eyes to look at her. It took a moment for him to focus on her face, but when he did he shook his head and turned away from her. Completely away. The message couldn't have been clearer even if he had spoken it.

Out of all the things that had happened to her, this was the most painful. Even now, even after she had gotten on her knees and saved his life, he couldn't look at her. He couldn't admit he was wrong.

"Hateful bastard," Christian spat. He didn't give her the

chance to be hurt anymore. He wrapped his arm around her, kissed her forehead and took her away from him.

She wouldn't see her father again, she decided. She'd done all she could do.

"You look like you could use a drink," Christian said to his wife when she walked out of their bathroom that evening.

"I could use two."

Her hair was wet. Slicked down to the back of her head. The nightgown she wore stuck to her body, telling him that she had barely dried herself off after her bath. She had been absent all evening. Not physically. She hadn't left his side since they'd gotten home, but mentally she was gone. Some painful place in her mind that he wished he could pull her out of.

Her father was a bastard. A shit. An asshole. He didn't know what else to call him that could encompass all the hurt he'd caused. But what he did today, how he'd turned away from Georgia, was enough to make Christian want to kill a dying man.

"I could go out and get you something. Liquor stores close late."

She gave him a sad smile and climbed into bed. "You know, I've never had a drink in my life. Maybe I shouldn't start now when I'm feeling so…shitty."

"I like it when my preacher's daughter wife cusses." He kissed her nose. "It does all kinds of things to me."

"It's the only way to describe how I feel."

"I'm sorry." He wrapped his arms around her and held her tightly against him.

"Why did he have to do that?" she asked softly. "Why did he turn me away again?"

"I wish there was a reason, sweetheart. He's just a bastard. He's a mean old man."

"He's never loved me."

"Georgia…" He didn't know what to say to that. It couldn't be true. Georgia was love. It would be impossible for him not to.

"He never even pretended to like me. He said I talked too much. He said I was too strong willed. I tried not to be. I tried to do everything to please him, but I couldn't. Nothing was ever good enough."

There were no words he could think of to make her feel better. Nothing he could say to take away her hurt. "They came today because they love you. Your siblings. You please me. You're more good than I deserve. Don't let him make you feel bad, Georgia. Don't make him doubt how good you are."

He felt the first spill of hot tears on his chest, then he heard the cry tear from her throat. He felt truly helpless. Worse than the first time he'd woken up after the blast. Worse than the first time he'd realized that nearly all his men had died. He had accomplished a lot in his life, but this was one thing he wasn't sure how to succeed at. He wasn't equipped to take away his wife's pain.

So he held her and kissed her forehead and whispered whatever words came into his head. He wasn't sure how long they stayed like that, but after a while her tears stopped and her breathing evened out. Poor Georgia had cried herself to sleep.

When Georgia woke up a few hours later, Christian's hand was underneath her nightgown, resting on the small of her back. To think she didn't have him a few months ago. Now she could hardly see her life without him. Besides Abby, he was her only constant. She knew his road was no easier than hers. She knew that life was a struggle for him, but he was there for her. She'd loved him on their wedding day, but somehow that love had grown even stronger. Life, she decided, would be no good without him.

She hoped he knew that. She hoped he believed her when she told him she loved him. But sometimes she knew words weren't good enough. She gently pulled herself out of his hold, causing him to roll onto his back. He did not awaken and she took the opportunity to study him in his sleep. His hair had grown even longer, a halo of light brown curls resting on the head of a man that looked anything but angelic.

She kissed his face. She kissed the scars she had fallen in love with as she pulled her nightgown over her head and straddled his body. She was naked, and she lifted his hands and ran them over her body, over her breasts and nipples. She then placed a hand between her legs, encouraging his fingers to explore her there. It was then he opened his eyes.

He said nothing. He did nothing. He just watched her with his sleepy eyes. It never took much for her husband to arouse her; just the feel of his hard body beneath hers sent her trembling.

"You do this to me." She slid her fingers through her wetness. "Every time. No other man could make me enjoy sex like this. I don't think you know how much of a gift you have given me."

She shifted her body down his and slipped him free from his boxers. He looked at her curiously, his eyes warming her skin.

She took him into her mouth slowly, watching his eyes as they widened and then shut in pleasure. She wasn't sure what she was doing, she just worked her mouth over him, taking little breaks to kiss down his thick shaft and to swipe her tongue over his head.

He hissed out a breath, his hands gripping the sheets as she pleasured him. "Georgia. Please."

She wasn't sure what he was asking for, so she looked up at him, taking him into her hand as she lightly stroked him. "What is it, sugar? What do you want me to do?"

"Come here."

She moved her body up his but she didn't give him the chance to take over, to guide her, because she slid herself down on him, not deeply, just enough so that she could feel fullness of him. Then she lifted herself up. A rush of hot sensation swept over her and she shut her eyes, unable to keep them open, unable to do anything but just feel him. He grabbed her hips but just held her there as she moved on him, but soon it became too much for him to lie passively. He thrust into her, but shallowly, the increased pressure causing her to cry out in pleasure.

"I need you closer." He rolled her over onto her back and slid all the way into her, but he just stayed there for a moment, not moving his body, only kissing her deeply and hard and slowly. Her toes curled, and then he started to move in her again, but this time his thrusts were shallow and quick and intense. It took her totally by surprise when the feeling started to build in her again. So quickly. It stole her breath and suddenly she was crying out. Her body shook uncontrollably.

Christian looked down at her, the smile spreading across his face so quickly and beautifully she was having a hard time thinking of anything more lovely. His smile melted away when he kissed her and he moved in her again. Pumping deeply. Filling her up. It caused her to spiral into another orgasm, but this time he came with her. It was the first time they had finished together. It was the first time she had felt this connected to him, inseparable from him. It was a feeling that she never wanted to go away.

She wrapped her arms around him, burying her face in his neck, enjoying the feeling of his thickness still inside her.

"Oh, God," he breathed after a few long moments. "That was… You came."

"Yes." She nodded. "It's been known to happen."

"Not when I'm inside you."

She frowned at him. "Why is that so important to you?"

"Because I feel as if I'm failing you as a husband when I you don't."

"Gosh, you're stupid."

He pressed a soft kiss to her mouth. "I know, but I can't help the way I feel."

"No." She looked away from him, too embarrassed to look into his eyes. "You're big. When you fill me up all the way it doesn't feel as—as intense, but sometimes I need to feel you that way. I need you to go slow and kiss every part of my body. I may not…react the way you expect me to, but I'm always satisfied by you. I never once felt as if I wasn't. And if you don't stop acting like a big insecure jerk I'm going to punch you!"

"Okay." He slid his lips along her neck. "Now let me make love to you slowly. Let me love every part of you."

CHAPTER 26

He had barely had been away from Georgia for four hours, but Christian was eager to see his wife again. He had just come from Howard and Helga's. It was different going there this time. Better. Everybody was over the initial shock of seeing him. They welcomed him. They were happy to see him. Things hadn't changed much in his long absence. Most of the people he had grown up around were still there. They begged to see pictures of Abby and asked about his wife. They all seemed so happy for him.

They told him that he should have come back earlier, and maybe he should have, but he wasn't sure that he could have returned before now. Georgia made the difference in his life. He came into the kitchen through the side door to see her standing at the stove.

"Hey!" Her face lit up and she left her spot to greet him with a kiss. "I missed you today."

"It's getting bad, isn't it?" He brought her closer and dropped a kiss on the bridge of her nose. "I used to think those three days when you were off when I was in the hospital were bad, but now I go a few hours and it's as though I'm craving another fix of you. I think I'm addicted."

She blushed prettily. "I think that might have been the sweetest thing you have ever said to me."

"Is it? Have you started to cook yet? I want to take you out to dinner tonight."

She nodded. "I would love to go to dinner with you tonight. And dessert. I had a dream about cake last night. Chocolate cake with lots of icing. I've been needing something sweet all day."

He studied her for a moment. Her face looked a little fuller, her eyes tired. She had been hungry the past few days, hungrier than usual, and it caused him to wonder if she was pregnant. She hadn't said anything to him, but she might be.

A little hope bloomed in his chest. He wanted another child. He wanted Abby to have a sibling, to have siblings. He wanted to grow their family. He thought back to his sometimes lonely childhood and how he'd felt so lost when his parents were killed. God forbid something might happen to him and Georgia, but if it did he wanted Abby to have somebody else to turn to. "There's a little place a couple of blocks over. We could walk there. It's a nice night."

A few minutes later they had grabbed Abby and were walking toward the little mom-and-pop café. "You never told me how your meeting was today. I thought about you the whole time you were gone."

"It went well. I'm glad I took Tobias and the general with me. They really helped me explain to Cliff what exservicemen needed. I can't always find the words."

"Tobias is great with words," Georgia said thoughtfully. "He called the other day while you were getting your oil changed and sometimes I forget he's only nineteen."

"He's been through a lot. It made it him wise. Cliff offered him a job today."

"He did!"

Christian smiled. "As a taster in the product development department. Since Tobias lost his sight, his other senses strengthened. He was eating some of the new candy the company is developing and he named all the ingredients in it. Cliff was so impressed he hired him on the spot. He starts training on Tuesday. They are going to send him to chocolate school in Montreal."

"Chocolate school? That's amazing! Do you think he'll be okay going alone?"

"He'll be fine. He'll have help. But he really wants to be independent and I applaud that."

She nodded. "What else did you talk about? I love hearing this."

"The company is expanding. We're going to need another plant in the next year. That's two hundred new jobs. We could hire a lot of former military. Cliff helped me sketch out a basic plan for the foundation. We could help a lot of people."

They turned a corner, leaving their quiet little neighborhood and turning onto a street populated with historic buildings and cute little shops. "I'm proud of you, Christian."

He shook his head. "I'm just doing what I'm supposed to." He took one hand off Abby's stroller and grabbed Georgia's hand. "How are you feeling? I know your sister has been updating you on your father. I know you're too nice to tell her that you don't want to hear it anymore."

"But I do want to hear about him. I know it's wrong, but I want to know how he is."

"It's not wrong, sweetheart. You love him. He's your father."

"He used to be a happy man. I was hoping that one day I might be able to see that man again."

"I'm so sorry your daddy is a rat bastard."

She laughed quietly. "It's okay. If he wasn't I wouldn't be married to you."

They came up to the Catfish Kitchen and were seated outside. They talked over dinner about their childhoods and fathers and life's happy times and its disappointments. Sometimes Christian lost track of what Georgia was saying because he was too caught up in staring at her.

He couldn't have gone back, even though sometimes the itch snuck up on him. He couldn't leave her. He would miss her too much.

"Have you ever had gelato? I saw it on TV this morning and have been dying to try it. You think we could find some of that around here?"

"Yeah, there's a place up the street, but I thought you wanted cake."

"I do." She nodded her head. "We can get the cake to go. I want gelato. Right now, and I do not care that my pants are so tight the button is going to pop off and shoot you in the eye."

He grinned at her, so glad that she had become so much more easy around him. He was starting to feel married, as though he had a partner forever. "Come on," he said to her after he paid their bill. "We can take our cake and gelato home and eat it in front of the television."

"They'll pack it up for us?"

"Yup. We'll take home a couple of pints."

She smiled beautifully at him. "That makes me so happy to hear. I love this town. You can get anything here. You know, I never had store-bought ice cream till I was twenty-one."

"What?"

"We used to make it at home, so there was never any reason to buy it. I was in college the first time I had it. It was soft-serve chocolate-and-vanilla twist. At the time I thought I had never seen something so amazing. The other girls I was with teased me unmercifully, but I had never seen anything like that before."

"Were you really that sheltered, Georgia?"

She nodded. "Just me and Carolina. He thought the less we knew about the world, the better. I don't want that to happen to Abby. I want her to know everything."

"We'll do right by her. I promise." He looked down at Abby in her stroller. She was calm, softly and happily singing to herself.

"I always planned on raising her alone, but I'm glad I don't have to. Daddies are important. She's been so happy."

He looked over at her. She was looking wistfully at their daughter. "I know these past few weeks have been crazy. I know I haven't been easy to love, but I want you to be happy, too. Are you happy, Georgia?"

She wrapped her arm around his and rested her head against him as they walked. "You bought me crab cakes. I'm about to eat cake and ice cream. I'm happier than a pig in mud."

He loved her. He had loved her almost instantly. He wondered if she knew, if he had ever told her that. Probably not. He hadn't said those words to anybody in so many years. Not even when his parents were alive. He had gotten stupid in his teenage years, afraid to say it for fear of sounding like a little boy. If he could go back, that was one thing that he would change. He would let them know how he felt. He should let his wife know.

He opened his mouth to do so but an elderly woman stopped in front of them. She looked sort of wild-eyed as she stared at Georgia. He thought she was homeless for a moment, looking for a handout, but she was too well dressed, and instead of asking she just stared, stared at Georgia and at Abby.

The woman lunged at Georgia so quickly he could barely react. She grabbed her face in her hands and started to sob. Christian grabbed her arm.

"Don't hurt her," Georgia begged. "It's my mother."

When Georgia left her mother that evening she found Christian in Abby's room. He was sitting with the freshly bathed little girl in the rocking chair by her window. He was reading the book *Goodnight Moon* to her.

Abby sat there, rubbing her eyes, but listening to her father's deep voice as he told her the story. Georgia was surprised to see them like that. With Abby sitting so still and calmly. She had been such a wiggly ball of energy lately. But then again she was always good for Christian.

Georgia wanted to be annoyed by it, by the fact that Abby was a daddy's girl, but she couldn't, because Abby's relationship with Christian was the exact opposite of the one she had with her father.

She sat on the floor next to the rocker and rested her head on Christian's knee as he finished the story.

Drained didn't describe the way she was feeling. It was more than that. She had been so worried about her mother these past few weeks. She'd tried to deny it. She hadn't wanted to think that anything bad could happen to her, so she'd tamped down those feelings and tried to think of other things. But Mama snuck into her mind in those quiet moments, when all her other thoughts fled. She had secretly thought that her mama just needed a break, a little time for herself. That was why she'd left Daddy. Yet she'd always suspected she would go back to him.

Her parents had been together since her mother was seventeen years old. Fiona Williams was one of those proud Southern women who always stood by their man. Sometimes that broke Georgia's heart.

Christian stood up and placed Abby in her crib, kissing her good-night, whispering, "I love you," as he did. It was something he did absently. Something he always whispered. They were words he never said aloud. Words he never said to Georgia, even though she knew he did.

He left Abby and scooped Georgia off the floor, taking her to the rocking chair and holding her like he held their daughter. Only his hand wandered up the back of her shirt and his lips rested against her forehead. "How is she?"

"Sleeping. She hasn't said very much. She hasn't told me where she's been."

"Is she okay? She seems…" He trailed off. Georgia knew why. He was trying to save her feelings. He didn't want to mention how broken her mother looked.

But it was true. Her mother looked broken. She had heard about her husband's heart attack.

He's been here in Charleston. All this time. I should have been with him.

"She's not okay. At least she's not the way I remember her. My mama used to be so beautiful. Now she looks so…"

"Guilty." He kissed her forehead. "She looks so guilty. I know the look. I've seen it in my own eyes a time or two. But she came here for you. She came to ask forgiveness."

"They've all come back to ask for forgiveness. I want to forgive. I want to forget, but I can't seem to, either. It seems to be drying up."

"It's not. You're just overwhelmed. It's all too much for you right now." He buried his fingers in her hair at the base of her neck and began to massage. "What can I do, Georgia?

You want me to send her home and whisk you away, banning all contact from anyone with the last name Williams?"

"That doesn't include Carolina. Her married name is Hammond. Don't forget about banning contact with her, too."

He smiled down at her. "Hammonds, too, but you don't mean that. If you did, I would do that for you in a minute. You want your family back. It might not be right now, but you'll want them around. I want to take you away from here soon. I want to take you to where I grew up. It's time for me to go back. Would you like to come with me?"

She nodded and lifted her head to kiss him. "I would love that, but right now I want you to take me to bed."

CHAPTER 27

"Mama?" Abby asked Christian the next morning as he dressed her in a tiny yellow-and-white dress.

"She's in the kitchen cooking breakfast. She's making French toast. Your grandmother is here. I don't think your mama can sleep very well now."

"Her mama can't sleep very well now, either."

Christian turned to see Georgia's mother, Fiona, standing in the doorway. The only way he could describe her was diminutive. She was tiny. Less than five feet tall, with tiny hands and delicate bone structure.

She looked much better than she had last night. The nearly crazed expression in her eyes had gone. She simply looked like an elderly woman at the moment. But he knew Georgia's mother was not old. It was just that some of the life had been sucked out of her.

"Georgia is downstairs if you need her." He turned back to his daughter, running his big fingers through her little ringlets. "There," he said after a moment. "You look beautiful now."

Abby clapped as she did every morning when he finished dressing her.

"You're the only one who ever claps for me." He lifted her up, holding her close to him. "That's why I'm crazy about you, kid."

Abby leaned in and kissed him with her sweet spitty baby kiss and his heart lurched, as always.

"She loves you."

Fiona's voice had taken him by surprise. He thought she had gone. "I'm her father," he said simply.

"Yes," Fiona said softly. "Yes, you are. She looks like him, though."

He was sick of hearing that. Sick of hearing that his daughter looked like his wife's rapist, even if it was true. "I don't care. I wish you Williamses would stop saying that. She is not a part of him. She is mine and Georgia's and I don't want him spoken of in this house again."

"I understand that. I even agree with it, but I think there are things you should know about him, about us."

"I know everything. Georgia keeps no secrets from me."

"You know her side."

"Her side is the only side that matters," he snapped.

"I know you are angry with us. With me. And you should be, but just listen for a moment." She sucked in a wobbly breath. "Robert was a good boy. There are some people you can tell are phony and no good, but he wasn't one of them. Maybe he had us fooled, maybe he changed, but I would like to believe that when we first met him there was some goodness in him. His parents were harsh with him, with everybody, really, but they treated him as though he was a servant and not a son."

"I could say the same thing for you and your husband. I know you worked your daughters like dogs."

"They had chores, but they were never not loved."

"That's not what Georgia thinks. She thinks your husband doesn't love her. He can't. He couldn't have, because he let that man get away with what he did to her. He threw her out, he called her a liar. She saved his life, right in this very room, and he wouldn't look at her afterward. He turned his head away from the only person who lifted a finger to save him."

"I can't explain the actions of my husband. There is no explanation."

"Then maybe you can explain yourself. You let him throw her away. You let her struggle. You let her bring this child into the world alone. What kind of mother are you? How can you look at yourself in the mirror knowing what she went through?"

"I can't!" Her eyes filled with tears. "I can't. I can't even look at her without feeling ashamed. That's why I'm here with you and not with her. But you don't know what it was like living there with Abraham Williams. You don't know what it's like to see the love of your life turn into an unfeeling stone of a man who was so depressed sometimes he couldn't get out of bed. Abel was his boy. His pride. They were close, and when he died so did most of my husband."

She drew a deep breath, and continued, "So did the church and the town. Oakdale is a dying place. It has been going ever since my son left this earth, but when Robert came to town he made my husband feel something. You think I would resent the fact that he couldn't find it in him to bond with his other children instead of a stranger, but when somebody you love is in such a deep, dark place like that you'll do anything to pull them out. So I let it be when Robert started coming over for dinner and sitting in Abel's place. I let it be when Abraham started helping Robert pay for school, because it made him feel good. I let it be when I noticed Robert's eyes starting to follow Georgia around, because I thought they might get married one day and make my husband happy. And I let it be when Abraham threw Georgia out because I knew that once he chose Robert over her that there was nothing left for her with us. I could have begged him to let her stay. I could have threatened to go with her, but in the end I knew that it would harm Georgia more than any good it would do."

"What kind of bullshit thinking is that?"

"She was the strongest of all my children. And the smartest. If anybody could get out, if anybody could make something of themselves, it was her. I could have gone to the police, but what do you say to the chief when the victim's own father calls her a liar? When the father is the pastor who has more power than the mayor. Georgia needed to go. It killed me to let her go, but I had to. She's so much more than she would have been if she stayed."

"So why are you here now, Mama?" Georgia came up behind her mother.

"I needed to see for myself that you were happy. Your sister said you were, but I needed to see you." She took Georgia's face in her hands. "You are happy. I can tell. I can tell just by the way you look at your husband. You're very much in love with him."

"I am."

"Then I'm not sorry for letting you go. I'm sorry for what happened to you. I'm sorry I couldn't help you more. I'm sorry I was such a horrible mother to you all after Abel died, but I'm not sorry I let you go. You deserved a better life than what we had planned out for you. You deserved better than us."

"Okay, Mama." She looked at her mother for a long moment. "Breakfast is ready. I made about a pound of bacon. It's maple glazed and just about the best thing I've ever eaten."

"Wait a minute," Christian said, bewildered. "After all of that, that's all you have to say?"

"No." She shook her head. "I guess not. What took you so long to come see me? You left Daddy weeks ago."

"I was scared to face you. Scared you wouldn't be happy."

"You weren't scared I would hate you?"

"No. I don't think you can hate, but if you did I would have deserved it and accepted it."

"Okay." She nodded and looked at Christian. "I just didn't want to hear another apology. I wanted to hear a why. I'm tired of being angry. I just want to move on. We've got this new baby coming and I don't want him or Abby growing up with us stuck in the past."

"What?" He took a step toward her but then stopped. His mind was reeling.

"I'm having your baby, Captain." She closed the distance between them and set her lips on his. "Thank you for giving him to me and thank you for not batting a lash while I have been eating like a pig this past week." She took Abby from him and kissed her curls. "Don't you look gorgeous this morning? Come on, baby. Let's get some food in you."

CHAPTER 28

Time heals all wounds. Georgia thought about that statement as she talked to her sister on the phone two months later. She wished that was true. It wasn't true for everybody. It wasn't true for her, but time did help. Time did ease some pain. She rubbed her belly as her sister talked about her own pregnancy and how she had only started to show in her final months.

Georgia wasn't so lucky. Her belly was round and stuck out beneath her shirts already, and she was only entering her fourth month. But Christian didn't seem to mind. He seemed to love it, talking to his unborn child every night before they went to sleep. He was so happy about becoming a father. Again.

She thought her pregnancy with a child of his own blood might change the way he felt about Abby, or at least the way he treated her, but there was no change. Abby loved her daddy and Christian couldn't get enough of her.

"You think you could come to my house next weekend, Georgia? All this unpacking business when I'm about to pop is quite annoying. But Miles really likes Charleston and I'll be closer to you, so it won't be bad. Mama said she would come, too. Miles said I should just stop being fussy and let him hire some people to unpack for us, but I can't. I don't want strangers touching my underthings."

"Carolina, they…" she began but stopped herself, knowing she would be wasting her breath trying to explain that to her sister. "I'll be there."

Things between her and Carolina was surprisingly wonderful. It was so nice to see her sister as an adult, preparing for motherhood, being a wife. She had loved Carolina as a child because she was her little sister and only friend, but now she liked Carolina as an adult because she was adorable and flighty and happy all the time.

Things with her brothers had not gone as easily, and she wasn't sure why. She didn't blame them for what had happened to her, but they blamed themselves, it seemed. Eli still could barely look her in the eye. Josiah apologized every time he saw her and Gideon was away, overseas in Germany serving his country. He hadn't spoken to any of them since the day of their father's heart attack. If she could change one thing, she would change that.

In the end her mother had been right. Georgia had needed to leave Oakdale. She wouldn't have had the life she wanted if she had stayed.

Christian walked into the kitchen with Abby in his arms. She was dressed more beautifully than normal. Her father was taking her to work with him today. He loved to show her off. The people at Howard and Helga's had really been kind to them since Christian had gone back. Christian could no longer say he was without family or friends. Now he had more of them than he could count.

He buried his face in her neck and kissed her there, moving his lips up her throat until she lost all train of thought and moaned.

"Georgia?" Her sister's voice rang through the phone. "Are you okay?"

"I'm feeling a little woozy. I'm going to have to call you back later."

She disconnected from her sister and wrapped her arms around her husband. "What's the deal with you kissing me like that when I'm on the phone? You know I go all kinds of crazy when you kiss me like that."

"I know. I wanted you to pay attention to me."

"Yeah!" Abby said.

"You going to work with Daddy today?" She grabbed Abby's hand and pressed it to her mouth. "They're going to spoil you rotten."

"They are. I'm only going in for a little while. We'll be back by lunch." He rubbed her belly and kissed her forehead. "I want you to take a nap while I'm gone. Just relax. No cleaning or gardening or cooking. Just grow the baby."

"Okay. Take tomorrow off and grow the baby with me. I miss you since you've been going in every day."

"I can't tomorrow," he said, looking guilty. "We're meeting with some potential employers who are interested in hiring some of our men. It's going to be a while before the plant is open, so it's important that I meet with these people. We need to place as many servicemen in jobs as we can."

"I know." She kissed his mouth. "But I still miss you."

"Friday. I'll take off on Friday."

"Thank you." She smiled at him. "Now hurry up and go so you can get back. You are taking us out to dinner tonight."

"Really?" He grinned at her. He loved to take her places. Sometimes she felt spoiled, but she knew that was important to him. He wanted to take care of her. "What are you craving?"

"Cheeseburgers with extra cheese and nachos with lots of jalapenos and butter-pecan ice cream on a waffle cone."

His smile widened. "Okay." He kissed her nose, her cheeks, then her mouth. "I'm going to stuff you so full you won't want to move. Then I'm going to love you all night. Because I love you. I love you, Georgia. Do you know that?"

"Yes." Her insides warmed deliciously. "I know it. You never say it, but I know you love me."

"From the moment I opened my eyes in Jericho and saw you."

"You asked me to kill you."

"Yes, but you brought me back to life and I love you for it."

"Go to work," she ordered, feeling ridiculously close to tears. "I'll see you later." She kissed Abby and Christian once more before she pushed him away.

"I'm going." He gave her belly a quick rub and left the house.

Georgia knew she was supposed to be relaxing. She had been a little more tired with this pregnancy. This baby was a little bigger, according to her doctor. He was taking a little more out of her, but she couldn't rest. She was still feeling tingly from Christian's words.

She pulled out the flour and all her baking supplies and prepared to make him the Mississippi mud brownies he loved so much. All she needed was more butter. She grabbed her handbag and stepped out the kitchen door to head to the little convenience store a few blocks away.

"Georgia." She heard a male voice call her name and smiled, assuming it was her neighbor, Tim. Christian had apologized to him and since then they had become friendly, but when she looked up it wasn't Tim. It was the last person she had ever wanted to see.

Robert.

She backed away from him and turned, unable to think. All her body told her to do was get away. She ran back into her house, but he ran after her, slamming his body into the door as she was trying to close it.

The force of the blow sent her reeling backward. She landed against the counter, hitting her side so hard it took her breath away.

"I don't want to hurt you," he said as he walked into her home and stood over her. "I just want to talk to you."

"Get out!" she screamed.

"No." He crouched in front of her, pushing his face too close to hers. It had only been two years since she had seen him last, since he had lied to her family, to her father, and claimed that she had tried to seduce him, tried to trap him into being the father of her unborn child.

He hadn't changed much. He looked a little older. He was in his thirties now, and his face had lost that handsome boyish charm that it used to contain. Mostly because he was sporting a black eye and his nose was crooked. "I need you to stop this."

"Get out of my house." She pushed herself away from him, scrambling to her feet. She would never feel beneath him again. She would never let him take anything from her again.

"You have to stop this." He followed her closely, trying to corner her. His eyes looked different, a little unfocused, but his jaw was determined. He had come here for a reason, but she had no inclination to find out what that was.

"If my husband finds you here he'll kill you."

"He left. On his way to work. It's far away, Georgia. It takes forty minutes to get there this time of day."

"How do you know that?" She swallowed. She had to get away from him, but she didn't want him to know how scared she was. She didn't want him to see her fear. She had lived in fear after he had hurt her the first time. Fear that he would find her alone, fear that he would force himself on her again, and then after her father had turned her away, she lived in fear that she wouldn't be able to feed her baby; she feared living in solitude forever.

Robert had too much power over her for all these years. She refused to let him take any more.

"I followed him. I needed to get you alone. He's a big man, and I really don't want any problems."

"Then go." She reached behind her on the counter, feeling for a knife or fork or something to keep him away from her.

"I just want to talk to you."

"Talk, damn it. Then get the hell out of my house."

"Georgia." His eyes widened a bit as if he was shocked by her language. "What has happened to you?"

"I'm calling the cops." She reached for the phone but he wrenched it from her hand.

"I didn't mean for things to happen the way they did. Your father wanted me for your sister, but I wanted you. I was going to marry you. I loved you."

"You raped me!"

"You wanted it. You took a walk with me. You came into that shed with me."

"You asked me to. I trusted you. My father loved you like a son. I never thought you would hurt me."

"I didn't mean to hurt you. I just wanted you."

"And then you lied about it. About me. You said I was a seductress. You called me a whore."

"I didn't mean that and I'm sorry for that, but what did you expect me to do? I loved your father more than my own. Your family was the only thing I had. I couldn't lose them."

"But you were okay with them losing me."

"Your life is fine. You married a rich man. You live in a

big house. You got everything you ever wanted. You should be grateful."

She closed her hand and slapped him as hard as she could manage. "My life was not fine. I was pregnant and homeless and alone because you raped me. I was not fine."

"Stop saying that word," he hissed. "That's not what I did. We had sex."

"You ripped my clothes. You forced me!"

He slapped her this time. Twice. On her cheek and across her mouth. She tasted blood on her tongue. Panic beat in her chest, but so did anger.

She was mad as hell.

"You're ruining my life!" he spat at her. "You have got to stop telling people that I did that to you. I lost my job because of you. My boss said I was a man he couldn't trust around his daughter. A rock was thrown through my window. My tires were slashed. My friends are gone. Look at my face!" He pointed to his eye. "Josiah did this to me. In the middle of the supermarket. It took two people to pull him off. He told me I had to leave town or he was going to kill me. I have no place else to go. Oakdale has been my home for the past fifteen years."

"And it was my home for twenty-one, but you never seemed to care about that," she yelled back at him, too angry to be scared of the consequences.

"Your father won't see me anymore! He banned me from the house, from the church. The whole town has convicted me. I can't take it, Georgia. You've got to go back and tell them you lied. I need Abraham. They beat me, you know. My parents beat me for everything I did. For no reason sometimes. I didn't deserve that, but your father took me in and it stopped. He was the only one who loved me. You've got to tell them I didn't do that to you."

"I won't! You did do that to me. You hurt me!"

"You will or you won't see the last of me." He turned away from her for a moment, pacing nervously. "That baby you had is mine. I have rights. I can take her from you. I'll make it so you have to let me see her all the time."

"You can't," she said, feeling panic rise in her chest. "They don't give babies to rapists."

"Who's a rapist? You didn't go to the police. I wasn't charged with a crime. I'm just a man who had his child hidden from him. You think a judge won't believe that?"

"I know it." She would kill him herself before she let that happen. "You're nothing but a fraud. A fake. You'll never get her."

"Maybe not, but a court case could take years, and you'll see me at every hearing. I'll be around you, hassling you, in your space, in your head until you give me what I want."

"No." She wasn't sure of many things in her life, but that much she was sure of. Robert would never touch Abby. She would die before it came to that.

"Then I'll take her. I'll take her and run away with her and you'll never see her again. She looks like me. I've seen her. I've seen her with your husband. He likes to take her to the park when he gets home from work. You like to shop at the farm stand on weekends. I know everything about your life, Georgia. I've been watching you."

"You're crazy!" She didn't know why she was shocked to hear what he'd been doing, but she was. She had felt so safe here. This was her home, her sanctuary, and he had been watching her and Christian and their family. She felt violated again. She felt dirty. "Why can't you leave me alone?"

"Because you ruined my life! I can't leave you alone until I get it back."

"You did this to yourself. You're spoiled and selfish and you deserve this. You think I won't call the police? You think I'll just let you haunt me? You think my husband will?"

He gripped her by the shoulders, digging his fingers into her skin. "I'll kill him."

His eyes had grown wilder, his face more determined. He was serious. "You're insane."

"No, I'm desperate and that's worse."

A funny feeling nagged Christian as he drove to Howard and Helga's that morning. He looked back at Abby, who was occupying herself with a board book in her car seat. She was fine, and the only reason he was taking her to work with him this morning was so Georgia could get some rest. She was tired all the time; some nights she barely made it to eight o'clock before sleepiness overtook her.

She needed to rest, but he felt as though maybe he shouldn't have left her alone.

For the past month, he had been working a lot—too much. He thought he'd finally found his purpose in life, to help the men that were so much like him, but he had to take care of his wife first. He'd told her the truth when he'd said she had brought him back to life. He wouldn't be here, he wouldn't be happy without her.

He turned the car around, calling Cliff to tell him that he wasn't going to make it in that day or the next and to ask the general to take his place in the meetings.

Dan worked for them part-time. It gave him something to do, he said, but Christian really thought that Dan needed to help the former troops as much as he did.

He pulled back into his driveway no more than twenty minutes after he'd left.

There was a black car parked outside of their house. A black Mercedes that he swore he had seen before. But then he had thought he was paranoid, that somebody had been following him. He jumped out of the car the same time their next-door neighbor came from his house.

"Christian. I think I heard Georgia scream."

The hair on his neck stood at attention. "Can you take Abby?"

"Of course." Tim nodded. "Go."

Christian ran toward the house, his blood pumping through his ears. The kitchen door was open, the doorjamb cracked.

"No, I'm desperate and that's worse."

He saw a man with crazed eyes and his hands on his wife's shoulders. He moved. Ready to charge, ready to kill, when Georgia lifted her knee and stomped on the man's foot, then kneed him in the balls.

He didn't know whether to be inordinately proud or homicidal in that moment, but the man dropped to his knees and that was when Christian saw his face.

He looked like Abby. *This must be him. This must be Robert.* He stopped thinking. He picked up the man by his shirt and slammed him onto the floor so hard that his head bounced up.

Christian had killed before, but in war, in a gunfight with terrorists. He'd used bullets then. He'd killed to fight for his unit and his country. He hadn't felt the way he did right now, this kind of cool calmness, this knowing that today he was going to end a life. He stomped on the man's testicles, causing him to scream out in pain, but the noise didn't cause Christian to stop, or pause, or feel the tiniest bit of remorse.

He picked him up and threw him against the wall. He slapped him. A punch was for a man. Not for this thing. This coward who raped and lied and got away with it.

He slapped the other side of his face, splitting his lip. His cheek was already swelling, and a little bit of satisfaction bloomed in his chest. "Hit me back. Fight for your life. Or are you too much of a pussy?"

The man did nothing but moan. The cold fury spread through Christian's chest, and he lifted Robert up by the neck and slammed him to the ground, stomping on the hand that had held his wife down, kicking his ribs, knowing they broke as his size-fourteen foot connected with them.

"Enough, Christian." Georgia grabbed his hand and pulled him toward her. "Enough. I love you too much to watch you kill him."

"He deserves to die. He hurt you." He glanced at her shoulders, where Robert's fingers had dug into the flesh. He looked at her face, which was marked by his handprint, her mouth that was messy with blood.

If he hadn't come home, if he hadn't walked in when he did, he could have lost her. That was something he couldn't face. It was something he wouldn't have been able to live with. "He had his hands on you. Let me make it so he can never hurt you again."

The police sirens blared, and he knew Tim had called the police.

Georgia looked at him. "He won't. They're going to put him away for this."

He cupped her battered face in his hands and tears welled in his eyes. His throat burned. He could have lost her.

He could have lost her, and he had only ever told her he loved her once.

"It's not enough, Georgia. I need for him to die."

"But I don't. The only thing I need is to carry on with my life with you."

Two police officers burst through the door, their guns drawn. "Holy shit," one of them said, putting his gun away. "Is he still alive?"

"Barely," another one said. "We got a call that there was an intruder. Is this man it?"

"Yes," Georgia said before Christian could say anything. "He broke in here. He's the same man who attacked me two years ago. I want him put away for good."

"Call an ambulance," the first cop said. "Call two." He stared at Georgia's battered face. "Tell them to rush it. The female victim is bleeding from her side."

Christian lifted Georgia's shirt. There was too much blood to see it clearly, but there was a large gash on her side.

"I'm fine," she said quickly, even though she was going pale. "He knocked me against the counter. I'll be fine."

She leaned against him with all her weight. "Get them here now," Christian barked. "She's pregnant. We can't lose this baby. We can't."

CHAPTER 29

Georgia had stayed in the hospital for two days after Robert attacked her. They'd wanted to monitor the baby due to Georgia's injuries. She had strained a muscle in her back and needed stitches up her side where Robert had thrown her into the counter, and on her lips where he had slapped her, but she was okay.

She was sore and bruised, but she was grateful to be alive, and that Christian had come home when he did, and that their family had survived the ordeal.

It had now been two months since that day, and Christian barely left her side. He worked from home. He had gone to every doctor's appointment. He cleaned. He barely let her cook. He helped more with Abby. He was doing it all. And she let him, because it seemed to make him happy to do so.

His super overprotectiveness wouldn't last forever. She hoped it would end before the birth of their son, right after Robert's trial was over. It was starting today.

Robert had been charged with aggravated assault, a crime that carried a sentence of up to fourteen years. They all thought he would take a plea, that he would go to jail and serve his time, but he pled not guilty, and it was like a slap in the face to Georgia. Till this day he denied what he did to her. He blamed her. He still called her a liar. But she wouldn't stand for it.

She was going to testify against him. She was going to be in that courtroom every day until the case was over. The prosecutor assured her it wouldn't take very long. He told her that they could make a case without her testimony, but it was important to her to face her abuser, to tell the whole world their history, to tell them what he had planned to do to her and her family.

Her life was good. She was happy. Now instead of hatred, the only thing she could feel for Robert was pity. He was going to die alone, unloved, uncared for. He was going to have nothing while she had the world.

That was a sad existence for anyone to face.

Christian pressed a kissed to Georgia's cheek as they sat in the car on the side of Charleston's beautiful courthouse. "Are you sure you want to do this? I'll take you away from here right now. I'll take you wherever you want to go."

She smiled at her handsome husband. "I want you to take me for waffles and those big link sausages, but after this. I'm going to this trial. I'm going to be here every day."

"You are so brave." He took her face in his hands and kissed her mouth softly. "I love you."

"I love you, too, Christian. I know it's strange, but I keep thinking that if it weren't for him I would have never met you. So I can't hate him. I just need to know he's out of my life for good."

"He will be. I'll make sure he is." He glanced out the window behind her. "I think your family is here."

They all were. She saw when they got out of the car. Her

mother was there. She had gone back to her father, but things had changed between them. Her mother was no longer broken. She was happier. Abraham no longer ruled any part of her life. Georgia and Carolina spent a lot of time with her. She drove down on the weekends and spoiled her granddaughters. Carolina had a little girl named Grace. She was there that day with Miles. They vowed to support her. And they had in every way they could.

"Hey, sis." Gideon had come home on leave from Germany to be with her. He was so handsome in his dress uniform. Georgia hugged him tightly. He was no longer a baby, but she still worried about him. Their family issues had taken a much bigger toll on him than she had thought.

"You look beautiful, girl." Eli hugged her next. He had moved out of state, out of the South, to a little town in Delaware where he could start over again. Being around them seemed too hard for him, but Georgia understood. Sometimes a person needed to break away to start over again.

Josiah didn't hug her. He was busy helping her father out of the car.

Her father had come? That shocked her.

She hadn't spoken to him since that day in the hospital, but she kept up with him. She always asked her mama about it. He was dying. He had heart failure. He looked older than she had ever seen, but he was there, with his oxygen tank hooked to his nose. He was wearing his best suit and had a determined expression on his face.

Christian gripped her shoulders lightly, pulling her back into his warm, hard chest. She shut her eyes for a moment, letting herself sink into him. She needed him in that moment. Seeing her father was harder than she'd thought. It was harder than facing the prospect of dealing with her brutalizer in court. Her father, in the end, had hurt her more than Robert ever could. He'd thrown away her love.

"Open your eyes, love," Christian whispered.

She did. Her father had stopped before her and then did something she never expected him to do. He fell to his knees before her, grasped her hands and brought them to his wrinkled mouth and wept. She had never seen her father cry before. Not even when Abel had died. She didn't know how to handle it. It was all too much. It was too hard to see. Too hard to hear. Too hard to take.

"Daddy...don't." She got on her knees and embraced him as hard as she could, as hard as she could stand.

"I turned away because I was too ashamed to look at you that day. I was wrong. I was wrong. I was so wrong." He sobbed onto her shoulder. His breath was coming hard and heavy, causing Georgia to worry, causing her to pray he would stop. "I cannot ask for forgiveness I do not deserve, but I'm sorry. I'm sorry and I love you. I need you to know that. I need you to know that before I die."

She didn't know what had happened to her in that split second, but as she heard those words, as his tears mingled with hers, she felt a heavy weight that she'd never known she was carrying lift from her shoulders, from her heart.

"I've always loved you, Georgia. I just forgot how. You saved my life when you should have let me die. That is more than I deserved. That is more than love. That is more than I've given to you."

"It's okay, Daddy." She pulled away from him and wiped his tears. "I listened to your sermons in church. I remembered those messages. I remembered how you used to love."

"Excuse me." The prosecutor was there when Georgia looked up. "We're getting ready to start. Are you sure you want to do this?"

"Yes." She tried to stand, but her knees were still weak, so Christian came to her aid. "I'm sure. I'm ready."

Her brothers helped their father to his feet and walked him inside. Christian hung back. He wrapped both of his arms around her and kissed her. "Can it be so simple for you? Can you forgive just like that?"

"No. It's not simple to forgive. Or easy. But it's something I have to do. It's something I need to do. Things happen for a reason. After all of this, I realize that. All of what happened to me, what happened to you, brought us together, and I wouldn't change that. I wouldn't change my life with you for all the do overs in the world."

★ ★ ★ ★ ★

ELKHART PUBLIC
LIBRARY
Elkhart, Indiana